Winter Harvest

WINTER HARVEST
Bob Dylan to Jalaluddin Rumi
Shems Friedlander

TIMAS PUBLISHING | 3962
Non Fiction-Memoir | 12

EDITOR
Tuğçe İnceoğlu

COVER DESING
Ravza Kızıltuğ

COVER PHOTOGRAPH
Bruno Barbey, *Magnum*

1. EDITION
November 2015, Istanbul

ISBN
ISBN: 978-605-08-2167-3
9 786050 821673

PRINT AND COVER
Sistem Matbaacılık
Yılanlı Ayazma Sok. No: 8
Davutpaşa-Topkapı/İstanbul
Telefon: (0212) 482 11 01
Matbaa Sertifika No: 16086

TIMAS PUBLISHING
Alayköşkü Caddesi, No:11, Cağaloğlu, İstanbul
Phone: (0212) 511 24 24
timas.com.tr
timas@timas.com.tr
facebook.com/timasyayingrubu
twitter.com/timasyayingrubu

Ministry of Culture and Tourism
Publisher Certificate: 12364

WINTER HARVEST

Bob Dylan to Jalaluddin Rumi

Memories and Illuminations

Shems Friedlander

TİMAŞ

ALSO BY SHEMS FRIEDLANDER

Year One Catalog (editor)
Wisdom Stories for the Planet Earth
Submission: Sayings of the Prophet Mohammed
Ninety-Nine Names of Allah
SunLight, Poems and Other Words (with Nuri Friedlander)
Rumi and the Whirling Dervishes
Rumi: The Hidden Treasure
When You Hear Hoofbeats Think of a Zebra

TURKISH

Toynak Sesini Duyunca Zebra Celsin Aklina
Kish Hasadi (Winter Harvest)

FILMS

Rumi, The Wings of Love
El Mahya, Come to Life
The Circles of Remembrance
Dream Water Does Not Quench Thirst
Homage to Hamza El Din
Faisal, Legacy of a King

MONODRAMAS

(performed at the Howard Theatre, The American University in Cairo)
Dream Water Does Not Quench Thirst
The Calligrapher's Daughter

EXHIBITIONS

PHOTOGRAPHY

The Wall, Cathedral of St John the Divine, New York
The Sony Gallery, Cairo
Gezira Art Centre, Cairo
The Empty Quarter, Dubai

PAINTINGS

Gotham Book Mart Gallery, New York
The Sony Gallery, Cairo
Gezira Art Centre, Cairo
Mahmoud Mohktar Cultural Centre, Cairo
CUBE ARTS, Dubai

You must leave now,
take what you need, you think will last...

Bob Dylan

I've noted down the day of my birth
And some events known only to me
Which occurred between that day and another
Which I will not remember or note down
But leave to others.

Jorge Luis Borges

Blessed are you that are so wise!
Blessed am I that I have fallen into your company.

Tripura Rahasya

To my granddaughter
Alia Rose Friedlander
Born 26/07/2014
"The Future"

PREFACE

Few are left who knew me when I was young or who now walk the streets and were on the planet when I was born. I realize that as the experience of my life increased, its length diminished. Every breath taken did not increase my life but lessened it by one breath.

When Emine Eroglu, the director of Sufi Kitab Publishing in Istanbul asked me to write a memoir I was hesitant. Although each life is unique, it is not necessarily interesting to others. When I glanced back I saw that I had met many spiritual teachers from divers beliefs, men and women filled with light, energy, and love who willingly transferred these qualities to others, and their stories would be interesting to others. I agreed to the task and went fishing for memories in the ocean of my past.

I remembered my boyhood in Boston, Massachusetts. I remembered my years in art school. I remembered being a reporter for the Boston Record-American. I remembered the Gurdjieff Work, Swami Muktananda's flying lessons, and Lama Chimi's folded paper. I remembered Sheikh Muzaffer, Safer Baba, and The Whirling Dervishes. I remembered music and scents. I remembered Istanbul nights, Cairo days and much more that I have scribbled onto these pages.

None of these memories appeared in the order of their happening. They jumped to the foreground as if I were in a game of hopscotch.

Although linked by the invisible skein of my life, each event was unique and pregnant with the possibility of a future, unlike a frozen photograph that expresses a moment but has no future.

This book like its many remembrances is not written sequentially, although the events are tied by the continuity of my time. Much like my thoughts of the past, these memories jump from the timeline of my life like pieces of a puzzle that belong to one man. Like a mirror in many shards lying on the floor with a reflection of a part of the whole in each section.

645 Million Breaths

These are unconnected impressions of the theatre of my life, with players who drift in and out of light and dark, clear and sullied moments, faded and acute images, that emerge in the present as muffled prayers, or jumbled visions, during a winter harvest of memories.

Like a dedicated farmer pruning trees so they may grow healthy, I have searched for the places in my life where seeds were buried, and sought the fruit that may have been born. At an early age I became aware of vacuity, but with little life experience, filled it with the toys of the world, rather than the Name of God.

In my daydreams I visited invisible cities, and used poetry and art as weapons to defray the enemies of mankind. In the nearly 645 million breaths I have taken, how many have been conscious, how many contained the Name of Allah? Far too few I am sure.

The Sufi sheikhs say that a breath taken in which the Name of Allah is missing, is a wasted breath. How much of this precious life have I wasted, dreamed away, clouded with confusion, crowded with meaningless or poisoned thoughts? Will I be written down as a man broken by the world, a life devoid of meaning, unfulfilled, or is there yet a glimmer of hope, the afterglow of a firefly's light?

The Sufi sheikhs tell us that to say once in one's life, *la illaha illa Allah*, is enough to enter Paradise. This can be said in one breath. Not just repeated, but said from the deepest part of one's heart, with every fiber of one's being, with every cell of one's body alight, like the firefly.

Perhaps we are given 600 million breaths in order to locate the one where the Name of Allah is hidden.

The Wedding Night

Anatolia is like embracing ice in the winter of 1972. Konya is cold. Nevertheless thousands of lovers of Mevlana Jalaluddin Rumi converge from various parts of the world, to honor "his wedding night" in December. The Whirling Dervishes turn each night leading up to the 17th of December; the day Mevlana met his Beloved, some 700 years before.

I arrive from New York, the city of a hundred thousand traffic lights, to Konya, a small city in the heart of Central Turkey, that has one traffic light. I didn't know it but this particular journey would change my life.

Salik, a friend from New York is my traveling companion. We struggle with our bags at the old, dingy, Yesilkoy Airport in Istanbul, then find our way to Uskudar, to the house of Mevlevi musician Nezih Uzel whom I had recently met when the Whirling Dervishes were in New York.

Houses in Istanbul are heated by wood or coal stoves and carry a night chill. Nezih is to play the *bendir* in the Mevlevi dervish ceremony in Konya. Sadettin Heper is the *kudumzenbashi,* Kani Karaca, the blind *hafiz*, will chant the *Naati-Sherif,* Kudsi Erguner and Aka Gunduz will play the *ney* and it is master *ney* player Ulve Erguner's last *sema*, as his face is swathed in bandages, the result of the cancer that is eating him.

We board the night train to Konya at Haydarpasha Station. The "iron horse," clatters, clacks and chugs its way through a dimly lit Asian landscape, occasionally covered by patches of snow.

Arriving in the chilled early morning, we take rooms in the Shaheen Hotel on Mevlana Caddesi, just down the street from Mevlana's tomb.

The following day, a burly figure accompanied by four men wearing overcoats and round white hats, enters the Hotel Shaheen's lobby. Everyone who is a dervish runs to kiss his hand. I am among them. This is Sheikh Muzaffer al-Halveti al-Jerrahi and his dervishes from Istanbul.

I greet him, he greets me, and that is where it ends… for the moment. That night after the *sema* there is a private *zikr* in a Konya apartment. Seventy or so people are packed into a tiny, hot, room. I am pasted against one of the oven walls. The sheikh and several of his dervishes are seated on their knees in a circle on the floor, surrounded by several standing Mevlevi musicians.

"I can't stay like this for hours." I don't know what encourages me to do it, but I move to the circle and sit on my knees between Sheikh Muzaffer and his *khalifa,* Safer Baba. Not invited, I nevertheless nudge them aside and sit down. The *zikr* begins and I repeat the Names of Allah and do the swaying movements, which is natural for me. It becomes a part of me. I feel as though my soul has returned home.

The circle of men performs various movements in this long *zikr* that continues for several hours. My heart is bathed in light. At the conclusion, in this space of sacred air, the sheikh looks at me and says, "You make *zikr* like us," and he kisses my eyes.

"I want you to come and see me in Istanbul."

"I'll be in Konya another week."

He meticulously writes down exactly where to go and when to come and see him. "*Insha'Allah,* I'll be there."

Whose dream could have unfolded these images of an American educated, son of Russian immigrant parents, sitting before a dervish sheikh, in a *zikr* circle in the ancient city of Konya, the laboratory of Mevlana Jalaluddin Rumi, in 1972?

Some World Conditions

In 1940 a new car cost $890 and a gallon bottle of milk could be purchased for ten cents. American President Franklin Delano Roosevelt requested wartime powers, and urged higher taxes for defense. Britain began rationing bacon, butter and sugar. Saudi Arabia had been a country for only eight years. Israel did not exist. Saddam Hussein was three years old, and Muammar Gaddafi had not yet been born. Kemal Attaturk had recently died. Kings governed Iraq, Egypt, Iran, Libya and Saudi Arabia. There was no television. Pablo Picasso had painted *Guernica*. The Cincinnati Reds won the World Series and Joe Louis was the heavyweight-boxing champion. These were some of the conditions of the world when I entered.

Born In The Sky

Sophie lay on the clean sheets of the Medical Art Center Hospital on Eighth Avenue and 59th Street in New York City. She was in an upper floor room of a high-storied redbrick building that could have easily been mistaken for an office or apartment building. I was born in the sky. I passed through the birth canal of awareness, into the ocean of consciousness to an unknown world, and Sophie saw to it that I knew no hunger. They named me Ira, and I was called by that name for the first twenty-five years of my life, and long after by some friends and family. My father Sam was a member of the electrical union and therefore was assured a good income. After living in Brooklyn, New York for two years my parents moved to Boston, to an area called Roxbury.

My mother looked like a Russian ballerina, but had a modern dancer's walk. Her raven hair was parted in the middle and pulled back tight into a bun that rested on the back of her head. She wore it that way every day of her life, along with the gold gypsy hoops about the size of a quarter that hung from her ears. She had a birthmark in the center of her forehead in the place that Indian women position a small circle of red powder called *kumkum*, to indicate marriage. Her name was Sophie, but everyone called her Sonya. Some two decades before, my mother was living in Montreal with her mother and sisters. Her father had died in Russia many years before. He sold meat to the military, and when the czar was overthrown he was arrested.

"They arrested him. When the communists arrested someone, you would never see them again, they would kill them...you understand. Papa would never come home, he'll be dead. But then somehow...he just delivered them merchandise so they let him go. He was in prison. When he came out his skin was grey, he was a good man, his hair was all white and he became sick. Papa died and they assembled our papers. So we came here without him. They saw that papa wasn't a general, he wasn't one of them. One friend had a house in back of the jail where we used to go. We would see how they let out the prisoners in the yard. We used to see papa but we kept quiet so they would not discover us. When the Cossacks went to the streets every week to dance and play music we ran to look for papa. There was a special place on the main street where the Black Shirts met. I remember. I do. I don't know why."

The clattering of horses' hooves on cobblestoned streets sent Sophie and her siblings scurrying beneath their beds. The family hid from the Cossacks, until they could gain passage on a boat for Halifax, and then on to settle in Montreal.

My mother's father was married to a woman in Russia who birthed six children. Somewhere in the batch were twin brothers. One drowned as an infant, in the milk of the woman breast-feeding him, who had fallen asleep and unconsciously pressed her peasant arms so hard against his back, that he couldn't release himself from the massive breast. His brother, at the age of eighteen, was swallowed by the Black Sea while swimming, his intestines scrambled by the sea, and soon there was no breath left in him. Neither got to comb grey hair.

My grandfather's wife witnessed five of her children pass through her birth canal into the world. When her sixth child made the journey to the ocean of consciousness she died. As was the custom of the time, her husband married Ethel, his wife's younger sister, who also gave birth to six children. One of them was my mother. This all happened more than a hundred years ago.

At fourteen, my father was a volunteer fireman in Moscow. A photograph of him with a helmet and uniform, printed on a metal surface, was displayed in my parents' home. He was handsome and feisty. In his twenties he jumped a ship to the west and followed an older sister, Annie, who had settled in Canada. When Sam arrived he spoke no English, but got a job selling sandwiches on the train that went back and forth between Montreal and New York. He memorized the names of the sandwiches and could make change, so he got along with his customers. He worked long hours, saved money, and sent for the remainder of the family who were still back in the U.S.S.R. It appeared that destiny offered him more. One day he disembarked the train in New York and never looked back. He found a cousin in Brooklyn who took him in, taught him the electrician trade, and eventually got him a union card. He became flush with money, had a car and lots of women. He visited Montreal periodically to spend time with his family.

One day, during one of these visits, he was walking with a friend on Esplanade Street in Montreal at the foot of Mount Royal. In a window of one of the wooden houses with a thousand steps, was a beautiful woman. My father, of course he wasn't my father then, was smitten. His friend asked if he was interested in the woman. He answered that he was, and the friend coyly said that he knew her. She was the sister of one of his friends. They courted, married in Montreal, moved to New York and then Boston, and I lived with Sam and Sonya until I left for the army in 1962, and then on to New York to follow a career in the arts.

Numbed By Love

A devout dervish was walking one day when he passed a house and looked up at a window, where he saw the most beautiful woman he could imagine. Her beauty mesmerized him, and he remained on that spot looking up at the window hoping to gain another glimpse of this beauty. Days passed into weeks. Nights of rain and cold passed. The woman noticed the dervish's vigil and after some time sent her servant to bring him to her.

Upon seeing the beauty of the woman, the man's heart swelled.

"What do you look for, standing day and night with your eyes pasted to my window?"

"Your beauty has numbed me with love."

"If you think I am beautiful," she said, "you should meet my sister, her beauty makes me look like a dwindling flower. There she stands now just to the right of you."

The man looked over his right shoulder but saw nothing.

"I see nothing."

"I have no sister, and if you really loved me you would never have looked toward another." With this she slammed the door in his face.

We say we love Allah, but we are constantly looking at the world.

Radio Days

I would often sit with my dad in the 1940s style kitchen of our Roxbury apartment. The wooden ice-cream-parlor chairs faced each other, and we would lean toward the brown table radio perched on the center of a wooden counter painted white. My father jiggled one of the large glass tubes in the back of the radio to clear the sound.

Our knees nearly touched, and our hearts jumped with anticipation, as we faced the radio, my ears straining to hear Joe Louis, the Brown Bomber, defend his heavyweight boxing title against all opponents on what seemed like every Friday night.

The radio warriors rested for one minute and boxed for three. During that minute, when the seconds and handlers were washing down their fighters in their respective corners, and the sure-handed cut men worked their trade like fine surgeons, King Gillette, a name not a title, sold us razors that promised clean-shaven faces in the comfort of our homes.

Our attention waned as I shadow-boxed my father right there in the kitchen, and he parried my blows. I felt like Joseph Louis Barrow himself.

These were our radio days. My last impression of the champ came years later. Joe Louis was a black hero in a white world of segregation and discrimination. He defeated everyone but the Brockton heavyweight Rocky Marciano, and only when he had become old and depressed, rolling in a wheelchair was he finally beaten, not by a man, but by the Internal Revenue Service. The taxman put a lien on his earnings and broke his spirit.

My imagination was diminished, and the blow-by-blow descriptions of the excited announcer slid into the past when, a few years later my dad bought a television set.

Now on Friday nights I would carry one of the wooden chairs from the kitchen into my parent's bedroom where we watched Carmen Basilio, the onion farmer from upstate New York, battle Carl "Bobo" Olsen, or Walker Smith, better known as Sugar Ray Robinson, pound for pound the best boxer in history and as slick as they come with his Harlem "do."

On some Friday nights we watched Kid Gavilan, the black Cuban who threw a devastating bolo punch that came from nowhere, like a steel stealth bomber that always landed on flesh.

On other Fridays we followed the movements of Emile Griffith, who reduced the square ring to the circumference of a nickel. I saw him knock his fist against the head of Benny "Kid" Peret so hard that Benny later died in the hospital from a brain turned to mush.

Marciano was the heavyweight champ. Built like a fire hydrant he took on all comers and left the ring, undefeated. Roland LaStarza was a foot taller and Rocky couldn't land the blockbuster. So for eleven rounds Marciano punched LaStarza's upper arms until the twelfth, when the challenger came out to battle but couldn't lift his dead arms. Rocky sent him to the canvas with a sledgehammer to the head that could have stopped you from reading books.

Boxing was violent, but as a boy I like what my dad likes.

Radio was my main source of entertainment and offered much more than boxing memories. I listened to the western, Gunsmoke, Amos 'n' Andy, and the Jack Benny Program, but my favorites in those early days were the detective programs with their intriguing introductions spoken by announcers with mellow voices.

"There he goes. He walks down the street. Steps on the scale... weight 300 pounds, fortune, danger... J. Scott Smart as The Fat Man," or "Friend of those who have no friend, Enemy of those who make him an enemy...Boston Blackie," but my all time favorite was, "While traveling in the Orient, Lamont Cranston learned the secret of how to cloud men's minds. Who knows what evil lurks in the hearts of men, the Shadow knows."

I slipped from my youth with radio on my mind.

Jack-Of-All-Trades

My dad wasn't an athlete, or even a good businessman. He was a jack-of-all-trades and could fix almost anything, especially if there was a second that he could use as a model. In those early years, when I was still a boy, my father struggled to support his family.

Iron Lungs

I often rode my Schwinn bicycle with balloon tires down the steep Cheney Street hill to get a pack of Kent cigarettes for my mother. They cost fifteen cents for the pack. I puffed the breath out of me on the way back so that sometimes I walked down the tree-lined hill from Maple Street. I held my breath until I passed Steven Fisher's house. He had polio and I think that not taking a breath as I pass his window might save me from the same plight. The disease is the fright of our childhood. We are not allowed to enter common swimming pools, or even go to the movies. Crowded places were avoided. Everyone knew someone in an iron lung or crippled for life. Others like Steven were lucky and made a full recovery. Although my friends and I admired the baseball players Ted Williams and Joe DiMaggio, Dr. Jonas Salk, who developed the first successful polio vaccine, was our true hero.

If we aren't on our bikes, we are roller-skating down Cheney and balancing ourselves as we quickly turn into Maple Street. It was daring and risky to ride the Cheney hill all the way down to Grove Hall at the bottom. Our roller skates were made of metal, and clipped onto the ridge at the sole of our shoes and tightened by a skate key worn on a string around our necks.

The Smokescreen Of Childhood

Perhaps my father was unlucky, but he was as honest as a July day is long. When I was a boy he was in the haberdashery business. He had a store in South Boston. His partner Nat was a retired army captain and a hero in World War II.

On Saturdays when there was no school my younger sister Vivian and I went to the store and dad would give us movie money. We'd then go to the Oriental Theatre and watch matinees of double features, cartoons, newsreels, and a thrilling serial that always left the hero in a dangerous position. The film would be cut with a promise to find out what happened in the next episode. All this in a movie house with a ceiling adorned with sporadic clouds that appeared to move in a starlit sky.

Tom Mix, Gene Autry (the singing cowboy), Roy Rogers (he had a taxidermist stuff his horse Trigger and kept him in the living room of his house), and Hopalong Cassidy, the cowboys of my youth, moved on the screen bigger than life, filling my Saturdays with dreams of adventure, the smokescreen of childhood.

Coal Men

The somber Boston streets of my youth in the 1950s often smelled of yesterday's rain. Maple trees with their million leaves that changed from green to red, yellow, and orange in autumn, lined the street where I lived. My mother called me and my sister to dinner from the painted streets, by ringing a cowbell out the window of our first floor flat.

Buildings were still heated by burning coal. Men with bituminous arms arrive at our brick apartment house once a month, and trucks that bend over, send pyramids of coal down to the cellar via metal chutes placed in the open basement windows. I would sit by the window, my face pressed against the glass, peering at the black coal sliding below and listening to its roar.

Horses With Wings

Finally my dad had to close the shop. His partner Nat was caught hijacking trucks containing expensive furs and sent to prison. My dad worked for years to pay off his business debts. His honesty kept his pockets poor but his heart rich. I don't remember much about Nat, except he once gave me a pair of professional boxing gloves.

My father was a licensed electrician and a good carpenter, so he went into the business of buying empty run-down stores that were auctioned in the Boston Sunday Globe, and rebuilding them for resale. He did this for a few years until an old friend of his with a clothing store near Dudley Station in Roxbury asked him to manage the shop. It was a tough neighborhood, and there was one night my father returned home pallid because thugs or junkies jammed a pistol at his ribs in order to force him to open the store's safe. There was never much cash in the safe, if any, but junkies dream of horses with wings and will do almost anything for a fix. After the incident of the pistol, my mother perched herself in front of our living room window every night, anxiously waiting for my father's old Plymouth sedan to turn into our street.

A Fist Full Of Greenbacks

A lot of characters passed through my youth leaving behind a unique picture of events I would never see the like of again.

Jerry Sutter was wiry and tough. He had a few run ins with the law and was compelled to join the Navy. Periodically he returned to the neighborhood on leave, adorned with Navy tats and a fist full of greenbacks. Jerry liked me so I had a sort of built-in protection plan which was good, since I was a skinny kid with little desire for street fighting, although my imagination served me well in many a battle. I was watching when Jerry kicked another guy's eye right out of its socket. Few were prepared to mess with him. Later I think he was either swallowed up by the Navy or prison… I lost track of him.

I also had more gentle friends. Barry who lived across the street must have been rich because his house was the first in our neighborhood to have a television set. His father worked for the government and he had an older brother Kenny who I barely remember.

I have been working since the age of fourteen. My first job was packing raincoats on Saturday mornings, in the basement of the Cable Raincoat Factory in Boston, and placing them into large cardboard boxes, then fixing them with a hand-binding machine that tied the boxes with metal strips.

Innovators Of The Moment

I am on Maple Street in Roxbury playing stickball, using the edges of parked cars and manhole covers as bases, and a sawed off broomstick as a bat. Once the ball is hit you race between an old Buick fender and the headlight of a 1948 Kaiser that looks somewhat like a leftover tank from the war, the platypus of cars. Games were invented. We were innovators of the moment. If a high bouncing pink ball broke, we carried on, now playing half ball. We collected cards with pictures of baseball players or battle scenes from World War II. Sometimes we waxed these cards by rubbing a candle on them so they would slide better as we flicked them along the sidewalk toward a brick wall. Whoever got closest to the wall won and owned the other player's card. No one ever beat Dickie Freeze at this game.

Every boy had a folding jackknife that fits snugly in the front pocket of his dungarees, and serves as the tool to mark out territory in the ground. We shot the knife into the earth with a flick of the wrist, and from wherever it stuck we drew a line, and now owned that property. Years later I learned that adults did a similar thing with countries in the Middle East.

Sophie's Game

Sophie sits at the kitchen table in Roxbury playing solitaire and roaming her thoughts. She has two children, my sister, and myself, and is far from the Kremenchuk apartment, north of Moscow, where she was a child. I watch her move the cards from column to column while sipping black tea from a tall, clear glass, through the lump of sugar resting on her tongue.

She ate a raw onion held in her left hand like a baseball, and sliced with a paring knife. A slab of dark rye bread followed. The left-over traditions of Russia.

First Sufi Lesson

My first introduction to Sufism came at the age of twelve, when I read a two-line poem that affected the rest of my life. It stayed with me through my youth, my teens, into college years and for years after. It simply read, "I cried because I had no shoes, and then I met a man who had no feet." It was credited "anonymous" at the bottom. Years later, in my late twenties, when I was studying comparative religion, I learned that the poem had been written by Hafiz, a Persian Sufi poet.

Meat And Vegetables

Hoja Nasreddin's wife was constantly complaining. "The only meat I see is in the butcher shop, and the only vegetables I see are on the grocer's shelves."

"Be thankful to God," said the Hoja, "for you could have been blind."

The Walls Of Roxbury Memorial

The music of the 1950s was Rhythm & Blues and Rock and Roll. I was a teenager living in Roxbury, a section of Boston, when one of the greatest music events of the decade took place at the Shawmut Theatre. It was pre-Elvis and the stage was occupied by the likes of Chuck Berry, Little Richard, The 5 Keys, Big Joe Turner, Fats Domino and others. We were dancing in the aisles and shouting the lyrics to songs that are now known as the Golden Oldies. Music history was being made. I felt the sound beat into my bones.

At Roxbury Memorial High School our annual Talent Show was the hottest ticket in Boston, because our students were the best of the best when it came to singing Blues and Rock and Roll. Racism existed, but not inside the walls of Roxbury Memorial.

White Flight

During the end of my high school years white flight had begun in our part of Roxbury, and within a few short years the middle class whites moved out making room for blacks. I had many black friends, including Josh the preacher's son, Roscoe Baker and Hewitt Joyner, two of my teammates on the Roxbury Memorial High School basketball team. At Roxbury Memorial we took our basketball seriously. When Tony Santio, the team's star guard, fell asleep in Spanish class, Mr. Bonner, the Spanish teacher had the entire class silently leave the classroom, so Tony could finish his nap before the big game that evening.

Social pressure mounted and we became the last white family on Maple Street to leave.

Art School

I am nineteen, in my first year of art school. We had moved from Roxbury to Brookline. Milk was still delivered in glass bottles by either the Hood or Whiting milk companies, and was renewed by my mother placing a rolled up paper in the empty bottle's neck requesting additional quarts. Personal notes to unnamed people. The empties were left outside the door of your apartment.

I like New England weather. Mark Twain was right. You only had to wait a minute for it to change. The summers are warm and the winters are snowy. I walk down Beale Street, then Longwood Avenue toward art school, listening to the crunch of dried leaves under my shoes. Autumn brings multi-colored leaves and spring promises a season of baseball. Once it snowed in April on Opening Day of the new season. The Boston Globe ran a photograph of a snow-covered Fenway Park, the home of the Red Sox. Although later I became a Red Sox fan, in the early days I rooted for the Boston Braves. They had a great pitching combination in Warren Spahn and Johnny Sain. The sports writers coined a phrase, "Spahn and Sain and pray for rain."

Satchmo

I lived with my parents and daily trekked the twenty minutes, like a postman in the heat, rain, cold and snow, to the Massachusetts College of Art where I spend four years with paint-stained hands and clothes, before I graduate and join the Army Reserves, hoping that President John F. Kennedy won't send me "over there" to help build the Berlin Wall. I watched it built and I watched it fall.

Our landlord in Brookline was a bandleader at "The High Hat," a famous Boston nightclub. One night he invited our family to the club for dinner and to listen to Louis "Satchmo" Armstrong the great jazz singer, trumpet player, and scat vocalist, which was the art of using sounds and syllables instead of actual lyrics. I stand before "Satchmo," bask in his wide smile and notice that the dedication and many hours of playing trumpet had left his lower lip hard as the back of a clam. If you want to succeed you have to work diligently at all costs.

Mr. Sullivan, my Boston Latin School English grammar teacher loudly proclaimed, "If it doesn't hurt, you're not studying."

Picasso's Restless Hands

At Mass Art I do all the things expected of art students in the sixties. I am sitting with my fellow students downing 10-cent glasses of beer at the local saloon and arguing whether an ink blob could be called a hand, or perhaps even art.

I read that Picasso had restless hands. In a Paris bistro he molded bread into little figures, held unusual objects at an angle then changed the angle, and made a design on his plate from the bones of a fish that he just ate. He would turn something into something else and make it his own.

During lunch in a Harvard Square restaurant, in January of 2013

Leo, a former classmate described me when I was an art student. "You were aloof to a system that you disagreed with and wrote poetry that none of us understood, but we refrained from telling you, out of the fear of losing your friendship. You were on your own trip, with your own interests, and nurtured those directives. You wandered the corridors rather than attend classes. Didn't like being told what to do and were desire driven. Poetry seemed to be the answer to the world's problems and you were hungry for a hidden knowledge." Leo added, "If we looked at what you've done all your life to this point and we saw it back then, none of us would be surprised. You know, you are the only Muslim person I have ever met." What a revelation this was to me. An intelligent seventy-year-old man living in a cosmopolitan city in the United States, had never met a Muslim. It is no wonder that the U.S. doesn't understand how to handle its Middle East policy.

I was guided in a direction beyond my control for my entire life. I was seeking something, and knew there was something different than what was presented to me, yet I was fastened to the world.

Reading Gurdjieff

Art school brought out strange traits in us boys. In life drawing class a beautiful nude model sits on a high stool in the center of the room, and we would look past her to catch a glimpse of what was beneath the skirt of the girl sitting across from us in the studio. After all we are explorers. Explorers of art, the culture, sports, women, spirituality, mind expanding drugs, anything that could give us some clue as to who we are and why we are here. With what seemed like great seriousness, we sought some purpose to our lives. We shunned television, and had no dreams of laptop computers or phones that fit into your pocket. I spend long hours in my room painting or reading *All and Everything*, by G.I. Gurdjieff. Then, at a certain moment I realized that I could not change the world, but that I could change myself, and at that point I started to look at things differently. So, it didn't matter anymore on a grand global scale what was happening. What is important is the realm of my being and how that related to the world outside of me as well as the one inside of me. The *zahir* and the *batin,* the hidden and the revealed.

On Tuesdays I cut classes and either drive or take the bus to New York, and make my way to the Lexington Avenue loft to listen as Willem Nyland talks about Gurdjieff, consciousness, and how to work on oneself to become a harmonious man. I never worried about the classes I missed, since one of those who made the trip was my painting instructor, George Lockwood. Others who often went along were the photographers Paul Caponigro, Marie Cosindas and a teenage boy, the nephew of Montgomery Clift, the actor, whose name was Bill, who years later moved to New Mexico, and photographed Factory Butte in such a way that it made you dream. After the "meeting" we made the five-hour drive back to Boston, arriving in the early hours of the morning, but before dawn. Although I was a few years older than Bill Clift, I couldn't have been more than twenty.

My first real girlfriend, or adult relationship, came at this time. Suzanne had been married briefly, so she was versed in certain physical arts that I had until then only imagined. Her long hair was the color of oats and she always had a sweet smell. Her apartment in Greenwich village was small, and decorated with handcrafts that she did in her spare time. We were together for several months, going to the Gurdjieff meetings and working on Mr. Nyland's land in Brewster on the weekends. She was a bit promiscuous so it came as no surprise that she left me for an older fellow in the group who was a carpenter. She left him also, and the last I heard of her she had become a "Weatherman," involved with the terrorist group that was making explosive devices on Eleventh street and wanted to sabotage the system. They began as the May 2nd Movement, then merged with the SDS (Students for a Democratic Society) a faction of which became the "Weathermen," taking their name from a Bob Dylan song.

"Keep a clean nose, watch the plain clothes,

You don't need a weatherman to know which way the wind blows."

I Wanna Be Like Mike

In college I played some basketball and once went to a game with a 104-degree fever and scored 32 points. My press pass allowed me free entry to the Boston Garden where I viewed Boston Celtics games, sometimes from the press box with the Record-American's sports reporter Bill McSweeny, who was my friend and mentor. He had been a hero in the Korean War, and was now a major in the Army Reserves. Just before I was to be drafted, I enlisted in the Reserves during my last year at the Massachusetts College of Art.

The basketball heroes of my day were Bob Cousy, Bill Sharman and Bill Russell, the nemesis of Wilt "The Stilt" Chamberlain, one of the great centers of the game. I saw George Mikan play for the Minneapolis Lakers, before the twenty-four second rule was introduced to force the game to go faster. At nearly seven feet tall he towered above the other players. He stretched his long arms upward and almost without his feet leaving the ground, dropped the ball into the basket. Those were the basketball days where the running was even-paced, and jumping was rare.

This was before the Chicago Bull's Michael Jordan changed everyone's perception of the sport. Jordan would soar into the air like a black angel floating toward the basket, and dunk the ball one-handed into the net from an altitude other players could never reach.

We admired the talents of our sports celebrities and forgave their indiscretions. They gambled, cajoled, were infected by HIV, bragged about their numerous female conquests, until finally we lost our admiration of them as role models for our sons. Heroes are hard to come by.

Untimely Death

My girlfriend in art school was an umber-haired local beauty queen. Years later she had married someone else, had two kids and was pregnant with a third, when she climbed a water tower in Revere clutching one infant and leapt. The results of an alcoholic father, an acquiescing mother, and rarely hearing a soft word in the family. The seeds of unhappiness are generally planted early in life. I read it in the Boston Globe while visiting my sister in Randolph.

The Birth Of A Leopard

I learned to draw and paint. The two art scholarships, to the weekend program at Mass Art and the weekday program at the Museum School that I was awarded in high school seemed to be paying off. My immigrant parents would have liked me to choose law or medicine as a profession, but I stayed with art, and fifty years later I'm still in that game.

It is 1958. I am sitting on a wooden chair in the Saturday morning art class at Mass Art. Light enters the room from the large glass windows on the Longwood Avenue side of the building. I am painting a watercolor of a leopard; concentrating on the ink, as it becomes black spots on the leopard's yellow body. I am present at the birth of the leopard.

Roxbury Moments

Blessings come in various disguises. In high school I was a decent basketball player and one of a few white boys on a mostly black team. Contrary to the belief of some, I could jump and had a decent jump shot, but being skinny as a stick I lacked stamina on the court. I sat on the bench watching my teammates glide over the slick wooden floor like gazelles. Those were the years when I first learned about jazz, smoking dope and gambling. I played basketball with Chico. We are hanging out on a Dorchester street corner with other friends, watching our teenage lives drift past us like a river gone sour. Eddie's older brother Charlie is in the mob and we all look up to him. Late at night he shows up at the corner in $50 shoes and manicured fingernails, and treats the lot of us to coffee and sandwiches at the G&G delicatessen on Morton Street in Dorchester. One day Charlie is found shoved in the trunk of his car with his genitals stuffed in his mouth, a variation of the Colombian necktie, where an incision is made in the throat and the tongue pulled through. This is a method that wise guys use for squealers, and to deter others from talking out of turn. Our admiration begins to wane.

We spend our youth "holding up the corner," debating the merits of the Boston Red Sox over the New York Yankees, and betting on which team would win. Our bets now included the Boston Celtics as we took the points or gave them, hoping our choice would be correct. The bookmaker took the vigorish, a piece of the action.

Monty, we called him that because his parents moved to Boston from Montana, was backing bets as a young bookie while still a teenager. His destiny seemed to be written. He had the uncanny talent of looking at a dollar bill for just a few seconds and repeating the serial number backwards. He could reel off the names of the presidents whose engravings appeared on all the bills. Monty would close his eyes, as if he saw these people in his head, and sing out, "George Washington, one dollar bill, Thomas Jefferson, the two, Abraham Lincoln, the fiver, Alexander Hamilton, on the ten, Andrew Jackson, the twenty, Ulysses S. Grant, the fifty, a non-president Benjamin Franklin, the one hundred dollar bill (we had seen all these bills but never the remaining ones), William McKinley, the five hundred, Grover Cleveland, the only president to occupy the office twice but not in succession, the thousand dollar bill, James Madison, the five thousand dollar bill and Salmon Chase, the ten thousand dollar bill." I don't think they print anything larger than a hundred today and I don't know anyone who has pocketed the others. Hanging on the corner with Monty was like entering a house with six doors.

Our crew has two corners. One in Roxbury and the other in Dorchester and each has its special flavor and attitude.

It is dusk. We are all hanging at the corner in front of Fast Eddie Dean's Pizza joint when Sheryl, blonde and beautiful (she was the dream of us all), but Chico's girlfriend, steps out of a car her dad was driving, and is sent flying twenty feet in the air, landing on the pavement, after being struck by a speeding Ford driven by a lame school teacher at dusk. We watch her lifeless body lifted onto a stretcher, later to be pronounced Dead On Arrival at Boston City Hospital.

The corner has its stories. Albie Farber is 6'6" and built like a line backer for the Cleveland Browns. He is as gentle as he is huge. They beg him to play football for the high school team but he keeps refusing out of fear of injuring someone. He knew his own strength. The coaches finally get their way and Albie suits up for his one and only game for Roxbury Memorial High. In the first play he sends three members of the opposing team to the hospital. That ends his high school football career. He simply quit.

Albie has another talent. Diagonally across from Fast Eddie's store is an old three-story wooden house. Albie takes a copper penny with President Abraham Lincoln's image engraved on it, balances it on his thumb and index finger, and with a flick of his wrist sends it soaring to the rooftop of the wooden house. I am not certain whether it is uncanny strength, magic, or a miracle. I have often wondered what happened to this decent giant of my youth.

Eddie Dean was already a broken man when he opened the Pizza joint on the corner of Humboldt Avenue in Roxbury. We called him Fast Eddie, a bit derogatory, in memory of the fastball he never could hurl when he pitched in the Minor League for the Philadelphia Phillies franchise. Now he was slinging pizza dough in the air and overseeing the three pinball machines tucked into the far corner of the store. In those days the pinball machines were a form of gambling. If you mounted a certain number of points, the house (Eddie) had to pay you a sum of money. The more points amassed, the more cash received. It wasn't easy, and we spent hours of the life we didn't know was precious, cheering our friends to nudge the machine just a little to the left or right to gain extra points without tilting it and crashing the game. Of course Eddie could whip a fastball harder than any of us, but he just couldn't make it in the Big Leagues. Sometimes one of us would don a catcher's mitt and he would slide a few quick ones straight into the pocket right there on the street amidst the traffic.

As weak a pitcher as Eddie was, that was how good Marty Garber was at making that baseball jump with speed as it left his right arm and took the quick journey to leather. Marty was a few years older than we were and a lot bigger. At 6'4" with a body like a boxer and a heart of gold he was destined for the Majors and stardom. The Cubs signed him one day out of high school and he went straight to the Class A League.

Someone said that in an exhibition game Marty struck out Ted Williams, the Red Sox star hitter who was the last ballplayer to reach a batting percentage of .406, and that was back in 1941.

Williams took a hiatus from baseball to become a fighter pilot in the Korean War. The day he returned to Fenway Park I was in the stands just behind the Red Sox dugout, when Ted emerged on the dugout steps. The news cameras flashed, and there I was in the next day's sports page of the Boston Herald Traveler, right behind one of the greatest hitters in baseball history, and the nemesis of Yankee slugger Joltin' Joe DiMaggio, who later married screen actress Marilyn Monroe. Ted had no idea at that moment about "Cryonic Suspension" or fifty years later when he died on July 5th, 2002 that his family would squabble about dipping his lifeless body in a tank of liquid nitrogen. But that is just what happened. "The Splendid Splinter," as he was known to all of baseball, became a pendulous form frozen in time, in a state of neuroseparation. His head was severed from his body and placed in a steel can filled with liquid nitrogen. Even after death one's fate is not always one's own.

We followed Marty's progress with news from his brother. About six months went by and Marty's fastball hopped past incredulous batters, and his curve danced around bewildered opponents, and the pen was dipped into Major League contract ink when we heard the news.

It happened somewhere in the South. Marty was pitching a no-hitter. It was the eighth inning when a minatory, drunken fanatic leapt from the stands, raced to the pitcher's mound, and slashed Marty's neck and arm with a razor-sharp Buck knife. He recovered from the attack but his career faded, the Major League contract ink dried out, and Marty never grasped the red stitching and horsehide again.

Hard Time

I went on to art school and left the corner for other friends. Years later I read in a book on the Boston Irish Mafia that Chico had become one of the smartest sports bookies in New England, had amassed millions in cash, which he secreted in a number of safe deposit boxes, and was continually plagued by both the FBI and mobsters, until he died of the Big C. Jimmy, another street corner friend, who had spent some "hard time," finally gave it up and went into the witness protection plan, emerging occasionally to attend the wedding of one of his children.

Cub Reporter

While at art school I worked for the Boston Record-American as a copy boy and later as a cub reporter. Joel Ostroff, one of my pals at Roxbury Memorial High had an in with the paper because his father was one of the photographers. These were the days of speed graphic cameras and flashbulbs that popped. One day one of the copy boys didn't show up and Joel called to ask if I was interested. It turned into a job and I stayed with it through my art school years. As a copy boy I ran errands, worked the wire machines linked to the Associated Press and the United Press International, hung out with photographers and reporters, and learned how to read metal type upside down while the pages were being composed.

The city room was filled with rows of metal desks that were occupied by unshaven, green visored men, a Camel cigarette dangling from the lower lip, shirt sleeves rolled to the elbow, pecking, with their index fingers, at lettered keys on black Monarch typewriters that sang out with the sound of a bell at the end of every sentence.

I stayed at the newspaper during my high school and art school years. Bill McSweeny was the leading sports reporter for the Record-American. Bill was a soft spoken, bespectacled, adept writer who could bang out a story on his black Monarch with the speed of a racer. He became my mentor when I was still a teenager and has been a friend for over half a century. His good humor, fairness, talent and consideration of others was a guidance in my youth and a model in my maturity. He went on to become an advisor to President Lyndon Johnson and then the President of Occidental Petroleum International.

Courtroom Artist

The editor learned I could draw, and assigned me to cover the Willem Van Rie murder trial as a courtroom artist. Van Rie was a handsome Dutch ship captain of the "Utrecht," who was accused of hurling a woman into the sea after an argument. He had flaxen hair and a mild composure that appealed to the jury. Because the ship was from Holland the story got international attention.

I attended the trial every day at Suffolk Superior Court in Boston and several of my drawings depicting the ongoing court procedures appeared in editions of the Boston Record-American. Insufficient evidence, the body was never fished out of the ocean, leaned the jury to allow the sea captain to fly back to Holland.

All And Everything

I attended class in the daytime and worked the Saturday night "lobster shift" and weekends as a reporter. In the police cruising car at night I rode with a seasoned reporter and met gangsters, celebrities, saw jumpers fished out of the Mystic River with tenterhooks, met John F. Kennedy when he was a young and lanky senator, talked to Bob Cousy in the Celtics dressing room, listened to plangent music, ate insalubrious food, became a voracious reader, read *All and Everything* by G.I. Gurdjieff, entered a world of comparative religion, became George Lockwood's apprentice in his lithography workshop located at the end of Public Alley Number 10 in downtown Boston, met Willem Nyland, a profound disciple of a great mystic, who became my spiritual teacher, and the photographer Walter Chappell who became my friend and mentor, and experienced many other things which have slipped out of memory and slid down the cracks of forgetfulness. It was an unusual college education.

November 22, 1963

The White House in Washington has had a resident psychic since the presidency of Abraham Lincoln.

Vincent Ragone had the gift of being able to see incidents that others could not. He was clean cut, in his mid-thirties, and was already advising Washington. John Fitzgerald Kennedy was the focal point of a parade in Boston just before the 1960 presidential election. Vincent Ragone was seated in the VIP area alongside the Governor of Massachusetts and the Mayor of Boston.

Kennedy stopped and greeted the VIPs. He shook hands with Vincent Ragone. Ragone smiled and greeted him as "Mr. President."

"Not yet," said Kennedy.

"I see it. You will win by a small margin."

That is what happened and Vincent Ragone was invited into the White House as a psychic advisor.

Two years later he telephoned Jackie Kennedy. "The president shouldn't go to Dallas. I've seen a black screen in Dallas." Jackie told her husband.

"I am the president. I must follow my destiny." He went, much the same as President Abraham Lincoln went to the Ford's Theatre, in April of 1865, where he was assassinated.

The next day, November 22, 1963, a bullet smashed into the president's skull while he rode in an open car in front of the Texas School Book Depository. Parts of his brain splattered from his head onto his wife's lap. Lee Harvey Oswald had pulled the trigger and within days was himself shot dead by Jack Ruby, a known gangster. I watched the first live murder on television. To this day there are questions and no clear answers.

It was the middle of a brisk autumn day. I was in a Boston restaurant when I heard the news about JFK. My food became tasteless, and my body was stunned. The pit of my stomach felt like the aftermath of a well-placed punch. The world was about to change.

The Destiny of JFK

I am in art school, working the night shift and weekends at the Boston Record-American. Five editions of the tabloid printed daily in order to report the sports and horse racing results.

John F. Kennedy is elected as the Democratic nominee for President of the United States in 1960. He is a Boston boy from a wealthy family but was born on Beale St. in Brookline in a simple wooden one-family home two hundred yards from where I live.

The nominee was returning home. I am assigned as one of the reporters covering the homecoming speech. Logan Airport is packed with well-wishers. They are anxious to hear Kennedy's tarmac speech.

I am on the tarmac in a press car with a photographer and a radio connected to the city desk. I am young, with little experience under my belt, or anywhere else. The huge crowd of Irish, Italian, Catholic, and Jewish faces in the crowd dismay me. JFK is their hero and they want him in Washington. He has become the great hope of the people.

It is an impenetrable crowd. How would I get close to the president-elect? I wouldn't. Something in me changed course and I deduce that in some nearby building members of the Kennedy clan would be waiting for embraces.

I discover his mother Rose Kennedy, a sister and cousins seated in a VIP room. I enter.

"An auspicious moment for the family and the country. Tell me how you feel. Did you expect this victory? A new page in your already crowded family album."

The answers flow and I scribble in my reporter's notebook as fast as they speak while the photographer snaps some images. I thank them and rush to the press car; phone in the story that is printed and on the streets before Kennedy's plane lands.

C. Edward Holland, a thin, distinguished, erudite man, whose grey hair is slicked back, is the editor-in-chief of the Boston Daily Record. When I return from Logan Airport to the city room, he walks me around its periphery with his arm around my shoulder. Typewriter keys are clacking and bells are ringing. Re-write men are composing stories. The continuous sound of the Associated Press and United Press International teletype machines join in the symphony of the newspaper city room.

"Your actions today were professional. When you graduate I welcome you as a staff reporter. But as a friend I advise you to stay in the art world."

He points out the dun faces of reporters and rewrite men perched before black Monarch typewriters. "The city desk is as far as you could go," said Holland. "You are destined for more. But if you decide on being a reporter after you graduate, the job is yours."

Obituary Of An Inanimate Object

Back in 1975, the Boston Globe published an obituary that indicated the beginning of a change in communications as powerful as the invention of moveable type by Gutenberg in 1450.

Typewriter Era Comes to End, Remembered and Mourned
The Smith Corona Corp., the last major U.S. typewriter manufacturer, has filed for bankruptcy.

Its clatter was the voice of the newspaper office at deadline, the typing pool at high noon and the dormitory at midnight. It was the doorway to the computer.

The typewriter was democratic. Mark Twain wrote on it. So did your older sister. If you aspired to be a writer, you took your first draft and, in a phrase that is completely meaningless today, put it through the typewriter one more time. It was also the medium of the ransom note and the anonymous threat.

The computer, with its discs and chips and operating systems and other gizmos, is mysterious and inaccessible. The typewriter had visible bolts and keys, and a ribbon and springs. The ink got on your fingers when the keys jammed, the bell sounded at the end of each line. All this was a reminder that the work of the writer is a craft, not unlike the work of the joiner and the carpenter and the watchmaker.

Embracing Reality

I saw Vincent Ragone in his nondescript apartment outside of Manhattan several times. Once I had a ticket to California in the inside pocket of my jacket. "You are travelling West," he remarked before I could even sit down.

Another time he advised me where to dig a well and how far down to go before we would strike water on a country property I had purchased in upstate New York.

Probably the most important meeting I had with this uncanny visionary was when my first wife Barbara gave her appointment to me. We had been having a rough time in our marriage but couldn't let go of one another. Vincent convinced me that the work we had to do together was over, and it was now time to release one another and move on. Somehow this conversation and his gentle demeanor reached me, and I realized that I could not cling to illusions but needed to embrace reality. Barbara and I have remained close friends for the nearly forty years since that day. Sometimes we marry women who should be our sisters rather than our wives.

Vincent slept little and at night went to children's hospitals to work and meditate on cancer kids as they slept. At the same time he attempted to balance the troubles within himself.

Public Alley Number 10

Behind Boston Police Headquarters on Boylston Street was Public Alley Number 10. George Lockwood, a young peripatetic artist, whose long silver hair fell over his right eye, opened "Impressions," a lithographic workshop for artists on the second floor of one of the loft buildings. Many of the local artists created lithographic editions of their work in this space. Public Alley Number 10 had a cleaner smell than the trafficked Boylston Street, and was flanked by loft buildings inhabited by artists and writers. You could hear the bells of the firehouse down the street. A few melancholy trees gave off the smell of green, and in winter a skin of snow covered the alley. Our footprints were evidence that we had been there.

Lockwood taught me painting at the Massachusetts College of

Art. The day I met him I knew he was different and would play an important role in my spiritual life. I was determined to be his apprentice at "Impressions." When summer edged out the school year Lockwood asked if I was still interested.

"More than ever."

Jim Forte, a sensitive music composer who ate nothing that had a face, and was a follower of a Hindu master, was the other apprentice at the workshop. We became fast friends and shared ideas about philosophy and meditation.

We were having coffee in a Harvard Square café in Cambridge one night when Jim suggested he call his friend Eduard and ask if we could visit. I had heard about Eduard, who had an ability to read one's past and see the color of auras that surround the body. I was interested. Eduard served us coffee in a dimly lit room decorated with oriental furniture and carpets. Jim and I sat opposite him. After greetings and introductions Eduard faced me and said, "Your grandfather worked with animals and in later life he was blind." I could not verify either comment as my father's father died when I was two years old. Eduard continued, "Your mother's sister had no children, everyone thought she was barren but it was the inability of her husband."

Eduard soon turned to Jim and made some comments about his life. The evening had worn on; we thanked Eduard and entered the dark Boston night.

The next day I asked my father about the profession of his father. "He was a tanner, he worked with the skins of animals."

"In his old age did he have trouble with his sight?"

"Yes, actually in his last years he became blind."

I asked my mother why my aunt never had children. "She wanted a child, but it seemed that her husband was not capable." Eduard was right regarding all his comments.

The Man Who Ate Flowers

Sarah was a tall gray-haired woman in her sixties who stood like a sapling. In my art school days I thought that was old. I met her through the Lockwoods. She had been a vegetarian for over forty years. "Isn't that difficult?" She looked at me through peaceful blue eyes and said, "Nothing is difficult if you believe it is right." She taught me a meditation and I would occasionally visit her when I needed calm and peaceful moments in my life.

During one of these visits Sarah told me of a sage she knew who wrote poems about food and only ate flowers. The smell of freshly cut apples on the kitchen table filled the room.

She said that the world could be rebuilt from the Names of God, then added, "If you have the Cloak of Faith, and do not use it, it becomes like a raincoat in the closet on a rainy day."

Chappaquiddick

George and his wife Margo, a poet, are vegetarians and follow the path of Ruhani Satsang, a spiritual group based in India, and led by the renowned Indian guru Kirpal Singh, who I met in Boston during his world tour in 1963. The Lockwoods will summer on Chappaquiddick, a small island off Martha's Vineyard on the tail of Massachusetts, later made famous when, on July 18, 1969, Mary Jo Kopechne, a twenty-nine year old teacher and political campaign specialist, drowns in a car driven into the ocean by U.S. Senator Ted Kennedy. He escapes and swims away from the underwater scene, leaving her behind.

Before leaving for the summer, Margo asks me to return Kenneth Walker's *Venture With Ideas*, to the library. I begin reading it on the streetcar home and finish in two days. I am filled with questions, and am anxious to see the tree whose fruit I can shake down.

Who is the mysterious G. in the book, and what are the hidden teachings he gave in London to the likes of C.S. Nott, A.R. Orage and other literary and artistic figures?

I am given P.D. Ouspensky's *In Search of the Miraculous*. A more tedious read, but now I know of Gurdjieff and *All and Everything, Beelzebub's Tales to His Grandson*. A door is opening.

That summer I spend a week with George and Margo in their rented Chappaquiddick cottage. There is no electricity. Fields of wildflowers, reeds, and a variety of tall grasses surround the house. It smells like the sea. We eat vegetables, drink herbal teas, read, sleep, talk of spiritual matters, and George and I make lots of drawings. I discover a large dead bird among the grass, and make a sketch that later becomes a lithograph drawn on stone. Among the flowers of sobriety, George and I became as close as honeysuckle to a fence post.

I am studying drawing and painting with George Lockwood, calligraphy and typography, anatomy and perspective drawing. The doors of my life in art are opening. There are spiritual talks with some of my art teachers, but it is George Lockwood who becomes my guide into a sacred world, where I still travel over smooth and rocky trails. George moved from Boston to the countryside in Pembroke, Massachusetts in 1968 and died of a heart attack a year later at the age of 40. Perhaps his work here was done.

Willem Nyland's Visit

A few weeks into the autumn that followed the Chappaquiddick summer George told me a man was arriving from New York to talk about the ideas of Gurdjieff. I am invited to be among the small circle of listeners that include George and Margo, the photographers Paul Caponigro, and Marie Cosindas, the artist Nina Bloom and the photographer Walter Chappell, who arrives from New York with Willem Nyland, and becomes my teacher and friend for almost forty years, until his lungs stopped working on August 8, 2000.

That night in Lockwood's apartment I hang on every breath and word that Willem Nyland speaks. I watch him attentively as he tamps his pipe, pausing occasionally to suck in smoke. At the end of the evening I feel as though I understand nothing, but have experienced a spiritual truth. I am hooked on Willem Nyland and join Paul, George and others who weekly drive from Boston to New York to attend the talks of Willem Nyland based on the ideas of G.I. Gurdjieff.

We Breathed And Remembered Ourselves

Walter Chappell was one of the most remarkable men that I met on this journey. He delivered all of his children, designed and built two houses from the ground up, moved around the country a dozen times and each time constructed a photographic darkroom. In northern California he had an outdoor bathtub in back of his house, and beneath a mountain. Submerged in water, he held conversations with the mountain and the sky. He was among the finest photographers and printers to have ever walked the planet.

When we sleep our three centers, the intellectual, emotional, and physical, separate. When Walter woke in the morning he would sit quietly on his bed allowing the three centers within him the time to fuse, as he became aware of his breath. He built a house in Wingdale, NY on a remote piece of land in the woods, a stone's throw from a rushing river where we used to bathe. Many of us from the Gurdjieff group would go to Wingdale on weekends and help Walter construct the house. We cleared land, sawed wood, put up walls and worked on ourselves. It was winter, I was in my early twenties in the Army Reserves, stationed at Fort Dix in New Jersey. During a long weekend break from my duties, I took the bus to New York and joined Walter.

We were covering the roof of the house with tiles. Row by row our bodies moved down the span of the roof in silence. We handed one another tiles and nails and always seemed to know what the other was in need of. We breathed and remembered ourselves. We hammered and remembered ourselves. When we rested we remembered ourselves. Hours folded behind us until we both looked at each other and laughed.

It was twilight and had been snowing for sometime. We were oblivious to time and weather.

Whenever we mixed mortar for any part of the structure we added musk oil, so that a gentle fragrance would be exuded when the sun shone upon that part of the building.

The Smell Of Paradise

It is told that Adam was cast down upon Nudh, a high mountain in India. He had the smell of Paradise on him, and it remained as a perfume on the trees and the earth on which he stepped. Even today the finest *oud* comes from India.

Build The House, Tear It Down

Before the Wingdale house was fully enclosed, New York State decided to run an electric line through the land in front of the house. Poles would be put up and the landscape disturbed. They took the land by eminent domain, and paid Walter a pittance. He decided not to continue and to move west. But first we would deconstruct the house. Over several weekends a number of us from the Gurdjieff group joined Walter, and razed the house that we had built. It was a strange feeling building a house and tearing it down at almost the same time. Walter packed his family, and as many possessions that would fit into his Saab, and headed toward California.

Although several years younger than the others, I felt like a member of a secret world of those who wish to know themselves. "Know Yourself, Always and Everywhere," was written in lapidary above the entrance to the ancient Pythagorean School.

Occidental

Walter, Donald, and I meet Mr. Nyland in Occidental, California where he has a group of followers. We are in his private room sitting on hand-hewn chairs. Mr Nyland greets us outside and walks us through a maze of corridors that leads to his room. His eyesight is poor, yet he walks with confidence and assuredness. Walter begins talking about ordinary matters. Mr. Nyland abruptly stops him. "Let us not waste our time. What are your questions about inner work?"

Decreasing Sobriety

On the stained yellow wall behind him scrawled in foot high block letters were the words, "decreasing sobriety." Walter Chappell's tall body dwarfed the wooden worktable in his Santa Fe studio. He parted his long grey hair in the center and wore it loose. It fell to his chest and rested above the horizontal scar, a remembrance of an earlier bout with tuberculosis. He scratched a match on the wooden beam just under the skull of the mountain lion. It was at this moment that I photographed him.

His mustache was tinged yellow from cigarette smoke. He thought of his life as scribbling on sand, and waited for seamarks to be all that remained. He had become a collector of images, and every silver image he had captured was now a part of him. An etched pain complicated his night sleep and often caused him to rest both his hands on his heart, and then trace the confiscated images of nature on his body. Sucking in smoke, he turned from the table, moved his shadow toward the door, and gazed at the dirt path. The mountain appeared as porridge, and a cold milky wind was eating the land in front of his house.

The Gurdjieffian Lessons

In the early 1960s Walter Chappell along with Paul Caponigro, Marie Cosindas, and William Clift start the Heliographers, a photographers' cooperative gallery in New York City. The space was a converted storefront on Lexington Avenue a few doors down from the loft where Willem Nyland talked about the ideas of Gurdjieff. I occasionally stayed in New York and helped Walter, a seasoned carpenter, design and build the gallery. Walter had spent a year with Frank Lloyd Wright at Taliesin.

Gurdjieff was a Greek Caucasian, a seeker of Truth, who travelled "hard roads to sacred places." From the Gobi Desert to mysterious Egypt and hidden terrains of Asia, the Caucasus, Russia, Turkey and Syria, Gurdjieff danced with dervishes, meditated with holy men and conversed through long nights with Sufi sheikhs. He emerged in Russia and then brought a teaching of self-knowledge, based on his experiences, to the West. In October of 1949 he was buried in the cemetery of Fontainebleau, outside of Paris. A stone monolith marks his grave. I once went there and introduced myself to him.

Willem Nyland's talks were salted with his personal experiences with the "ideas" as presented by Gurdjieff. Mr. Nyland sits before us in the Lexington Avenue loft, his unkempt silver hair falling over the right side of his forehead, his blue eyes like pools of peace, and his mellow, authoritative voice convincing. The tobacco stained fingers of his right hand use a small tool to tamp "Captain Black" into the bowl of his pipe. It is the end of March in 1962.

"When one facility is impaired, the others grow stronger and come to its aid," said Mr. Nyland.

He recalled what the architect/philosopher Buckminster Fuller said about the phrase, "A chain is only as strong as its weakest link."

"This statement which we accept is not true," Fuller said. "The chain is as strong as its whole; as its total strength."

"The same can be applied to man," Mr. Nyland said between tamps.

"You must grow vertically, in a different way. We are caught up in the horizontal. Every morning for two weeks wake up and try to be aware of yourself. Sit, relax, know your arm moves, you open your eyes, close your eyes. Say to yourself, I am opening my eyes, I close my eyes, I am aware that I touch my knee, I am aware that my arm moves. During the day you will recall these moments and you will see yourself. Do this for fifteen minutes each morning."

He began to speak about the necessity of relaxation. "Sit, drain your head of its thoughts. Let them flow downward, as they reach your face, relax, let your mouth fall, do not be tense, let the tension flow down through your arms, your body, always relaxing down through your legs and out your toes. By this time your upper limbs will be tense. Start the process again. It is as if your body is filled with a fluid that is receding until it goes out your toes. This is relaxing.

"You are all adults. You have a purpose in life, to yourself, as a mother, a father, a friend. You must be able to answer that you have done your best. Do not concern yourself with nonsense. Nonsense must be taken care of. Let someone else do it. Do not concern yourself with television, with bad reading, with intellectual canned food. Enough of this kind of candy. Become a serious person. Set aside time for yourself. Work at your job but leave some time for yourself. Inner work is not easy. Make an effort to be aware of yourself."

I Draw Lines

In the 1950s the American architect Frank Lloyd Wright came to Istanbul with his wife Olgivanna. They met Muzaffer Efendi (this was before he was the Halveti Jerrahi Asitane Sheikh), spent time in his bookstore in the Sahaflar Caddesi, and asked to purchase Islamic calligraphies. Wright went through stacks of them and always chose the best ones. He bypassed many, occasionally selected one, and placed it in a pile on the right of Efendi's large wooden desk. Muzaffer Efendi asked, "How do you know the best calligraphies," and he answered, "I draw lines, so I know how to look."

As they spoke Wright said he had visited the Suleymaniye Mosque, built by Mimar Sinan, one of the great Ottoman architects, but it was crowded and he would have liked to see it when no one else was there. Muzaffer Efendi reached into his jacket pocket and pulled out a key. He was the *imam* at the mosque during Ramadan. A solo visit was arranged. Wright trembled with amazement as he walked around unimpeded by the vibrations of others.

They went to the Sultan Ahmet mosque, which had been built by two of Mimar Sinan's students. Wright examined every detail. Muzaffer Efendi asked, "Could this be built today?" Wright answered, "Revive the architects from their graves, invert this dome, fill it with gold and it could possibly be done."

Wright had known the esoteric teacher Gurdjieff, who visited

Taliesin, Wright's workplace and school, and probably gained an interest in the East and Islamic calligraphy from him. Olgivanna Wright was a student of Gurdjieff and taught "the movements" at Taliesin. Gurdjieff, who travelled throughout the East, had lived for a time in the Pera district of Istanbul. When I went there in the 1970s the two elderly women who owned and cooked in a Russian restaurant off Istiklal Street, said that they remembered the enigmatic Gurdjieff.

Death Of A Bird

Willem Nyland studied with Gurdjieff and was trusted to be in his inner circle. At one point he disagreed with the way the "work" was taught at the New York Gurdjieff Foundation and disassociated himself from them. I remained with him.

On weekends we drove to Mr. Nyland's property on Gage Hill in Brewster, NY to gather in a large group for spiritual and physical work, listen to music, share deep talk, and practice the "movements," a conscious dance based on dervish movements in *zikr* circles that Gurdjieff had witnessed during his travels. Ruthie, a short emotional girl with straight brown hair, taught the "movements."

We lined up in even rows in the barn, trying to be aware and listen to the sound of the piano as it guided us through the steps. Being tall I was in the back row next to Walter. Until the beginners got the hang of it we all appeared like insects on the barn floor going in all directions. It took immense concentration and many months of practice to gain the experience of "harmony, breathing and consciousness" in the "movements." Many esoteric schools in the past taught a form of movement or dance to balance the occupation of the mind.

After a late-night coffee we drive the long road back to Boston, stopping once on the Berlin Turnpike in Connecticut for another cup and arrive in the early hours of Monday. The car was filled with artists so we talked about art, poetry, life and the harmonious development of man.

We build a music room over the barn, work on the land, cook and eat meals on large wooden family tables that we constructed. When the music room was completed, Donald, Walter, Paul, Bruce, George, Bill and I carry the black grand piano up the dirt hill, raise it with pulleys to the barn floor and place it in a corner.

"You look like a huge centipede," observes Willem Nyland.

That evening we all sit on the floor of the new music room and listen as Mr. Nyland improvises on the piano. He jumps octaves, manipulates melodies, and strikes notes that correspond with the sacred places in our bodies. At the end we sip French Armagnac, as Gurdjieff had done, and drink bitter coffee from tin cups.

Although we all lived as ordinary people, these times of awareness introduced a sacred aspect into our lives.

I reported to Mr. Nyland that I had found a dead bird at the entrance to the men's sleeping room.

"Go and bury it. Think of it as yourself as you place it in the ground."

I dig a hole about a foot and a half deep with a blue trowel. The bird is lying by my right side. Silent, motionless.

My body wrapped in a white cloth is lowered into a dark earth pit. My face is turned toward Makkah. Breath no longer nourishes any part of my physical being.

I cradle the still bird in my hands and gently place it in the hole. The head falls to the side and its pale yellow beak points towards the southeast.

Wood is arranged about my corpse and earth is shoveled to fill the cold, black hole. There is a hollow sound of finality and promise.

I cover the bird with earth and pat it down with the back of the trowel.

Men are repeating the Name of Allah over my grave.

The Way To Rest Is To Change Your Activity

Donald and I are scrunched in a crawl space under a building trying to fix some plumbing. We have a difficult time manipulating our bodies so as to turn the pipes with our wrenches. We gasp and finally rest. Walter comes by. We explain our problem. "If one cannot do it, and two cannot do it, then you call another." He squeezes his 6'3" body under the floorboards with us and we become a human pretzel. Somehow the three of us in this incredible position manage to open the valve. The work must be done.

Another time my task is to chop down a tree with an axe. The work is tiring, the day hot, and I am not succeeding. Bruce comes by and sees me sitting on a large rock.

"The tree is not complying with the demands of my axe. I am resting and thinking about it."

He brings a large two-man bow saw. We begin the rhythmic dance of sawing down the tree. In between heavy breaths Bruce whispers, "The way to rest is to change your activity."

This was advice I have used my entire life.

Tired, with earth-stained hands and a glow in our eyes we all retire to the music room as the sun disappears yet again. We are drinking coffee from our flower-patterned tin cups when Mr. Nyland appears and begins to talk of Gurdjieff in a solemn tone. As he speaks he unfolds a cloth revealing a death mask of Gurdjieff. We are all stunned. The room falls into a zone of silence and has a smell of adrenaline.

I moved from Boston to New York. Along with my daily routine as a fledgling New York graphic designer, this was how I spent my time between the ages of nineteen and twenty-six.

Bob Dylan's Dream

It was the 1960s. A gruff-voiced young folk singer who scribbled his own songs drifted to New York from Hibbing, Minnesota. Bob Dylan quickly became the voice of a dissident generation, and no one realized at the time that he would become one of the greatest poets of our time.

It was the time of the Beatles, Bob Marley, fast lanes and drugs that led to the early demise of many young musical talents.

Dylan's first major concert was at New York's Town Hall on April 12th, 1963. I went with artist Tony Price and poet Peter Zett, two of the Greenwich Village attendees to the Gurdjieff talks. Tony was into *The Book of Urantia* and other esoteric readings that were mind expanding. Peter wrote songs for the Grateful Dead, deep poems that would have made the poet Hart Crane cry, and shared his time between New York's lower east side and a Buddhist monastery in Thailand. Years later he became a farmer of mind-altering plants in the California hills.

Dylan's manager Albert Grossman was standing in front of Town Hall "papering the house," so the media would review the event.

Finally this skinny kid wearing jeans, a neck brace harmonica, and carrying a simple guitar meanders onto the stage, and without a word begins the cacophonic singing of what would turn out to be some of the great folk songs in history. Within minutes *Hard Rain, Highway 51, Bob Dylan's Dream, Blowin' in the Wind* and rambling talk about Dylan's hospital visit to Woodie Guthrie mesmerized the audience. Town Hall tasted of adrenaline. He told our story in poem and song. We were the rebels. The dissidents under thirty who did not want to participate in the Vietnam war or be like our parents. Bob Dylan gave voice to the anti-Vietnam war movement. After 50 years on stage, the rambling road a long ribbon trailing him, he is perhaps the greatest entertainer of our century, and has my vote for the Nobel Prize for Literature.

John Hammond Jr. is probably the best white blues singer ever. In the early sixties he had a house on MacDougal Street in the heart of Greenwich Village. He was a tall, good looking young man who wore cowboy boots and spoke with a stutter. One night a bunch of us found ourselves at Hammond's house consuming pot and pizza. When the joint reached me I declined. Mary Mary, a beautiful long haired blonde and the subject of Dylan's song "*Just Like A Woman*," looked over to me and said, "Don't worry you will." She was right.

Later that evening Hammond picked up his guitar, sat on a high stool, closed his eyes and sang the blues for hours. Besides his authoritative voice, the remarkable thing was that in all those hours of singing, he did not stutter once.

Tomato Soup

One of my own drawings is taped on a broken plastered wall of my room on 88th Street and Amsterdam Avenue. The room could have told stories, but for now it protected me from the brisk winds and rains of autumn in New York. It was an "affordable" room with a lock on the door to keep out the junkies, would be artists, musicians with their *ganga*, and mid-western women who ran out of money in their quest for a job or a taste of fame in the Big Apple.

It was my first residence in New York City. The bathroom was down the hall. The one window looked out to the street four floors below. A landlord designate came to the door every week to collect the rent. My job was to get a job, and every morning I went to the coffee shop on the corner and scanned the help wanted page for a position in graphic design. Sometimes my funds were really low and I would order a cup of hot water, stir in some ketchup and call it a tomato soup dinner.

Eagle had the room two down from mine. He drew charcoal portraits on Sixth Avenue in Greenwich Village. I never knew his real name or his story. He was a middle-aged black man who made his bones on the street, and took me under his wing at the residence.

In Movement There Is Blessing

I paced the streets of New York, used public telephone boxes in the back rooms of bank lobbys to make appointments with art directors until I finally landed a job in a small studio for fifty-five dollars a week. I stayed there just long enough to learn the language of the design studio and moved to a better job. A month was long enough before changing jobs and becoming assistant art director of a small magazine. The publication folded in two months' time, and I went back to the streets.

Lou Dorfsman was to graphic designers what Daniel Day Lewis is to actors. Dorfsman is the art director of CBS. To art students he is a legend and to the industry a reference. CBS was located at 485 Madison Avenue and I was determined to have Dorfsman look at my portfolio. His secretary was a pleasant, matronly woman who took a liking to this naive kid. "I'm sorry, Mr. Dorfsman is already in his office and won't see you today."

"When does he arrive?"

"He takes the train from Long Island and gets into Grand Central Station at 8:45 am, walks from there and is at the office at 9 a.m."

"I'll be here tomorrow."

The next day at 8:45 a.m., I am sitting in front of his secretary. Dorfsman enters, glances at his pink slipped telephone messages, glances at me and continues walking to his office.

"He won't see you today."

"Okay, I will be here tomorrow."

The next day, same time, same sequence. Dorfsman glances at his

messages, then at me and continues to his office.
"Sorry, he won't see you today."
"That's okay, I will be here tomorrow."
This identical scenario occurred each day for two weeks until finally Dorfsman arrives, glances at his messages, glances at me, begins to walk to his office, looks back and says, "What are you doing here kid?"
"You are known as the best graphic designer. I want to show you my portfolio, and I am going to be here every day until either you die or I die."
"Okay, okay. Come into my office."
I trail him down the long corridor and enter his office. The cream-colored walls are covered with design awards. He looks at my portfolio. I felt like I am an art student showing Pablo Picasso my drawings.
"What do you want?"
"To work with you and learn from you."
We agree on a price. One hundred and ten dollars a week. I would have worked for free.
"When do you want to start?"
I take off my coat. "Right now."

Dorfsman takes me upstairs and puts me in the care of Peter Bradford, a seasoned designer who later becomes a friend and colleague. So began my career as a New York graphic designer. Years later I found out that Dorfsman began every conference and university lecture he gave with this story.

There were many fine designers working for Lou. He saw me one morning and asked, "Where were you? I was looking for you at 9:30 last night." Then he answered his own question, "You probably went home at six. You have a normal life."

Years later soon after my son Nuri was born I met Lou on Sixth Avenue. I was eager to share that I had a son.

"I don't know my children. I left for work before they were

awake and came home long after they were asleep. For sixteen years I barely saw them."

The New York minute takes away a lifetime.

It was difficult to leave CBS and Lou, but this was a business that you had to change jobs in order to advance. The Arabic saying, "*fi'l haraka baraka*," (in movement there is blessing), applied. A year later, after soaking up more design knowledge than I received in four years of art school, I was told of an assistant art director position available at the esteemed magazine *Architectural Forum*. I took it and worked for the art director Paul Grotz for another year. The large format heavily pictorial *Holiday* magazine was next. Len Jossel the art director, made me associate art director with my own office, and taught me the fine art of magazine production.

Il Est Mort

President Nixon was making a mess of America. My friend David Lyle was taking his family out of Manhattan and transplanting them in a small village in the south of France. I decided to join them. I gave all my books and clothes away, told some friends I was leaving my apartment and dragging a bag on wheels up 91st toward the south of France, I threw the key to 5B high in the air and didn't look back.

After a long ocean voyage that took us to Naples, we boarded trucks loaded with all our possessions and drove to Entrecasteaux. My room was a cave on the edge of a farm called Les Breguieres. Its last inhabitant was a German prisoner of war. There were no traces of him and if any memories lingered on the earthen walls I could not retrieve them. I tied two ropes to ceiling hooks, looped the ends, slid a plank through them and had a shelf for clothes and books.

David Lyle had been the Foreign Articles Editor of *The Saturday*

Evening Post, a monthly magazine whose offices in the Curtis Publishing Building were one flight below *Holiday* magazine, where I was associate art director.

Becca, Sarah and Stevie were his children when he and his wife Cecily adopted an American Indian boy. None of us knew that two decades later Jamie Lyle would die driving his car too fast on a Santa Fe back road.

I pulled out old photographic slides of us all in Entrecasteaux and gave them to David. Jamie was only five when he played among Van Gogh trees and blue-armed French farmers with shirt-sleeve tans, under a steel-blue mare's tail sky.

I mostly worked on the land, read and rode a motorbike to nearby cities. At night I did my best to avoid scorpions and sleeping spiders that also inhabited my cave.

"*Il Est Mort*!" We saw the news in Le Monde. Bobby Kennedy had been shot and killed in Los Angeles.

It was May 1968 and a strike hit the whole of France. Transportation was snail-paced. I decided to go to Paris. Between hitchhiking through a dark night and luckily finding a bus, the Eiffel Tower appeared at dawn. I took a room with a wash-basin and a shared toilet down the hall in a small hotel on the Isle St. Louis, for eleven francs. After a few hours sleep I wander the city. It begins to rain. One of those famous Paris rains where everything is soaked. I don't know why but I am shaken to the bone by the news of Bobby Kennedy's assassination. Was America coming apart at the seams? I buy a light raincoat and a newspaper. His death shouts from the first page. Rain soaked, I sit on a bench in the Tuileries and read the story. It feels like a punch in the chest. I fold the masthead page and force it between my sock and the sole of my shoe where a hole the size of a quarter has worn through the leather, and continue walking in no particular direction.

Lunch With Krishnamurti

I carried thoughts of Bobby Kennedy's assassination like an extra book in my stuffed backpack. From Paris I took the train through green mountains, and fields of cows grazing under a ceiling of white billowing clouds, to Gstaad in Switzerland, to attend the summer talks of Krishnamurti, that were annually held in Saanen.

Each morning several hundred followers of Krishnamurti's philosophy crowded the huge tent set up in a field in Saanen. It was a mixed crowd, but mostly Europeans and some Americans from the two coasts. Musicians, artists, poets, Gurdjieffians, and students of yoga were among the audience.

A single wooden chair was placed in the center of a platform, where Krishnamurti, immaculately dressed in slacks and a shirt open at the collar, shoes glowing (he shined them himself daily), spoke on the condition of man in relationship to himself and the universe.

I knew some of the inner circle and was invited to a private lunch with Krishnamurti. He was staying in an immense chalet on the same mountain where I had a small room in a farmhouse. After lunch he suggested we walk a wooded path on the mountainside. There was a fresh, clean smell to the air. It was mostly a quiet walk, feeling the presence of one another among the trees and clean air. His lean, brown body floated along the earthen path. Looking toward the sky he interrupted the silence.

"Sir, have you ever taken the time to look at the clouds?"

Later, as I walked down the trodden path to the village below, I mused as to how such a simple statement could contain an entire philosophy. Books have been written about the essence of this statement.

Willy Fleckhaus's Pages

It was a long walk from my tiny corner office down the corridor to Allen Hurlburt's large office at *Look* magazine. I had to pass a number of editors as well as Will Hopkins' office that was next to the art department housing the paste-up and mechanical artists who took our designs and made them camera-ready. Today all this is done by computer, but in the 1970s a magazine was designed and produced manually. An illustrator's representative had told me about the *Look* position and I made an appointment to show my work. *Look* and *Life* were the two most important pictorial magazines in the world. Will Hopkins, who had spent two years in Germany working with Willy Fleckhaus, possibly the best editorial art director to have ever danced on the planet, was being groomed for the position of *Look's* art director when Hurlburt retired. Will and I were the only two designers *Look* had hired in ten years. Will was a tall mustached man who wore Edwardian suits and was to emerge as one of the best magazine designers in the world. I was pleased to not only work with him but also later, after *Look* folded, become his partner in a New York design studio.

Although Will had worked directly with Fleckhaus, I was also greatly influenced by the Munich master and consider him one of my design teachers. Fleckhaus designed *twen* magazine, a monthly German publication directed toward young people before they hit thirty. Each month on the day of publication, I would be at Rizzoli bookstore to purchase my copy. I ran to my office at *Holiday* magazine and browsed the issue gleaning design moments. Then I took sheets of tracing paper and carefully traced the layouts on every page so I understood how Fleckhaus cropped pictures and used type. He illuminated words, became my teacher and I became a better editorial designer because of him. I never had lunch with him.

Songs From A Room

In 1969 I was the art director of Columbia Records, a division of CBS and happened to be in San Francisco when Johnny Cash was giving a concert at San Quentin Prison, and was invited backstage. The concert was being recorded and would later be released. Cash was a tall man, dressed in black, with his guitar slung over his shoulder like an AK47, and had the presence of a rebel onstage. There were two thousand prisoners in the audience. When he sang the lyrics, "I shot a man in Reno, just to watch him die," the entire audience jumped up, applauded, hooted and yelled in approval. So much for rehabilitation.

Leonard Cohen wanted an image of himself as an old man on the cover of his second album, *Songs From a Room*. We discussed how to create this phenomenon in my office at Black Rock, the CBS building on West 53rd Street. We agreed that I would work on the cover, and show Leonard a mock-up in a few days. But first we went to the street and took a number of photographs of Leonard in his blue raincoat and Greek fisherman's cap.

I selected one of the prints, sent it out for a photostat to the size I envisioned for the cover, and asked that a high contrast print be made that dropped out all of the gray tones. I prepared a dummy cover with type and positioned the image in a small square surrounded by a lot of white space. With the gray tones eliminated, Cohen looked older. I wanted to try one more cover. I sent the high contrast print out and asked for it to be made into a mezzotint. The print came back with some of the small dots of the mezzotint print seeming to erode the image. Leonard Cohen looked like an old man.

When he came to my office the next day he placed an empty black film canister containing the finest grass on my desk. I showed him the high contrast cover. He liked it but still wanted to look older. I showed him the mezzotint cover and he said, "That's it, you did it." The cover was exhibited in the New York

Art Director's Club annual show of the best designs.

A few years later a Roberta Flack album cover I designed for Atlantic Records was chosen as one of the thousand best cover designs, and published in a book by Taschen.

Roshi's Stick

The crack of a flat stick on my right shoulder brought me out of the imagined scenes of imagined dreams that I had somehow slid into. I sat facing the white wall in the *zendo* on East 68th Street in New York City and came to a moment of consciousness as the Roshi passed to the next meditator.

I wanted to avoid living a quotidian life and found the awakening moments in *seshin* and *zen* practice helpful. Henry David Thoreau said it well in *Civil Disobedience*, "Most men lead lives of quiet desperation..." I was a seeker who at times was unaware of what was sought. All doors could be entered, meditations practiced, drugs taken, relationships experienced, gurus, swamis, roshis, and Sufi sheikhs embraced. The tools of my search were poetry, painting, photography, writing, and filmmaking. I knew the road was travelled by many and in those days I had a burning desire to be one of those who arrived.

Mevlana Rumi wrote,

You've only been here a few days
And you've become so friendly with life.
I can't even talk about death anymore.
You're on the journey home
And your donkey has fallen asleep
In the middle of the road!

Rumi understood that the signs were on the horizons, but the secrets were within one's self. The spiritual energy from the East had arrived and we embraced many paths and were multi-disciplined.

Rumi wrote, "Be as you appear, Appear as you are."

A Sufi sheikh was asked how he became a sheikh. "I was walking in my village, by the open window of my neighbor I heard my name mentioned. The men inside were saying that I was trustworthy, a good friend, and that whenever they were with me they learned something, and were always reminded of Allah by my speech and actions. They also said that they would be honored to trust me in the teaching of their children. In that moment I decided that I should be what they saw, and soon became a sheikh."

Zen meditation on Thursday, *zikr* on Saturday, a lecture on Hinduism, the Gurdjieff work or Tibetan Buddhism on Monday, all this and more dotted my calendar for the week, and somehow I shoehorned a job or some freelance work into the day.

Spiritual Rain

I met a lot of spiritual teachers. I was fortunate enough to be in the West at the time that the spiritual energy from the East was being transferred to the West and teachers from various paths were flocking to the states. I was a player in the heart of it all in New York City. Buddhists, Sufis, Hindu gurus, Yoga masters, Rabbis, Jungians and Tibetan monks fell upon the West like a spiritual rain that flooded our hearts and minds. We gave them our attention and they poured out teachings from the East that altered our consciousness and opened the eyes of our hearts.

I was involved for many years with Pir Vilayat Khan and the Sufi teachings as presented by his father Hazrat Inayat Khan. Pir Vilayat led meditations in the Swiss Alps where we did personal retreats. Once I took him to Konya to meet Mevlana, and then to Istanbul to see Sheikh Muzaffer. They got along fine. As if they were governors of different states. Muzaffer Efendi used to say, "I like Pir Vilayat. He prepares people for me."

My life was more spiritual than physical. I felt trapped in a physical body and was learning to adjust to living in it while still maintaining my spirituality.

Lama Chimi's Paper

I am in the mountains in Chamonix at a Sufi camp. Large white tents, in which we slept, ate, meditated, and listened to discourses, dot the mountain. Among the teachers is a Tibetan named Lama Chimi. He gave a talk that was interesting enough, although I wasn't overly excited about it. Afterwards, I approach him. "I would like to speak with you if you don't mind."

"So, you thought my talk was good?"

"Actually, I wasn't that moved by it. I thought it was interesting."

"Then why do you want to talk with me?"

"Because I watched as you folded the piece of paper at the end of your talk, saw that you were totally conscious in folding the paper, and that's what I want to know about."

He said, "Come along. I've had students for years that have never seen that."

We sat on two large rocks on the side of the mountain and could almost touch the clouds. He taught me a breathing exercise and how to be present to the moment.

After so many years of input and output of information, of teachers, of masters, sheikhs, gurus, of interest in spiritual work, I did not think I would sit on a rock in the wilderness and ask someone if they would teach me how to fold a piece of paper.

The House Of Inayat Khan

Pir Vilayat Khan is sitting in Fazil Manzil, his father's house in Paris. It is the 1960s. I have known him a long time because he stayed at my house whenever he came to New York. He was living in a cell-like room at the Tudor Hotel in New York, and giving lectures to middle-aged women with some spiritual interest, when we were introduced. I was living at the coach house on 84th street and insisted he come and live with me. This was the beginning of our relationship and my deep interest in Sufism. Each morning before dawn we sat in meditation as he taught me how to invoke the Name of Allah. His following grew. He was a master of meditation and introduced a generation of young seekers to the Sufi path established in the West by his father.

We are in the prayer room of his father Hazrat Inayat Khan who had died long before but had breathed *zikr* and prayed in this room, and his *baraka* permeates the space. Pir Vilayat feels something stir in him and says, "I've got to initiate you, I have to, my father is telling me to.... "and he initiates me as a sheikh in the Chishti Sufi Order. Then he says, " Shamsuddin, that's the name that's coming to me."

He gave me that name and I spent a year or more without ever using it because I felt that it was ominous and something I had to grow into. A spiritual name is like a Sufi cloak. It never fits you. It's always too big and you have to grow into it, because it doesn't shrink.

A Meditation From Hazrat Inayat Khan

The Closing of the Gates meditation is done just before going to sleep and the first thing in the morning.

1. Take a deep breath–close ears (with fingers)–hold breath five seconds only–listen to the sound HU.
2. Close eyes after deep breath–see the Universal Light, the beauty of life.
3. Close nostrils after deep breath–breathe through right nostril–hold one minute–absorb total of life–fragrance of life.

4. Close mouth–symbol of peace–open mouth–sorrow, destruction. Mouth speaks the Name of God–lips closed retains Name. Close all gates–seated on left heel which closes the anus, experience the light and sound of the entire universe. Breathe three times.

Basic Three Day Retreat Schedule

A – frame wooden structures that can house one person pepper the side of the mountain at Chamonix. They are used for three–day retreats.

Six–seven a.m. Purification–five times each breath.

Inhale through the nose, exhale through the nose–feel the magnetic energy of the planet enter you through the soles of the feet.

Water–Inhale through the nose, exhale through mouth with closed lips pressing the air through as if it rains upon you–shake your hands by your side.

Fire–Inhale through the mouth with closed lips feeling the coolness of the air as it goes down and fans the flames of your heart *chakra*. Exhale through the nose sending light through the heart *chakra* and *sahasrahar*.

Air–Inhale through the mouth, exhale through the mouth. As you inhale, arms outstretched, (disintegrate), allowing all the poisons in your system to depart through all your pores. As you exhale, move arms towards your heart center and breathe in new energy through all your pores.

Filtering practice with the sun–drinking in the sun's energy.

Meditation on immaculate state-image of snow, water glistening in sunlight, state of being before becoming. Immaculate source of life flowing into you.

Seven–eight a.m. Rest.

Eight–nine a.m. Meditation on Light. Surround yourself with a protective shroud of Light.

Nine–eleven a.m. Repetitions of the Names of Allah.

1. Say aloud
2. Think the word
3. Think the meaning

Each step is repeated 101 times.

Ya Hu–God Absolute

Ya Alim–Omniscience

Ya Kadir–Power of God in the heart-to all cells of the body.

Ya Adhim–Divine Glory

Eleven–three p.m. Rest

Three–four p.m. *Zikr*

Five-six p.m. Buddhist meditation. Meditate on the Buddha rising above all things, thoughts, emotions while watching yourself in the world from a high seat.

Six–eight p.m. Rest

Eight–ten p.m. Gates to the Head meditation. Three times. Then meditate anyway you are led. Do this exercise three times.

The third day of the retreat introduces a slight variation.

Four–five a.m. Meditate on the Masters

Five–six a.m. Rest

Six–eight a.m. Purification

Eight–nine a.m. Rest

Nine–eleven a.m. Meditate on Light

Eleven–twelve p.m. Rest

Twelve–two p.m.-Repetition of the Names of Allah

Two–three p.m. Rest

Three-five p.m. *Zikr*

Five–six p.m. Rest

Six–eight p.m. Buddhist meditation

Eight–nine p.m. Rest

Nine–eleven p.m. Gates meditation

Note to the reader. This was the retreat schedule at the Sufi Camp of Pir Vilayat Khan held during the summer in the 1970s in Chamonix.

Muktananda's Flying Lessons

Swami Muktananda was a guru from India who looked like a jazz saxophone player. He took me out of my body, gave me flying lessons and showed me different realms within the universe.

This was in upstate New York in a place called Big Indian. A friend of mine, Donald Harrison had written me some postcards from Swami Muktananda's *ashram* in Ganeshpuri, India. When he returned to New York he phoned me, "You know Swami Muktananda is here." I said, "Okay."

"Come and see Muktananda, we're going to Big Indian." There was an antique dealer in New York named Albert Rudolph, also known as Swami Rudrananda, who had gone to India many years before and was the disciple of Swami Nityananda, the teacher of Muktananda. Big Indian was Rudi's *ashram* in upstate New York. Years later he would die when the small plane he was in crashed into the side of a mountain.

Muktananda was going to stay in New York for some time but Donald kept insisting that I go right away. "No, I think I'm not going to go, you can borrow my car if you want. You can drive to Rudi's *ashram*."

Finally my resistance was broken. Donald and my wife Barbara convinced me to go. She didn't want me around because we were having problems and finally I said, "Okay, all right I'll go," and I drove with him into the mountains. We came to the parking lot at Big Indian. Muktananda was walking below and Donald said, "Here he is, here he is, let's go."

Donald bowed down, touched the swami's feet, and I thought, "God what's happened to my friend?" So, I did a hesitant *namaste*, put my palms together greeting him, and thought that was sufficient.

He looked like the jazz musician Thelonious Monk. This dark

guy with a funny hand-woven colorful hat, and a swagger stick was meandering. Later we found that there was no place for us to sleep so we slept on the floor of the meditation room. About three in the morning people are mumbling and moving around and jostling one another and I said, "What's going on? We can't sleep."

Someone said, "Muktananda promised to meditate with us, where is he?" He never showed up and it was time for breakfast. We had breakfast in a large hall with a lot of people. When we came out Muktananda was standing there and Donald said to him, "This is my friend from New York." Swami Muktananda grabbed my arm at the forearm, greeted me, kept holding my arm as he spoke, and then left for a walk. Professor Jain, Multi, Draupadi and a few others of his Indian entourage always shadowed his steps.

He strolled to the big lawn where people were doing *Tai Chi* or *Qigong*. He observed them and every once in a while he sort of looked back at me, but I was a good distance, maybe thirty yards away. When he looked at me I thought, "You just stay there and I'm going to stay here and things will be okay."

He had left something in me that I wasn't aware of when he had held my arm. I realized there was something happening between us. Then, without another glance, he strode to his room for a rest. I was outside sitting on some wooden steps, enjoying the sunshine and feeling good when Donald came and said, "I was just inside with Muktananda, there are a few people there, you want to go in and sit next to him?" I said, "Not particularly. I'm happy here, the sun is shining I'm feeling okay."

He went again and then came back ten minutes later and said, "He wants to see you." I said, "Come on, I'm…" He said, "Come on guy." So, I took my shoes off and entered the room with an undefined trepidation. I sat behind about eleven people who were sitting on the floor in front of me. Muktananda was sitting on a bed, cross-legged facing everyone. He was talking, answering questions and then all of a sudden — he looked at me, he didn't say anything, didn't touch me but I felt another presence in my body. I felt like he was there with me. I had known other people could fit into my body through my thoughts and dreams, but this was different, Muktananda was part of the space I had always considered my own.

I told myself that it was okay and soon I began feeling as if I was in deep meditation. So, I sat there, it was peaceful and calm, my eyes were partly closed, and I was half listening when somebody asked Muktananda, "How does one recognize one's guru?" He answered, "When the time is right you will know." For example, I don't even know his name," pointing to me. "He's never talked to me or asked me a question yet I know he's my disciple and he knows I am his guru." It went on and on like this and all the questions were answered and by then I was in a meditative state. I couldn't even move on my own. At one point I reflected that I could die like this. I accepted, let go of my thoughts, and entered even deeper into the meditative state.

"Take him," he said to my friend Donald, "Take him outside, put him near my meditation couch and sit him there." Donald had to help me stand and walk me to the outside room where I sat in meditation. Suddenly while seated I was doing the dance of Shiva with my arms, and entering *mudras* that I had never seen before.

I was travelling further and further outside of my body and at a certain point my hands dropped into mid-air. I wasn't there anymore but felt there was a tiny reference of breath that existed, giving me the confidence that I could return. I was out there, seeing colors that unfolded before me and beautiful scenes, Buddha and Christ and other amazing beings. I glanced to my side and Muktananda was flying next to me.

After some time, I have no idea how long, but I'm told later that it was over an hour and a half, a cyclone entered my chest and with a thud and a jolt I was in my body again.

Prior to that I heard music a long distance away. As if it emerged from deep in the woods. I saw fifteen or twenty people dancing and singing just ten feet away. Muktananda was standing next to me, put his hand on my head and I grabbed his leg and hugged his leg as he lifted me up. He was eating a banana, took half the banana and gave it to me and said, "Eat this." I ate, and then he took a piece and gave it to Donald saying, "That's for bringing him here."

"You've just been reborn, we are born twice. Once from the semen of our father and once from the grace of the *guru*." Then Muktananda strolled to his room.

"I want to come with you."

"No, not necessary, you will never lose what you've just been given, no matter what happens in your life, it's yours. It doesn't belong to anyone else, it is yours."

"Yes, but can I come in while you're resting and hold your big toe?"

"No, it's not necessary you're okay."

So, he entered his room and that was the beginning of my adventure with Muktananda that lasted for several years.

On Monday morning at dawn I am at Rudi's meditation hall on East 10th Street in New York. Muktananda placed me there. I sit in meditation for seven hours until Donald takes me upstairs to sit next to the swami. For the next month my life is occupied by dawn and evening meditations with Muktananda while I attend my day job as a New York art director.

He gave me a pair of his shoes before he departed to India. A special gift, as the feet of the *guru* are considered holy.

I held meditation classes in my house at 502 East 84th. The first years were good. The meditations were deep and several people came to the studio each week to play music, chant the *Guru Gita,* (Song of the Guru) read from Muktananda's book *Chitshakti Vilas,* drink *chai* and soak in the well-being that was surrounded by the energy of the *guru*.

During this time several people went to India and returned with a permission to teach meditation in the name of the *guru*. This dissipated our group and caused uneasiness within me. Of course I only saw from my limited point of view and didn't know the deeper meaning of Muktananda's intentions of "stirring the pot." My ego edged to the foreground of my being and soon after finding the path to Sufism, I began a cat and mouse game that finally ended with my leaving Muktananda. This was difficult to do as I loved him dearly, but all things are written, a few erased, and one is left with a palimpsest of a soul that has taken the shape of a temporary body.

I never got to India. Muktananda kept writing me saying, "Why don't you come?" Every time I tried to go for some reason I would get sick, and never understood why, but I never went, and he once said at a dawn meditation, "You're like my son and you didn't visit me."

Burying A Black Dog

I was never scared. There was one time that I was returning home from a Muktananda meditation in New York and felt a sharp pain in my chest. I'm walking the street near my house pausing every ten steps to exhale the pain. At that time, Barbara and I had a black Labrador retriever, a really beautiful dog, but I didn't like dogs so much because as a child, a large dog jumped at the carriage I was in and placed a fear in me for life. But this Labrador was so gentle it was impossible not to be its friend. I made it to my house carrying this pain and fell into bed. I had just been with Muktananda the entire afternoon, came to this moment and said, "Okay, if I'm going to die, I'll die."

I either slept or entered a state, but I wasn't conscious and the black Lab stayed by me the whole time. When I opened my eyes and sat up, it was thumping its tail on the floor. I felt completely renewed. The dog had become my friend and when she died of old age I dug a grave on a rainy day and buried her myself on the country property of a friend.

Tolstoy's Bicycle

When I heard that Tolstoy took his first cycling lesson at the age of sixty-four, I decided at seventy-three I could learn to swim. Years earlier I had almost drowned in a friend's swimming pool in Woodstock, NY. It was the deep end. I always feared the deep end, had slipped under the surface, panicked because I could not swim, bobbed up and down several times gasping for air, until Barbara ran to the pool from the kitchen and threw me a rubber float. Barely breathing, I grabbed for it and with what felt like my last breath, hoisted myself onto its flat surface.

I took swimming lessons in Istanbul from a woman who speaks no English. But if Tolstoy can ride a bicycle, I could swim. By the end of the tenth lesson I could swim the length of the pool, but still fear being in water that is above my head.

The Magician's Sleeve

Rudy Wurlitzer and I met in a lunch line at a Muktananda retreat in New York. While in California a few months before, Richard Weschler, a mutual friend, gave me Rudy's name and number and told me to contact him. Either I was shy or procrastinating but I never made the call. As we waited for our brown rice and vegetables Rudy and I struck up a conversation. When he told me his name I reached into my wallet where I had kept Richard's paper and showed him his name and number. Rudy reached into his pocket and withdrew a paper that Richard had given him with my name and number. He hadn't used it either. We became friends, and to this day I consider Rudy Wurlitzer my friend and teacher. He is one of the best writers of our lifetime and has a magic way with words that is rare today. It's as though he pulls phrases from a magician's sleeve and has created a use for language that equals the inner octaves of music, and the palimpsest of painting.

Postcards From The Saints

In June of 1972 I have my first exhibition of drawings and watercolors at the Gotham Book Mart Gallery in New York City. The Gotham was the most famous literary bookstore in the city. Its walls were adorned with autographed photographs of such noted authors as Ernest Hemingway, F. Scott Fitzgerald, and the poets of the Beat Generation.

The exhibit coincided with the Harper and Row publication, *Year One Catalog, A Spiritual Directory for the New Age,* that I edited, and was my first of several published works.

This was about the same time that I became disturbed with the amount of junk mail stuffed into the metal mailbox with my name scratched on it, which was in the downstairs entranceway to my coach house in the city. Whenever I met a sheikh, guru, or zen roshi, I had them write a message with their own hand and sign it. Then I placed a photograph of them on a corner, printed thousands of them, and created, *Postcards from the Saints*.

I gained access to several mailing lists and sent them out randomly so that people could get a positive message along with their junk mail. Some of those included were the Tibetan teacher and author, Lama Govinda, the Sufi teacher, Pir Vilayat Khan, and Zen Buddhist and author, Alan Watts.

Dream

In October, 1980 I have a profound dream of Swami Muktananda. We are outside, talking, he says he knows why I left and that I was right to do so, and he will tell me the deeper meaning. He feels the love I am emanating to him. His eyes go deep into my soul with love and kindness. Muktananda touches my eyes and forehead and I feel *shaktipat* (spiritual energy).

Akagunduz, the Mevlevi *ney* player appears. He shows Baba Muktananda a belt that is perhaps a foot wide, with coins imbedded within it in certain places. They represent events he won in becoming the best *ney* player.

Muktananda is on a stone platform. He comes to the edge and whispers something in my right ear, then holds my head next to his and three times says something in a language I do not understand. He dies in my arms. I carry him all around. He has little weight and looks young and angelic. Some people are present and a paramedic comes. I lean on his leg while he breathes deep into Baba's mouth. Still in my arms Baba opens his eyes as if coming out of sleep but immediately closes them to show he does not want to stay. He is now weightless. Some people are preparing a place for him to lie down for I am carrying him all this while.

Death Of Fahreddin Efendi

Safer Baba and I are sitting in the garden of his house in Uskudar overlooking the Bosphorus, on a balmy Istanbul day in March 1982. We are eating watermelon and white cheese. In a soft voice he recalls the death of Fahreddin Efendi.

During his last days he said, "Don't leave me." Until the moment of death *shaitan* can be present and that is why Fahreddin Efendi, the *asitane* sheikh of the Halveti Jerrahi order of dervishes, asked not to be left alone. Safer Baba approached him and became aware of a beautiful scent so powerful that it made him swoon. There were times that Fahreddin Efendi could hold back that scent. When they went to the Turkish bath together Safer Baba was aware that a beautiful scent had permeated the sheikh's undershirt.

Fahreddin Efendi looked up from his pillow and addressed Safer Baba, "Did I ever tell you that I was the *Qutb Alim*? Did I say something like that (he intimated that he had not). Safer Baba remained silent. He refused to answer.

"I did not say that. I never said that I was the *Qutb*. I only said that the *Qutb Alim* is the station over there in the Yeni Camii and I told you how to get there but I did not say I was the *Qutb*."

Fahreddin Efendi closed his eyes. When he awoke he asked Safer Baba, "When did you arrive, how long have you been here." As if Safer Baba had just arrived. This occurred a day or two before his death. He wanted Muzaffer Efendi to wash his body. Safer Baba and Kemal Baba would pour the water and Hamdi Efendi was to heat the water. He gave instructions that Safer Baba and Kemal Baba would place him in the grave and that the *wird* should be proclaimed when he was about to die. When he heard this he would know it is time. After that *Yasin* could be recited.

On the night of his death, he ate watermelon, white cheese and bread. That night Muzaffer Efendi told Safer Baba not to go home, and to stay with Fahreddin Efendi. Later Fahreddin Efendi's wife also asked him to stay. All the women of the family were present.

From across the room Safer Baba saw Fahreddin Efendi's hand raised and thought that he was calling him. He rushed over and began rubbing his swollen leg. Fahreddin Efendi opened his eyes and said. "I have put on my shoes to journey to the other world." Safer Baba didn't want to believe it, but in a few moments Fahreddin Efendi closed his eyes and began a steady heavy breathing of *Hu, Hu, Hu*. A wonderful scent was emanating from him. Safer

Baba knew the time had come and began to recite the *wird*. Safer Baba closed his eyes and repeated the *tawhid*. He was aware of movements in the room and heard many voices invoking the *tawhid*. He opened his eyes and saw Kemal Baba and Necdet Baba making *zikr*. Later he asked Kemal Baba how he knew.

"I was invoking the Name of Allah after night prayer and became aware of a beautiful scent. I immediately left home and rushed here. As I approached the *tekke* the scent got stronger, and I ran faster. The kerosene lamps around the *tekke* went out. I entered and joined the *tawhid*."

Fahreddin Efendi had passed. His eyes were open. He died on the third day of Shabban, the month of the Prophet Mohammed. The next month would be Ramadan, the month of the Believers.

They washed his body according to his own instructions and placed him for the night next to Pir Nureddin Jerrahi in the old part of the *tekke*. The funeral was on *jum'a*. It was a grand funeral with dervishes and sheikhs representing every order present. You could read pages from the "Book of Grief" on the faces of the ones who loved Fahreddin Efendi. There were three *zikr* circles. After *jum'a* prayer his body was carried back to the *tekke* and placed in the grave.

Seven years before that Friday of loss, Fahreddin Efendi ordered his own grave to be dug and covered with a stone.

Safer Baba and Kemal Baba lowered him by the ties of the shroud that were around his head, feet and waist. His body was soft. Rigor mortis had not entered. They opened the shroud to place the head facing the Ka'bah and saw that his head had already been moved in that direction. Safer Baba wanted to move the earth stones from his eyes but they were glued on. He pulled and blood came from the eyes. Muzaffer Efendi shouted, "Enough! Let it be!" They closed the grave.

On the underside of the flat stone a message had been written seven years earlier in the wet cement by the gravedigger. "Please

Sheikh Efendi do not forget me in your prayers."

There was a man named Adam who loved Fahreddin Efendi very much. When he died Fahreddin Efendi placed earth from Karbala on his eyes. As he did this the dead man cried tears of blood.

The Fragrant Name

Bishr al-Hafi saw a piece of paper lying in the mud at the side of the road. His eye fell on the Divine Name written in one of the sentences. He lifted the paper, cleaned it, bought some scent, perfumed it, and placed it in a cavity of the wall of his house. That night he heard a voice say to him; "O Bishr, you have made My Name fragrant in this world and I will make yours fragrant in this world and the next."

Muzaffer Efendi reminded us many times, "Why don't you cry when you hear the Name of Allah? And if you don't cry why don't you cry because you don't cry?"

The Sacred Pen

During my first trip to Istanbul in 1972 I experienced Islam each day through all of my senses. My ears heard the call to prayer. My eyes saw beautiful calligraphies written on the walls of mosques and other buildings, and I walked amidst architecture that represented man and his Creator. Viewed carpets woven with reminders of Allah that were placed in homes. I tasted flowers and delicious foods, and meditative experiences and prayer often brought the scent of the Prophet. Beauty was part of my day and beauty reminded me of Allah. In *Phadreus* Plato wrote, "The contemplation of beauty enables the soul to grow wings." Plato describes this as being identical with love.

Calligraphers wrote the *basmala* or *ayats* from the Qur'an and kept the shavings from every reed pen. They asked their students to burn these wooden shavings to heat the water used to wash their body when they died. The pen was sacred, and there existed an *adab* for the tools one used in writing the Name of Allah.

On the back of a tea-stained envelope I wrote:

Beneath the skin of dreams
And unkept promises lives love,
Like a word in a muffled prayer,
A poet's pen lost among distant thoughts.

Embracing Islam

The bus journey from Konya to Istanbul over two-lane blacktop takes twelve hours and passes through a night whose landscape of darkness is opened by yellow headlights. In Istanbul I make my way to Nezih's house in Uskudar.

The sheikh owned a religious bookstore on Sahaflar Caddesi, at the fringe of the bookseller's corner in the covered bazaar. I arrived in the late afternoon and he told his *khalifa*, "Take Shems, give him some dinner and bring him to the *tekke* tonight." Safer Baba brought me to his house and later we went to the *tekke*. As I entered the *sohbet* room, Sheikh Muzaffer stood, raised his arms and said something in Turkish.

I found out what he said on a bus, ten years later. Some dervishes were travelling and Zulfu Baba turned to me and said, "Have you ever wondered why you've been accepted here, and you've been one of us since the day you walked into the *tekke*, and that you are our brother?"

No one at the *tekke* ever asked me about my profession. They didn't know my last name they didn't care what my position was in life.

I said, "I guess I was curious for a while."

"When you entered, Sheikh Muzaffer stood up and announced, 'This is our brother. You will treat him as such. He is one of us.'"

I was working in New York City as an art director and designer and every time I had a vacation I would hightail it to Istanbul. Sometimes I travelled to Konya to visit Mevlana Rumi and Mevlevi Sheikh Suleyman Dede, but I would always go to Istanbul to be with Sheikh Muzaffer. I was planting seeds whose fruit would be Islam.

After three years, I realized that this door to Sufism was not going to open any further unless I embraced Islam. I understood that the natural evolution of Sufism came through Islam and realized that there were no Sufis who were not Muslims. To be a Muslim doesn't mean you have to be a Sufi but to be a Sufi meant you had to be a Muslim.

I felt I had learned more from Sheikh Muzaffer than any other person in my life, so I embraced Islam. I came to Islam through *tariqa* rather than *sharia*. This was the gate for many in the West. We were first drawn to the spiritual, the esoteric, and later embraced the religion. I make no distinction between Sufism and Islam. They are one.

Spiritual masters do not care who you are physically. They see something else. In a way I feel I've been blessed that I've never known what they saw. But I've had many experiences where spiritual masters see me and I'm drawn to them, and they are drawn to me, I don't know what this thing is but it's there. Perhaps my need is evident.

Rumi said: "The thirsty man seeks water but water also seeks the thirsty man."

Names and professions may be revealed later. They're not really important. What's important is the essence of your heart, the light that comes through your eyes, something where someone recognizes that there's something behind that façade that they're viewing.

Pages From A Journal, Istanbul, December, 1972

It is cold but we surround Muzaffer Efendi in a small outdoor cafe in the shadow of the Beyazit Mosque. The hot tea is endless.

"We do *zikr* to open the eyes of our heart. It is important to see with your heart eyes as well as with the eyes in your head. If you can see through your heart you will know all men, all things, you will see like a telescope with a wide lens, you could see America from here. If you only see with the eyes of your head you are no different than an animal. An animal has a head, eyes, nose, mouth, skin, and ears. It is like you except you have the ability to also see through the eyes of your heart. When you see with your heart eyes all space opens for you."

I taste the possibility of the circle widening and maps drawn for the journey to inaccessible places.

The Prophet's White Cloak

It is the middle of an Asian winter in the early seventies when Tosun Baba, Safer Baba and I drive with Sheikh Muzaffer to Uludag, a mountain above Bursa. Safer Baba is doing his *tesbih*. At ninety-nine repetitions he turns and gives me his beads. "For you," he says. We leave our car on the first level of the ferryboat and climb the metal stairs to the passenger level to enjoy the sea trip. Muzaffer Efendi grabs two empty wooden boxes, stacks them to make a table and orders four Turkish coffees. He lights a cigar and begins a *sohbet*. It was at this moment that my camera recorded what was to become a famous photograph of the sheikh. The three of us are sitting on the edge of wooden boxes listening to the words of the sheikh.

"One must never travel alone, neither in the material world or the spiritual world. One does not know what may happen. There could be sickness, hunger or even death. You have to be careful in choosing your fellow traveller. When ordinary people travel the test is easy. You should eat the same food, have interest in the same things, do not walk quicker or slower than your friend and share an interest in business.

"On a higher level the test is more difficult. You should laugh when your friend laughs and cry when your friend cries. If there is pain that pain should be shared. You are like one person. His friend is your friend and his enemy is your enemy. If he is sick you take care of him. If he is poor you help him."

At this point Efendi interrupts the *sohbet* with a story and another bitter Turkish coffee. "Uwayys Karani worked hard his entire life. He was a shepherd who carried loads on his back up mountains until his shoulders were bent from the chore. He lived with and cared for his aged mother. One hot Yemeni day he said, "I would like to go and see the Prophet Mohammed."

His mother answered, "All right. Go first to his house and if he is not there then come directly home to me. If he is there, visit him."

The journey took two months before he reached the door of the Prophet. He knocked. A woman who helped in the house opened the door and informed Uwayys that the Prophet was at the mosque but would return soon. She invited him to wait, but he told her that he had to go home to his elderly mother. He made the long journey back to the mountains of Yemen.

When the Prophet returned he saw a light on his door. He asked who had come and was told it was Uwayys Karani. Upon hearing this, the Prophet looked into the eyes of the woman who had seen Uwayys Karani. He then went to the square and called all around him and said, "Come and look into the eyes of the one who looked into the eyes of the one who saw Uwayys Karani."

When he was dying the Prophet told Hazrati Ali to give his white cloak and woolen shoes to Uwayys Karani. Hazrati Ali and

Hazrati Omar travelled the long distance to find Uwayys. Upon entering his village they asked where they might find him and were told, "Somewhere on the mountaintop." They climbed the steep mountain and found him praying. He finished his *raka'at* and began a *dua'a*. An hour passes, then another, and the visitors are agitated after such a long journey. Hazrati Omar says, "Excuse me." Uwayys turns abruptly and says, "What do you want? Why do you interrupt me?"

"The Prophet has died."

"I know this."

"He asked us to give you his shoes and cloak."

"Still you should not have interrupted me. I was asking Him to free all men from sins. He just said yes when you interrupted and broke the connection."

Uwayys Karani asked Hazrati Omar if he had ever seen the Prophet.

"Of course."

"Then describe him to me."

Omar began the description. "He was neither brown nor very white. His hair was sometimes combed over his ears and the amount of white hair in his thick beard did not exceed seventeen. He had a wide forehead and long arched eyebrows."

Ali was asked if he agreed with this description. "Yes."

Uwayys said, "You are wrong, for you have only seen a little part of the Prophet, you have not seen his greatness."

Uwayys Karani kissed the shoes made of camel hair and placed them on his head. This is the origin of the dervish hat made from camel wool.

"How did you love the Prophet Mohammed?"asked Uwayys.

"When I heard he had lost his tooth in a battle I went and broke all my teeth on a rock, and he showed his mouth full of chipped and broken teeth. When I heard that he was wounded in battle, cut on the face, I took a knife and slashed both sides of my face.

This is love. Did you love him this way?"

Efendi sips his coffee and continues speaking. "When Allah tells Moses to invite the Pharaoh to his religion Moses asks for a loyal friend to accompany him, and is told to take his brother Aaron. Only Allah has no need for a fellow traveller. Everyone who says the Name of Allah has a travelling companion. Relate to the needs of your friends. If they are sick, visit them. If they are busy, help them. If they have forgotten, remind them."

We approach the shores of Bursa, replace our "chairs and table," and descend the metal stairs to the car.

In Bursa we check into the hotel that Kemal Ataturk used to stay in, and after a short rest and *mahgreb* prayer we pile into the car toward an unknown adventure. Tosun drives a battered Chevrolet that he named Duldul.

The sheikh directed us up this windy, turgid, dirt road, flanked by snow three feet high, to a restaurant that had sheep hanging from metal hooks in a cold room. We choose the sheep we wanted to eat, they bring it out, cut it up and cook it on a *mangal* by our table.

We were forced to eat the entire sheep. There were four of us and it was difficult to consume that much meat. Huge plates balanced mountains of lamb chops and hills of rice and salad. Sheikh Muzaffer kept insisting that we eat and finally, his *khalifa*, Safer Baba, who became the sheikh after Muzaffer, answered Tosun who was complaining. "What's the big test? In the old days, a sheikh would ask you to do things that you could die from. Here, your sheikh is just asking you to eat a meal."

It was a real teaching. We went back to the hotel in the dark of night. Muzaffer Efendi had the car weave around the rough dirt road and stop at a local mountain farm where he bought some honey. "This is the best honey. It is from Vakfikebir on the Black Sea. This honey can cure illness, can sweeten thoughts, one taste gives ecstasy, one taste freedom, it is the cream colored honey given to the women of Vakfikeber to make them more beautiful than sunsets, that makes their thighs sweeter than the pain of separation." Then Muzaffer Efendi passed the honey around and we all tasted what is indescribable. "Pray that your sons marry a woman whose heart is the honey of Vakfikebir."

Tosun Baba carefully maneuvered the car through the moonlit night. Efendi began a *sohbet*. "The bear lives in the forest and loves honey. He can smell a beehive from a great distance, puts his paw into the beehive, and tries to quickly pull out the honey. The bees rush out and begin stinging the bear. They are angry and sting the bear on his body, his paws and his face. In spite of the pain, the bear stays with his task of obtaining the honey. His tongue and face are swollen from the stings. The bear puts up with the pain, for he loves the taste of honey.

"The world is like the stinging bees. You will have pain here. You will have problems here. But, is not the sting of life worth the honey of Allah?

"The intelligent bear grabs the beehive and throws it into the river. When the bees fly away, he picks up the hive and removes the honey. The intelligent person in the world accepts the pain of life, but does not give it a place in his thoughts. He does not give it a room in his body.

"All your actions are tenants of your body. They live within this cage of flesh and bones. If you realize this you will live according to the conduct brought by our beloved Prophet. Do not allow room for sorrow, laziness, or deceit. Thoughts produce sorrow and loneliness. Then you must give them a room in your house."

We get through the night and the next day, then after sunset Muzaffer Efendi directs the car back up the cold, hard road, to the restaurant at the top of Uludag Mountain, for another lesson in obedience to the sheikh. During that meal, Tosun who is my friend and the sheikh of New York whispers to me, "I can't do anymore. I can't eat anymore."

I whisper back, "Look, it's okay. If he's a real sheikh, nothing's going to happen to us, and if he's not a real sheikh, we'll die. So what? Just eat. That's what he's asking us to do." We continued and we begged not to eat any more for the rest of the trip. On a platter in front of us there seemed to be a hundred lamb chops and a tray of salad that could feed a village.

A large flabby hunk of meat, or intestine, or jellied mass finds its way to Tosun's plate. He was cleverly moving it around so as not to have to eat it. Muzaffer Efendi looks over to him and asks, "Don't you like that part?" And with a flick of his fingers pops it into his mouth with great relish. I shuddered at the thought of my having to consume this part.

One of Tosun's favorite meals is fried calf's brain, so he was an intrepid eater, and no stranger to eating the unusual. The next day among muffled complaints, the sheikh took us for a huge Adana Kebab lunch. Adana Kebab is meat laid out on pita bread swimming in yoghurt and tomato sauce.

Uzbek Tekke

I am standing on the flat roof of the two-story stone house in Uskudar with the dervish musician Nezih Uzel. He lives on the upper floor with thousands of books in several languages, and several kinds of musical instruments. His elderly mother moves between her bedroom and the kitchen on the lower floor.

Nezih is filming me with an eight-millimeter camera as we talk. It's March, 1975 and as white clouds emerge from our mouths, snow descends. The Turkish saying, "In March the peasants set fire to their farm implements, and the rich burn their furniture," is understood on this frigid afternoon. We leave the snow to the trees and the street. The warmth of the living room is welcome. Nezih picks up a *bendir* and begins to sing *ilahis*, poems that praise the Prophet Mohammed.

Years later Nezih digs out the reel and plays it for my son Nuri. He barely recognizes me through the long coal-black hair and beard.

On Sunday night Nezih and I walk the winding hilltop streets of Uskudar to the Uzbek *tekke*. We are greeted by the musicians Kudsi Erguner, Akagunduz Kutbay and Sheikh Necmeddin's two sons, and are served from a never-ending pot of Turkish tea. The music and *zikr* go on into the early morning.

The Instantaneous Moment

Kadiri Ane was a tall, stately looking woman in her eighties who emanated *baraka* through her presence. I met her in Istanbul. Nezih took me to her house in Kadikoy in the Asian side of Istanbul. She had cared for a Kadiri sheikh for over forty years and was a universal mother figure to all who came near her.

She sat on a long couch covered by a *kilim* from Van, an area in Central Turkey. Her slender fingers floated through the air as she emphasized a phrase. Mostly she spoke on the necessity of inner peace and how the remembrance of Allah can alter states of consciousness.

We sat cross-legged, facing the couch, on the carpeted floor. I took the small Leica camera from my bag, held it for a minute, adjusted the aperture and shutter speed, and placed it next to me on the carpet.

After a while of just sitting in her presence, the room felt different. I lifted the camera and looked toward her. She acquiesced. I matched my breathing to hers and clicked three shots, then returned the camera to my bag.

As we left she stepped before each of us and passed her hands from the top of our heads to our torsos. Her energy entered each of us causing a mild tremor within our bodies.

Breaking Fast

Ramadan in Cairo is unique. Abdallah and I are walking through the Khan Khalili to the small mosque next to Sayyidina Hussein. The *Lovers of Hussein* have set up numerous tables and feed *iftar* to the community. We give them some of our *zakat* and weave our way around the pots and huge skillets of steaming food, to a table covered with plastic, in the back room.

Skinned carcasses of sheep are carried into the kitchen. The smell of raw and cooked meat is pungent. Local people bring large empty pots and bowls to be filled with meat, soup, vegetables and sweets.

The moment the call to *maghreb* prayer is heard we drink the water before us and eat a few dates, then enter the main part of the old mosque, and pray the sunset prayer on ancient, musty, carpets, in a space that masks the breath of hundreds of years of men praying.

After prayer we spoon soup from plastic bowls and eat a mound of rice topped with a hunk of boiled meat. Sweets, coffee, and then we give our *selams* and enter the crowded area around the mosque where hundreds of people from Cairo and the villages have spread large cloths on the ground, and sit in long lines breaking their fast. A number of tents have been erected. Each one houses a different Sufi order. We move through them all stopping to make *zikr* with each of them. There are thousands of people in the area and hundreds in each tent, swaying and chanting to the direction of a sheikh.

I have been in Cairo two years and Abdallah has introduced me to all the local sheikhs and *zikr* circles.

Silent Meal

I first met Reshad Field at a Sufi retreat in Fazil Manzil, Pir Vilayat Khan's residence outside of Paris in the late sixties. He had been a member of a successful British musical group but now he turned toward the esoteric. Pir Vilayat initiated him as a sheikh in the Chishti Order of dervishes and later Reshad studied with the enigmatic Bulent Rauf whose interest in Sufism, and in particular Ibn Arabi, drew a number of seekers toward his circle. It was at this time that I met the American actress Ellen Burstyn who was studying Sufism and was called Hadiya.

Years later Reshad visited my studio in Manhattan and pulled from his vest pocket a photograph of a white haired, white bearded man who appeared to be glowing.

"He is a master of the Universal White Brotherhood and has a group in Frejus in the south of France. His name is Omraan Mikhael Aivanhov."

I knew that I had to meet him. Barbara and I were visiting the painter Paul Jenkins in Paris that summer and I wrote asking to visit the *ashram*. When we arrived in the evening we were brought to separate cell-like rooms and told that there would be a sunrise meditation at the top of the mountain.

A hundred men, women, and children woke up in the dark, and silently, in single file, climbed to the mountain's peak in the grey of pre-dawn. We sat on the eastern side of the slanted earth on large rocks and waited for a golden rim to appear. When the sun became a yellow orb that danced upon the hunter-green mountain, and the night was behind us, we walked in a different state of being, down to the flat land where we took breakfast and then participated in work details.

Aivanhov created a set of movements that were done both severally and collectively; its purpose was to raise awareness of the bodies in which we lived. Slow, measured movements were done in a state of awareness. Hands moved along the extremities of the body, brushing them with light.

He was called *Le Maitre* (The Master), by his mostly European followers. I met with him in a green garden that smelled of sweet flowers and we spoke of the practical philosophy of dancing on the grass-side of the planet. I photographed him in his white suit that complimented his beard and long hair, and then joined the entire group at an extraordinary lunch.

Three round tables covered with white cloth and set for a meal were placed on a raised platform. *Le Maitre* filled the chairs with disciples chosen from the group of followers who sat at tables facing the platform. Everyone sat facing *Le Maitre* and his guests. Before sitting, he greeted us and when he raised his hands the smell of roses wafted throughout the large room.

The extraordinary part of the meal was that all courses were eaten in silence. Not only was there no talking, but also attention was taken so no utensils, plates, and bowls made any sound when moved or placed on the table. This required the height of awareness on the part of the one dining and gave me the sense of meditation in action.

The movements reminded me of the Malaysian sheikh whose feet imprinted the *tawhid* on the sand. The meal was a high meditation that could be practiced in daily life.

Consider how the quality of our lives would increase if, while cooking we write *bismillah* on the food with a wooden spoon; and while eating in complete silence, meditation is introduced into the meal.

In the circle of remembrance we say the Name of Allah whenever our foot is placed on the floor. What beauty could be introduced into our lives by remembering Allah with every step taken? Better than white cheese and watermelon, *kaymak* and honey, or a healing recipe from the Egyptian Spice Market in Istanbul.

Ramana Maharshi's Cave

Michael Moloshek was at the fringe of ninety when I met him in Los Angeles. He was at a gathering of the followers of Omraan Mikhael Aivanhov where he spoke about the harmony of food. I had been reading the *Mazdaznan Science of Dietetics*, one of their main teachings was on the harmonious combination of food, so my interest peaked when Moloshek broached the subject.

The next day I was invited for lunch with him at his mountain cabin in the hills of Malibu overlooking the ocean. He told me his story over a lunch of white cheese and purple grapes.

"At sixteen I overheard my parents talking about me in our European home. It seemed I had an incurable disease having to do with an inability to digest any food containing milk products. On the spot I decided to travel to America, a dream country at that time, and at least encounter an adventure before my demise. I left the next day by ship and after weeks on the ocean arrived at the port of New York. My illness was treated by internal medical specialists and after considerable time my body was cured and given a new life. I took this life to India and went to the *ashram* of Ramana Maharshi."

"What was it like to be with Ramana Maharshi?"

"He would sit in a cave and meditate for hours each day. I would enter the cave and sit next to him. He taught me how to balance my breath and leave my consciousness in my third eye, which he said was in the center of my forehead. He said that through these meditations I would learn to see not only with my two eyes but also with this third eye, and that would be like seeing with my heart."

"What did you feel while in meditation with such a great being?"

"When I entered the cave he was sitting cross-legged with a golden glow encircling his body. As I sat next to him this glow expanded and encircled my body as well. It was the experience of living in the moment in the light of God. I arrived at the *ashram* with the name Michael and when I departed to go back to America I was called Swami Shantananda."

After lunch he suggested that I join him on his daily two-mile walk along the mountain trails. The only sound was our own breath and the lapping of the ocean upon the shore below.

When we parted he said, "You are the sum and substance of the universe. You will never be more or less realized than you are at this moment." I watched him disappear into the forest.

Ramana Maharshi sits on white down,
Indian cloths, jars of herbs and oils,
Electric light, gray walls, leathered bare feet,
A light glows from his eyes,
A purple flower grows from his chest,
His alarm clock says ten after three.

Death Of My Mother

The Angel of Death complained that he was given an unrewarding job. "When people see me coming for them, they will eperience fear and hate me."

Allah told Azrael not to be concerned with this as He has created illness, and mankind will be concerned with their illness, and will not be attentive to his presence.

I am living in a coach house hidden behind a brick building at 502 East 84th street in New York City. Years before, my friend and graphic design partner Bob Cato turned it over to me when he moved to a large house in Pelham, NY.

I had a design studio in New York with Will Hopkins when cancer entered my father's body. We mainly did editorial design on magazines and books. Mostly because of Will's talent and business acumen, we became known as two of the best magazine designers in the city. When I wasn't involved with graphic design, my time was spent painting, drawing and writing. I was thirty-seven.

My father can no longer live alone; my mother died two years before, and he moves in with my younger sister Vivian (nicknamed Cookie since childhood) and her family in Randolph, Massachusetts. My sister is burdened with an aphasic daughter and the worry and etched lines of grief that permeate her days. She became the caregiver to my father. Her two older daughters Deborah and Jackie help, but her Russian heritage has placed the weight of sorrow on her shoulders.

I would fly into Boston on the weekends to be with my dad. During the next year or so that became the pattern of my week.

My father's body slowly deteriorates. The pallid look to his already alabaster skin and the pain that just didn't want to cease, finally brings him into the Beth Israel Hospital. The same hospital where my mother was taken with the cancer that slipped into her body four years before, and later caused her to die along a hospital corridor of tears, that could never wash her free of the constant pain, whose only relief was to exit the body.

My mother is dying between two white hospital sheets. I am sitting on a steel blue plastic couch at the edge of the corridor of tears. I wade into her room. It smells hospital green, and a slight breeze as if a winged being were encircling her bed was present. I whisper; "There is no god but God," into her ear. Repeatedly. Repeatedly. Maybe a thousand times, I am not counting.

She reaches out a bony hand with long yellowed nails attached to ringless fingers that could barely hold the paper cup of water I give her. Her right hand lay motionless, a puffed purple mass that once made lace, sewed trouser buttons, candled eggs, working its way from youth to uselessness. I was certain it would have known the doctor's hacksaw if she were not dying.

We smelled the rain together. Then she slept as her burning forehead pushed into cold sheets, stained yellow by three days of drizzled micturition in plastic tubes. I stared at the crevices in her feet that would never walk again. She danced on a Russian lawn, and saw the fog as it crept through autumn trees retracing her thoughts to an icy plain, where she had left her youth, so precious to a dying lady. Attempting to regain the lost images of childhood she breathed one measured breath onto a sheet of snow. There was no shadow behind her eyes and her head was empty of dreams. A last spurt of blood jumped from a blue vein, trickled down her arm and hung for a moment on the faded nipple of her sagging breast.

I watched her fly above the joy of making babies, dancing on the planet, yellow phlegm hiding in her lungs, sweet and sour in her mouth, above the light of grandchildren's smiles, past all weights, and the fear of death.

Suddenly a loud bell with the straightness of an arrow, comes from a screened box to the right side of her bed, and rings against the walls. My voice fills the corridors. Several nurses race to the room.

Shortly after dawn, they move your body from this stranger's room, to an unrefrigerated metal box, soon to be bonehouse underground. Your cold posthumous head browsing among unfinished thoughts, no longer at the mercy of your mind, pushing up through a dress of white lace into the blackness of time caught between end and beginning. This tin planter, with earth seeping through its uncaulked seams, where flowers will live and fragrant lilies will grow from the hinges of your bones, wedged between your thighs, like some garden gate to an ancient home.

I trembled with the admittance of the first day without her.

The night before, my father and I return from the hospital to his Beale Street apartment.

"Dad, I think you should do whatever you do to prepare yourself. Mother is going to die."

"How do you know?"

He could have been pounding his fist against the wall but it came

out in his voice.
"I just know."
The smell of loss was in the room.

This was the same hospital where I lay as a twelve-year-old boy on bloodstained sheets, hemorrhaging from my throat after tonsillitis surgery, waiting for snail-paced nurses to respond to my summons, because I had become "the boy who cried wolf," asking too many times for a glass of water.

Appointment In Samarra

Rumi asks us if we think we can flee from anything. Can one escape God...one's destiny?

One morning a servant came running to his master in great haste. His lips were blue from fright and his countenance pale. The master asks him, "What is troubling you?"

"I saw Death in the marketplace, he jostled me and looked at me with rage and vengeance. O master give me your fastest horse to carry me to Samarra where my soul may be saved."

The master gave him his swiftest horse. "Ride through the day. This steed will get you there by nightfall." The horse flew like the wind to far off Samarra.

The master pondered the situation, then went to the marketplace where, in a remote corner, he indeed met the cowled figure of Death.

"Why did you frighten my servant?"

"It was I who was taken aback, and stared at him in wonder," said Death, "as I have an appointment with him tonight in Samarra.

The Bath

When he was in the hospital my father and I would talk on the telephone. Whenever the doctors wanted to explore, invade, test or otherwise place him in more discomfort he called me in New York. His voice was fragile.

"What do you think son? They want to perform an epidermal. Should I let them?"

They did what they could and sent him back to my sister's house. Who can erase that which has been written? I continue to come on weekends.

My father needs a bath. He is too weak to bathe alone. My sister cannot do it. I walk him slowly to the bathroom. He no longer walks with authority. He takes little steps and places what is left of his weight on my body. I run lukewarm water and carefully sit him in the tub. Then I undress to my shorts and step in with him. I wash him. Soap him and wash him again. I wash his once muscular arms down to his hands with their puffed grey veins. I wash this body whose sperm I came from. This body that had worked for me my entire life, prayed for me, fed me, cared for me when I was sick, and comforted me when I was confused or distressed. My father bathed me in the beginning of my life, and I bathe him at the end of his life. Full cycle.

I stand him up, wrap towels around him and carefully lift him from the bathtub so he can sit on the seat of the toilet. Gently I brush him dry. In a whispered voice he says; "You are a good son."

"I would not be a good son if you had not been a good father."

Fishing In Canada

I reach my ten-year-old hand through an imaginary time and hold onto my father's powerful hand. We leave Boston behind, and are moving closer to Montreal, listening to the steady sounds of the train lulling us to sleep as our bodies sway in the shaking carriage. I remember the tobacco smell on the once blue velvet seats as we approach White River Junction, Vermont, and I fall asleep on my father's lap.

In Montreal we visit relatives, then go to the Laurentian Mountains where my father's older sister Annie has a summer cottage at the edge of a railroad line. I stand in the tall brown grass and wave to the engineers as the train rattles by sending shivers through the old wooden house.

My father and uncle take me out on the nearby pond to a place where fish are supposed to be abundant. Reaching to his limit, my father breaks a branch from a tree, winds some fishing line and a hook onto it, and fashions me a rod. We are in a small, rickety unpainted rowboat. I catch nothing, but learn that sometimes you can fish for relaxation.

The Turkish Bath

A poor, tired, winter traveller decided to go to a Turkish bath. He had no place to stay and he only had a few Turkish *lira*. He intended to rest there a long time so he bought a piece of candy that contained opium. This was normal in those days. He borrowed a loincloth and lay down on a large concrete slab in the public section of the hot room.

He soon saw a man who looked exactly like him, except that he had servants, a silk loincloth and soaps and scents. The man lay down in the private area and his servants left him. He could not believe his physical resemblance to the man. He thought that perhaps his father had visited the place where this man came from. The resemblance was uncanny. Curiosity overcame him. He had to see and talk to the man. Peering inside the door, he realized that the man was dead. There were no signs of life. So he decided to change places with him. Unnoticed, he dragged the lifeless body to the public area, and quickly sat in the private place. Soon the washers came, bathed him and put oil on his body. His servants brought hot towels. They gave him tea and he rested. After a while they brought his silk clothes and fur coat. In his right pocket was gold and in his left was silver. He distributed generous tips to the bath attendants who formed a line before him and bowed to his kindness.

He still did not know who he was but thought that he must be someone important. A beautiful carriage drawn by white horses waited for him. From inside the carriage he watched the man who died as he was carried out of the *hammam* like a dead animal.

His home was the palace. Servants asked where he would like to go. He feared he would be identified if he asked to go to his general living quarters. After all he must have a wife, perhaps more than one, and they would surely recognize him as an imposter. So he asked to be taken to his private quarters. For the next few days he quietly tried to find out who he was. Although his life was so rich he was miserable because he couldn't find out his identity.

One day the sultan called for him. It seemed he was a minister being called back to duty. He gathered as much as he could carry and fled to a mosque. He hid in the storage room for the coffins. He climbed into an empty coffin. Soon he heard a noise. Squeezing a look from a crack in the coffin he saw that thieves were in the same room dividing their loot. His stomach felt as if he swallowed a stone. The thieves discover him and chase him around the room and up the minaret stairs. He lost his balance, fell from the minaret and hit his head.

When he opened his eyes two burly bath attendants were in the Turkish bath shaking him. They said that he had been asleep there for hours. This is the extent of life. A little opium in a candy... you sleep, fall on a stone and wake up.

Death Of My Father

Some weeks after my father was returned to the hospital I bolt upright at 5 a.m., as if from a dream. My father is lying on his back and I witness the soul depart from the center of his motionless body. This is clear and profound. I had been sleeping on the floor of the studio part of my coach house in New York because the boiler broke in the frigid basement below, and there was no heat.

If we live in a dream, then who is dreaming us?

"I'll let you be in my dreams if I can be in yours." Bob Dylan said that.

I wait a while before calling my sister. Her husband answers the phone.

"She was called to the hospital." He didn't know more.

I telephone the doctor. "I am in New York, should I come?"

"Perhaps it would be good." He was noncommittal.

"Let me put it another way. When I come should I bring a suit?"

"That would be good."

It is 1978, one of the coldest, snow covered Februaries in Boston's history. Traffic is at a standstill. Abandoned cars are sprinkled on the roads. Failed batteries, tires that can no longer touch the road because of the snow that is Buffalo deep. You can read spoken words in the air. At the cemetery they can't open the grave. The ground is frozen. A backhoe cannot manipulate the area. Days pass. Uncomfortable days. Finally I go to the office of the director of the cemetery.

"If you do not open the grave by tomorrow I will come myself and dig it with a mattock and a shovel."

They manage to break into the stubborn ground, and on the coldest day in February that can be remembered, we lift the skin of snow and place my father's body into the frozen, unwelcoming earth.

One Hundred And Five Summers

Six months before she died my father's mother was still travelling around Montreal by autobus. The drivers all knew her and allowed her to disembark in front of the old wooden house where she lived with her daughter Riva and her family.

Then she fell and struck her head but did not lose consciousness. The hospital refused to keep her overnight. She was okay but too old. After this incident she was afraid to walk and confined herself to the bed. Lacking any exercise her body began to deteriorate rapidly. Her skin became translucent. Her words danced around her wrinkled face while her mind remained keen.

Grandmother had seen one hundred and five summers before she lay, half-motionless in the winter of her life thinking the soft thought that told her the winter sun was a lie.

She pulled my face close to her parched lips and whispered that she had just seen an angel with six hundred wings who was so vast he covered the entire sky like a ceiling of light. Later, staring at a flower in the corner of her room, she died.

I took the brown wool blanket that she had carried from Russia, and sat on it during meditation for several years before the hundred-year-old wool strands unraveled and deteriorated, as the body it had once covered.

The only time I saw my father cry was at the funeral of his mother.

"Dad, she was 105 years old."

"Yes, but she was my mother."

Some years later I wrote a poem for my grandmother.

A face that peers through earth veils
Towards a light that casts no shadows and gives no warmth,
This is Anna's face,
Time licked lines of age forming crevices of skin

That dance to the sound of her voice,
Hands with skin worn through in spots,
Softly rubbed clay plates, then paused
To send grey eyes across the room and touch mine gently,
Eyes that saw a hundred summers now rested on my face,
Lips that kissed dead lips now kissed mine,
Decaying bones wrapped loosely in skin touch my hands…
O Anna,
How you've watched your sons and daughters die,
Allowing one tear for each to travel down your wrinkled face,
They, who were drawn from your womb,
You felt the seed of each life,
Watched their bodies growing past your own,
Now they are dead and you, Anna,
Live within the body of an old woman
Whose soul has been touched by God.

Dervishes In America

After my father's death I stayed in Boston for a week helping my sister close his apartment, and prepare the necessary paperwork for the state. We went through all his papers and books and collected his clothes, and the remaining clothes of my mother and brought them to a thrift shop for distribution to the needy. I kept his favorite cap, that I wore for a while, on cold winter days. It is not easy to die in America.

Muzaffer Efendi was in New York at the Spring Valley *tekke* of Tosun Baba. It was his first visit to America. The room was crowded. It was winter outside but the hundred or so people, sitting knee to knee, that gathered in the *sohbet* room gave the space a warm glow. I make my way to the front to kiss the hand of Sheikh Muzaffer. As I climb over and around the people sitting on the floor Efendi's voice bellows out to me, "Everyone comes and everyone goes." At first this strikes me as a cruel comment. Later, when I thought of it, I realized that it was a profound teaching that came at a perfect moment for I was open to hear the message.

The Academy Award

The actress Ellen Burstyn was a friend of ours. She was performing in a hit Broadway play called *Same Time Next Year*. It was the night of the 1975 Academy Awards. Ellen had been nominated for her performance in *Alice Doesn't Live Here Anymore*. Of course she couldn't be in Los Angeles and New York at the same time and since her house was a distance from the city, she decided to stay the night with Barbara and I and watch the awards on television. There was an explosive shout of surprise and joy when her name was announced as the recipient of the Academy Award for best actress.

Dinner With John And Yoko

I got to know John Lennon through my friend the actor Peter Boyle who also lived on East 84th street in New York. We never hung out together but John and Yoko did come to dinner a few times. My wife Barbara was a master chef of vegetarian food and at this particular time Yoko was pregnant with Sean and was interested in a healthy diet. John was trying to quit smoking and it helped the evening that the house was smokeless.

EST (Erhart Seminar Trainings) had captured the interest of New Yorkers. These weekend seminars aided one in a conscious look at one's self and one's actions, and being non-religious, found popularity among New Yorkers who were swimming in the pool of "teachers from the east."

Whenever John was asked for money by any number of people that were out of sorts, he would send them to an EST weekend at his expense.

The evening went well. We talked about health foods, looked at some of my photographs of the dervishes, exchanged eyeglasses temporarily, and at dinner John broke into song, *Goodnight Irene*.Whenever we met on the streets of New York John never failed to stop and chat.

Years later one of my students at The American University in Cairo, who was an avid fan of Lennon's, found out that I knew him. I mentioned the dinner and to my surprise he asked if I kept the silverware. The idea of celebrity had spread to Egypt.

Meeting The Sultan

Mullah Nasreddin heard that the sultan was visiting a village near his own. He told his friends at the local café that he was going to see the sultan. In three days he returned and was sitting at his favorite table in the coffee house when his cronies barraged him with questions. "Did you see the sultan?"

"Not only did I see the sultan, but he spoke to me."

"Another coffee for the Mullah," shouted one of his pals as their interest peaked. "What did the sultan say to you?"

"He walked right up to me and said, 'Get out of my way.'"

Fame and success belong to the one who has worked for it. It is not transferable through osmosis of the elbow.

The Painter

In 2011 when I tell my friend Dr. Ann Coxon, an important British voice for Islam, that my paintings are getting some recognition, she remarks over cappuccino in London, "You've put in your ten thousand hours, perhaps you will now find overnight success."

Initiation

My heart is fluttering like that of a small bird in an invisible cage. Sheikh Muzaffer al-Halveti al-Jerrahi is initiating me as his *khalifa* in a sacred ceremony. I have arrived in a white *tennure* tied by a *kamer*, and wearing a white *dul araki* on my head, representing silver, the step before being given the golden crown of a sheikh. I have taken full ablution and have repeated seventy thousand *tawhid, la illaha illa Allah,* the phrase of unity. Salik is by my side. We are being initiated together.

Hafiz Ali and Lutfu Baba are my *rehbers,* the guides that lead me in the four steps that bring me before the sheikh. Leading with my right foot I repeat, *as salamu aleykum ya shari'a*. Muzaffer Efendi beckons us forward. I say aloud, *as salamu aleykum ya tariqa*. Again the sheikh indicates us to move forward. *As salamu aleykum ya haqiqa*. And with the fourth step I repeat, *as salamu aleykum ya marifa*, and stand at the edge of a white sheepskin in front of the sheikh, who is seated on a sheepskin atop a Turkish carpet. I kneel on the sheepskin that once belonged to a sacrificed sheep, and wonder what I am sacrificing.

My knees are touching the knees of the sheikh, and with a firm hand he grasps my right hand with his right hand. I have joined the unbroken golden chain of hands that go back to the hand of the Prophet Mohammed.

Concentric circles of a hundred dervishes from Istanbul and New York witness the ceremony. The room smells of roses, as if an angel's wing has stirred, causing a sweet wind to permeate sacred air.

A coal-black cloak is placed around my shoulders. Sheikh

Muzaffer looks into my eyes and repeats a prayer from his heart. Then he places the golden *taj*, wrapped at the base with several layers of green cloth, on my head. A green tail of this cloth is left hanging over my heart, like a snake, to remind me to protect my heart from making idols of the world.

I repeat *astafigrAllah* eleven times, then *la illaha illa Allah*, seven times moving my head from side to side, leaving Allah in my heart. After the last *tawhid*, Efendi says, "*Mohammed ar rasul Allah*" and releases my right hand. He gives me a *sebha* made from the pits of dates that had been eaten by dervishes during Ramadan, the month of Fasting. I kiss the sheikh's hand, with Allah's Names symbolically written on them, and am lifted from my sacrificial seat. Sweet tasting tears moisten the lids of my eyes. Perhaps they are the "tears of healing" that were spoken of by Ibn Arabi.

Dervishes crowd around me and kiss my hand, welcoming me as Muzaffer Efendi's *khalifa*. Among them are Sheikh Tosun Bayrak, the renowned Arabic and Turkish translator Muhtar Holland, and Imam Feisal Abdul Rauf.

I am initiated into a four-hundred-year-old Sufi Order as a sheikh, in 1981, in an old firehouse on Mercer Street in New York, that has been redesigned into the Masjid al-Farah, a mosque inspired by Sheikh Muzaffer of Istanbul.

Is Everyone Born On A Bed That Their Father Built

My son Nuri was born at home on August 8th, 1979, on a bed that I had built. It was on the first floor of the coach house behind 502 East 84th. Lex Hixon (Nur), had constructed a similar bed and when I expressed an interest in building a "four-poster" he volunteered to help.

I made a rough sketch showing dimensions. We ordered the lumber pre-cut to size, and spent an entire day in the front yard constructing the bed. We used a hatchet to skim slivers of wood from the vertical posts to give it a rustic look. Then we stained the wood a walnut color and assembled the bed inside the house.

Nuri's Birth

Ramadan, Istanbul August 5th, 2013

The Mevlevi sheikh bows to Halveti Sheikh Tugrul Inancer seated in the *sohbet* room and gains a silent permission to begin the *sema*. Men in black cloaks slowly enter "the hall of celestial sounds," collectively bow to the Mevlevi sheikh, then form a line and drop their cloaks (their worldly attachments). They pass before the sheikh who stands on the red post, bow again and like fledgling birds begin to unfold their arms and turn toward their hearts, right palm up, left down, subvocally repeating *Allah* as they whirl. At the same time, in a large room attached to the room of turning *semazens*, the Halveti sheikh is leading a hundred men in a seated *zikr. Allah Hayy, Allah Hayy,* begins slowly and then like a rushing train gathers momentum and sound and the Name of Allah is repeatedly directed to the chest, like a saw cutting through the hard crust of attitudes covering the heart.

As an elder of the Halveti Jerrahi Sufi Order I am sitting on a carpeted bench next to the sheikh with a full view of the circle of dervishes invoking the Name. Sheikh Tugrul Efendi leans close to me, and looking at my son Nuri says, "Long time before, your beard was black like his."

"Yes Efendi, but grey in one's beard is a light from Allah."

"*Inshallah.*"

What a blessing in this chaotic world to have been given the gift of the Name of Allah, whose repetition assures peace in one's heart. It is said that Allah is secretly hidden in His Name. Tugrul Efendi is a master of *zikr*.

Nuri is kneeling in the first circle. He arrived to Istanbul with his angelic wife Krystina who is in the crowded women's section upstairs repeating the Sacred Name. I observe Nuri as he loudly proclaims the *zikr* and think that thirty-four years before, he was preparing to enter the world. Three more days and Allah would allow him to depart the dark, moist cave that has been his abode for nine months, and be untied and released to the planet.

"Don't worry Nuri, we will care for you, feed you, love you, pray for you, teach you, attach wings of understanding to your back so that one day you may fly from the nest and become a harmonious man in this world."

Ana stirred away from her dreams. The child within her kicked and caused a sharp pain just below her heart. Her breasts were swollen with the anticipation of milk. The need of the child will fill them with his nourishment. From her bedroom window she glimpsed the trees in the garden and in a calm moment knew that today she would spread her thighs wide and allow the being in her body to be released and begin adjusting to life on the planet earth. With this premonition Ana decided to fast.

At mid-day she experienced an abdominal pain followed by another. They continued periodically. She called me into the room and proclaimed, "I am in labor." She managed the words just before another pain caused her to wince. I was anxious. I had never seen a birth. Ana sat on the couch upstairs that was covered with a *kilim* that I bought in Turkey. I sat next to her and began noting the time between pains. This was our first child so we settled in for a long labor. Ana's heart felt like a dervish drum when she thought of the process going on in her body. Mine felt like two dervish drums.

I telephoned my friend Dr. Arif Rechtshaffen and after some time he and his wife Elizabeth, who was a midwife, arrived at the house. We had previously agreed that barring any unforeseen circumstances the birth would be at home. It was also agreed that I would deliver the baby with the guidance of Arif and Elizabeth.

Ana was still seated on the couch listening to a tape of an Istanbul *zikr* and attempting to control her breath between persistent breaths. For nine months she had listened to *zikr* and Beethoven. The long dark rivers of her hair cascaded over her breasts concealing the rainbow heart painted on her white shirt. I sat before her and calmed her with my eyes, then descended the grey-carpeted stairs to the bedroom, stripped the bed, placed pages of the New York Times on the mattress and covered them with a white cotton sheet. The newspapers would absorb the blood and afterbirth and not ruin the mattress.

Ana showered, then climbed onto the bed, and propped herself against the pillows. She said the Name of God aloud and closed her eyes at the start of another pain. She knew that as the pains grew sharper she was closer to birth.

She labored for nearly ten hours as Elizabeth helped balance her breathing.

"Is he coming? Is he coming?" Ana's words leapt out with the pain and the moan of her cries.

"Soon, just hold on for a second, don't push."

"Ah, Ah, Ah… this time he will come out." Her face was beet red from pushing when the child crowned.

"I can see the head."

Arif was beside me. The room was filled with particles of excitement. When I saw the purplish crown I cried, "*Bismillah*, now push." As she did my son slid into my waiting hands. His cry was strong and filled the dimly lit room. Our hearts were filled with the child's presence. My heart was filled with a sacred joy. I placed my son on my wife's stomach. She was fatigued, and glowing. I was relieved. After a few minutes when the umbilical cord thinned, I unfolded the Arabian pocketknife given to me by a dervish sheikh from Syria and cut my son's cord. I tugged at the other end until the afterbirth appeared, a huge organic mess that looked like an overgrown liver.

Gently I placed my son into lukewarm water and bathed him. He was smiling. Elizabeth wrapped him in layers of soft white cotton cloth and we placed him in the center of the bed. It was almost midnight. I hoped I would be a good father. Arif and Elizabeth went home, and Ana and I on propped elbows, lay on the bed looking in awe at our son until we all drifted into a satisfying sleep.

In the morning I phoned Sheikh Muzaffer in Istanbul with the news. There was a short pause, "Name him Nureddin…Nuri, the one who comes from Divine Light."

On his twelfth birthday I gave Nuri the pocketknife that cut his umbilical cord.

Krystina's Forty-Week Journey

January 4, 2014. Spring Valley Tekke

Nuri and Krystina drive down from Boston over snow patched roads, to meet us at the Spring Valley, NY *tekke* of Sheikh Tosun. Hatice and I are spending the weekend here before going back to Boston with Nuri. New York is like an ice station. Boston will be colder.

Nuri grew up in this *tekke*. When we lived in New York, before going to Cairo, we came to *zikr* here every Saturday. Now we are two grown men in the same circle of *zikr*.

I am sitting on the carpeted bench next to Tosun. Nuri and Krystina approach.

"I am glad to have you both here. I have news. Krystina is pregnant."

"*Alhamdulillah, mabrouk*."

My heart is joyful. *Inshallah*, I will be a grandfather, another distinguishing factor in the process of ageing. I think of Krystina with two hearts beating in her body.

In four days, *Inshallah*, I will be 74, an intrepid septaguanarean, and in seventeen days Sheikh Tosun will be eighty-seven. We have known each other for over forty years.

The Final Seshin

It is the late sixties and New York is the melting pot for spiritual energy. We were a generation surrounded by swamis, music and marijuana.

Baba Ram Dass (Richard Alpert) had returned from India and brought home meditation and the grace of the *guru*. He filled us with *mantras* (spiritual words that focus your attention on higher states of consciousness), and *asanas* (seats of spiritual comfort). We were learning prayers from the East and introducing Sanskrit words into our daily conversations. We were thirsty to enter the world of meditation and leave the greed of the world.

Zen master Shunryu Suzuki Roshi came to New York City. Dick Baker was an American from San Francisco who had gone to Japan, studied Zen Buddhism for years and was initiated as a *roshi* by Suzuki Roshi.

I was at the talk he gave in a small church on Park Avenue. There were two podiums, one on either side of the stage. Baker Roshi introduced his teacher to the audience. Suzuki Roshi was leaning against his podium. He was in repose and his eyes appeared to be closed. A window was open on the opposite side and as Baker Roshi was introducing him, a piece of paper flew in the air from his podium.

As it came in front of Suzuki Roshi, who we thought was sleeping, he slapped his hand down and the paper was brought to rest on his podium. The zen master remained in his reposeful state.

Suzuki Roshi had a *zendo* in San Francisco and another in the mountains of Tassahara in Monterey County. As he was departing

the mountain retreat on his way to the city he was asked, "Do you like it better in San Francisco or Tassahara."
"When I am in San Francisco, I am in San Francisco. When I am in Tassahara, I am in Tassahara."
During his last days in 1971 he used what little strength he had to lead a final *seshin*.

Are You A Man?

There is a story of the Buddha after he was enlightened. He was walking down a path. His being, effulgent, glowing, he was *munawwir*. A man was walking toward him and was so taken by this light that he asked, "Are you a celestial being or a god?"
"No."
"Well then you must be a wizard or a magician."
"No."
"Are you a man?"
Again the answer was "no."
"Then what are you?"
"I am Awake."

Be Here Now

The spiritual energy of the East continued moving West. Zen masters, Gurdjieffians, Sufi sheikhs, Swamis, Gurus, Hatha, Prana, and Raja Yoga teachers, teachers of meditation using sound, light or silence, a thirteen-year-old Guru from India who sat on a throne, Korean chanters, Sufi dancers, along with anyone who thought they could sell spiritual snake oil to naive westerners.
Professor Timothy Leary experimented with LSD, a mind expanding drug, along with his Harvard colleague Richard Alpert,

who later, after meeting Neem Karolie Maharaj in India, became Baba Ram Dass and encouraged a generation of youth to "Tune In, Turn On, and Drop Out."

The idea of the time was to "Be Here Now," and Ram Dass was floating in an Ocean of Love. "You just love," he said, "until you and the Beloved become One."

Hinduism and Sufism came together when Ram Dass and Pir Vilayat Khan met in my studio at 502 East 84th Street. Ram Dass never let me forget that when he was waiting downstairs in the meditation room a mouse calmly loped across his lap.

After Swami Muktananda gave me "flying lessons," I returned to the city and continued with my life. Except...I felt different... and even looked different. I had been a dusty light bulb that had been cleaned by the spiritual energy of the *guru* and was now effulgent. In Greenwich Village strangers approached me and said that I looked like the Sufi Master Meyer Baba. Finally, I cut my long hair to dispel the comparison.

El Topo

Alejandro Jodorowsky was born in Tocopilla, Chile to Jewish Ukrainian parents in 1929. He is an artist, filmmaker, author, and stage director, who brought his surrealistic western film *El Topo* to New York in 1971. The film became an instant success with the New York artist scene and gathered the interest of the city's intelligentsia. It was shown for months at midnight screenings downtown at the Elgin Theater.

El Topo was based on Sufi stories, Zen *koans* and tales, as well as the personal experiences and thoughts of this brilliant director whose life and work is a continuous trek on the path to enlightenment. He used unorthodox techniques such as giving women male voices and men female voices. The main character, the man in black, conquers four masters in the search for his inner freedom.

The concept of conquering a master to gain understanding or move past him is not new. The New York painter Robert Rauschenberg found it necessary to erase a drawing by Willem de Kooning in order to move past the master of Abstract Expressionism.

I was designing a publication about the film "El Topo" for Douglas Productions. Alejandro and I first met in the New York office of Alan Douglas who was promoting the film and producing a book of the screenplay and a lengthy interview with Jodorowsky that would come out in a special publication promoting the film. Our parental backgrounds were similar and my involvement with Hinduism, Buddhism, and Sufism interested him so we spent a day wandering the streets of Manhattan and ended up at my studio on East 84th Street.

Pandit Pran Nath, the Indian vocalist, brought eight *tambouras* from the East. I had one and was learning to play the drone instrument. I sat with Alejandro and showed him how to play. Being a musician and composer he picked up the technique quickly. We sat for a long time under the double skylight of the studio chanting Sufi poems.

Jodorowsky once followed a dog around a Spanish city in order to see and experience unknown streets.

The Man's Dream

Seven hundred years after the *mureeds* of Mevlana found him in the early morning in meditation, with his beard frozen by icicles to the cold ground of the mosque in Konya, Yusuf had a dream in Istanbul.

It was an early winter's morning when he had one of seven consecutive dreams. Mevlana came to him in the air and above the sea. At the end of the seventh dream Yusuf woke and turned 1001 times with one breath. He had never done the Mevlevi turn before.

Six months later, Hassan Efendi, a Mevlevi Dede from Yugoslavia, came to his shop and they talked of Mevlana. After three days he invited Yusuf to his home to teach him *sema*. Yusuf had not told him of his dreams. When he turned, the Dede stopped him and said, "I cannot teach you anymore. You have the Light of Mevlana." He initiated him by the holding of *sebha* as they sat knee to knee, and confirmed the dream.

Yusuf's Halveti sheikh also confirmed the dream and a green *tennure* was made for him. In Konya he was given the gift of an old *sikke*.

Now, each morning Yusuf awakes, swings from the bottom bed of bunk beds, and performs ablutions. He finishes as the *mue'zzin* begins his call to prayer. Yusuf makes his morning prayer and then turns eighteen times. After this he reads *sura Yasin* and prepares himself to go to work in his shop.

The Woman's Dream

A non-Muslim woman married to a Muslim, had a dream. She was in a village with her husband. Everyone in the village died except the two of them. An angel appeared to her. She asked, "How does one get to Paradise?"

"I don't know," answered the angel. "But the secret is hidden in the five prayers."

The woman became a Muslim.

Tell Your Dreams to Your Sheikh

I am sitting with Safer Baba drinking hot *sahlep* in a Beyazit café."Between *heh* and *wow* there are twenty-six letters. All the

Names of Allah are between these letters. The alphabet has twenty-eight letters in all.

"You must continue doing 70,000 *tawhid*, and *salat* (the prayers five times a day). Do not break the continuum and you can become a sultan in the other world.

"You may have a dream, or Efendi may have a dream, then you will wear the *dul araki*. Write your dreams and tell them to Efendi.

Nuri is a child at the time and Safer Baba gives me a healing formula to repeat at times when he may not be well.

Fishing for Gold In Rivers of Sand

In 1997 on a flight from Cairo to New York, I scribbled a poem while in the clouds.

Fifty-seven years have passed
through this body–tall,
but not as tall as youth.
Dreams these eyes have seen,
evaporated in memories
difficult to recall.
Postcards from the saints,
now gone,
like the silken rivers of your hair.
Unwritten poems
unspoken words.
Deaths of those I loved,
births of those I love.
The prayers of sheikhs,
the Prophet's house,
the sand upon which Abraham walked.
His footprints left in stone.

Where are those hearts
which once pressed close to mine?
Unspoken prayers
like molten gold which shapes
one word that no man speaks.
Layers of lies,
mountains of truth.
A distant memory of youth,
as if it always belonged to another,
I did not know then
It was on loan to be replaced by age.
Like this body now on loan
to be replaced by death.
Sweets prepared with frankincense
will lose their taste,
and the light of Madinah
will fade into a sea of clouds.
These years fit into this
moment alone...
which is all that is left,
except the secret word
which has no sound.

I know nothing but this word
which I cannot say,
and the scent of the rose
which belongs to Attar's garden.

Istanbul Notes

A Wednesday in December of 1979. Notes from a pocket journal.

I leave the hotel in the late morning and walk through the rain and mud-soaked streets to a little restaurant in the covered bazaar, stopping at a pharmacy to purchase a package of Vicks and two packets of Kleenex. A cold has entered my body. The lady behind the counter was two *lira* short, and seeing my condition, gave part of my change in aspirin rather than the usual chewing gum.

Ibrahim, who works in Efendi's bookshop, was at the restaurant. After we eat he slips away and pays for my lunch. It is a short walk from this part of the bazaar to Efendi's shop. After an hour there I excuse myself and go to the *dergah* to help with the preparing of *ashura,* the pudding Noah made after land was sighted. The dervishes make it in huge three-foot deep pots and stir the contents with four-foot long wooden oars. It takes two days to prepare. I am paddling across "the sea of life" opposite the *zakir bashi,* Kemal Baba. Tomorrow at the *dergah* hundreds will eat the pudding.

I am in bed writing this at 10:15 p.m. It rains outside. I invent a new sleeping costume. Long underwear (pants), socks, heavy tee shirt, cotton turtleneck, wool sweater and woolen cap, combine to keep out the bitter cold.

Thursday.

I go to the *tekke* to help with *ashura*. Kudsi Erguner came early with the intention of recording but two brown-outs cancelled his plans. A few of us had an early dinner at the *tekke*. The *zikr* is good but not too strong. I take the first ride to the hotel at 1:30 a.m. We drive through two inches of snow that is still falling.

Friday.

A night of rain eliminates whatever snow accumulated leaving the streets mud slicked. I feel a bit better so I go to Efendi's shop then to the mosque for Friday prayers. After prayer we go to the wedding ceremony of the son of one of the dervishes. I ride in the car with Efendi and after we drop him at his shop Ahmet takes me to buy dervish slippers from a man recommended by Safer Baba. Return to the bookstore until it closes at 6:30 p.m. I walk to Sultan Ahmet for some food and a night of rest and reading at the hotel.

Saturday.

The absence of light often makes mystery of the commonplace. At 12:30 a.m. Hafiz Ali picks me up from my hotel in Laleli and we go to coffee with Muzaffer Efendi. The management must think me mad. If I don't return at 3:00 a.m., I am leaving at midnight. Efendi meets every night with a small circle of dervishes at the Koska coffee and *nargile* house. A few nights before as we sat in a *sohbet*, the street was riddled with machine gun blasts and the meeting place was changed to a five flight walk-up salon in Beyazit, owned by one of the dervishes. There was unrest in the streets, students were unhappy, people were poor and depressed and anger flourished everywhere, it was a cold and dark time for Istanbul.

Bitter coffee was invented for dervish conversation. Words that reach deep into the night need a stimulus to keep the listener awake.

We arrive and find the group already there and after greeting Efendi partake of the plates of fruit and glasses of tea. After several teas and some coffee Safer Baba mentions the time. "It is 2:00 a.m. Efendi says: "Good," and lights a cigar. The room we are in is a small smoke-filled office with a circle of chairs and nine men all focused on the sheikh who makes never-ending conversation, in which Sufi stories are interjected. Not as pleasant an atmosphere as the outdoor café but safer at the moment.

It is 3:00 a.m. and the dervish talk continues. Efendi breathes smoke from his freshly lit Marlboro and says: "A person coming into this world is like a blind man. He is in darkness. Without faith he spends his whole life like a blind man. That is why God says that the blind in this world will be blind in the hereafter also.

"A person without faith is like a man who arrives at the marketplace after dark. In the darkness, this man cannot tell what he is buying. There are all kinds of people among the sellers. He pays his money and stuffs whatever they give him into his sack. He does not examine what he is getting. That man paid his money, but he has no idea what he bought. Back home, he empties his sack. He thought he had bought a rope, but finds he has a snake. The honey proves to be tar. The meat is a stinking carcass. All his money has been wasted, and he has bought himself a heap of trouble in the bargain. The human being entering this world is like the man going to the market in the dark."

To market we came
from our mother's womb.
We bought a shroud,
then back to the tomb.

He continues with a story by Mevlana. "Several blind people were brought into a tent, where an elephant was kept. They were told that they could now find out what an elephant is. Each blind person felt a different part of the elephant's body. After they came out of the tent, one of them was asked: 'What does the elephant resemble?' From the reply; 'The elephant is like a pillar,' it was clear that this blind man had felt the elephant's leg. 'No,' said another, 'the elephant is more like a wall.' A third disagreed, saying: 'Like a curtain,' while a fourth cried: 'Like a snake.' Each of them was right. The one who had felt the elephant's belly compared it to a wall; the one who compared it to a curtain had felt its ear; the one who said it resembled a snake had felt its trunk... The elephant's body did have all those parts, but they were not the elephant."

Efendi explained further. "Those who are dogmatic in matters of faith and belief are like the blind men describing the elephant. Each is right up to a point, but the whole truth emerges only if they get together and harmonize their conflicting views, instead of criticizing one another and fighting in the dark."

Efendi sees that it is now 4:20 a.m. and dismisses us. Istanbul is cold and dark at this time. The few men on the streets are like lost sheep. A cool blue light emerging from the headlights of cars illuminates the needlepoint *minarets* of the Beyazit mosque. Several soldiers at fixed bayonets on their automatic rifles, stand at the side of the road like an apparition forming a before dawn silhouette.

The Calligrapher's Ink

It is a rainy Istanbul winter day in 1980. I am pacing the steep cobblestoned street from Sirkeci to Gulhane, making my way through the stone alleyways and gusts of cold wind, before coming to the stairway that leads to Hattat Hamid Aytac's small flat. I came to ask him to write the Ninety-Nine Names of Allah for a book I was preparing. He was sitting on a broken chair in his little room stacked with rolled calligraphies of all sizes and stages, wrapped in plastic to protect them from the rain that seeped through the fissures in the ceiling. He wore two sweaters and a jacket to keep the cold from his body. As he wrote the Names of Allah for me his concentration was intense. He only breathed after the pen stopped. When his reed pen slid down the page to create the *alif,* he was aware that all letters could attach themselves to the *alif,* but the *alif* stood alone not needing to attach itself to any other letter. The *alif* represented Allah. When he drew the diacritical marks using a special green ink, he remembered his mother telling him that she used this green calligrapher's ink as *kohl*. "It healed my eyes and gave them an extraordinary look, as if they contained the letters of the Name of Allah, and a soft light would touch whoever saw them. Like the light in the eyes that saw Uwayys Kerani."

Hattat Hamid had written the Names of Allah numerous times and also wrote an entire Qur'an that was published. Between words he paused, looked up from the page, and said: "The words of the Qur'an contain *baraka*. Blessing and *suras* used to be woven into shirts and coats. Weapons were engraved with Qur'anic inscriptions, and soldiers sometimes wore clothes with the complete Qur'an sewn into the cloth."

A *hadith* states that: "He who writes the *basmala* beautifully, obtains innumerable blessings."

His was a hard life. The small broken room he lived and worked in was cold in winter inviting both wind and rain. He slept in a chair with another facing it on which he placed his feet. Water bubbled and boiled for tea that seemed to never end. We wrapped our hands around the small Turkish glasses filled with hot tea to keep warm.

The calligrapher continued speaking. " The calligrapher's hands must become wings and not be restricted by the constraints of daily life. My father once gave me a fistful of coins and told me to buy watermelon. I went to the market, wandered around and hours later returned home. 'Where is the melon?' My mind was so occupied with the shapes of letters that I completely forgot about the melon. I have been writing and cutting reed pens since I was a boy. My first teacher taught me. But in my old age I have come to understand that all this writing is just a sign that leads to the Book of Man. Man is a book of actions whose pages have been blackened by his sins with water-soluble ink. The Black Stone at the corner of the Ka'bah first was white, and then turned black from the constant touching of it by the hands of man."

Hattat Hamid then placed an uncut reed into the palm of my hand, its length resting on my wrist, and taught me how to cut the bamboo and transform it into a pen.

I recalled a passage from Shakespeare's King Lear.
THE EARL OF GLOSTER (blind)

The trick of that voice I do well remember.
Is't not the king...O, let me kiss that hand.

KING LEAR (mad)
Let me wipe it first; it smells of mortality.

"There is a possibility of washing off the blackness of one's own book with the water of one's tears and a solution of *Tawhid*. The world is a book whose understanding changes with the understanding of the reader."

The old calligrapher motioned for me to come closer. He had written the name of Adam, the first prophet and the first man. He showed me how the letters *alif, dal,* and *mim* represented man standing in prayer, seated in prayer and bowing.

"In the name of the first man Allah placed a secret of how to live. I keep the shavings from the numerous reed pens I have cut and have asked that these wooden flakes be used to heat the water that will wash my body when I die."

I saw Hattat Hamid a few more times and sensed the harsh Istanbul winters were catching up to him. He died in May of 1982 having seen ninety-one of them.

The Sheikh's Dream

A Malaysian sheikh had a dream. This night was 200 years ago. In the dream he was shown various movements that were done slowly and looked almost like a dance. The next day the sheikh began to do the movements that he was shown in the dream. Some around him said that this was not Islam.

He continued the complex movement that seemed to take his entire attention. He turned toward his heart. When he stopped, in the sand imprinted by his feet was the sacred phrase *la illa ha illa Allah*. These movements have been forgotten.

A grey-bearded dervish remembered his father teaching him the first movements. There was also a way to hold one's hands and fingers that spelled "Allah" and was similar to the way the Qadiri dervishes of India hold their hands during their seated *zikr*.

Passing The Baton

For Nuri's twelfth birthday we go to Istanbul. We are staying in Uskudar at the house of Nezih Uzel, a Mevlevi musician whose presence keeps together several dervish *tekkes* that are at the brink of decline.

Nuri is bonding with Safer Efendi who has taken him under his wing. They are walking a dirt road in Derseke toward the mosque at Akbaba. Tosun Baba and I trail them by about twenty feet.

"I used to walk with Safer Efendi like that. Now it is Nuri's turn. The baton is being passed." Tosun Baba agrees.

Near the tomb of Akbaba, a fifteenth-century Naqshibandi sheikh, grows an ancient tree whose roots stretch above ground like the fingers of a giant hand. Safer Efendi, Tosun Baba, Nuri and I are sitting on a wooden bench that circles the tree. Another bench faces the trunk. To the left of the tree is a cemetery whose stone markers reach to the top of a steep hill. In front of the tree is the old wooden mosque of Akbaba, and to its right at the bottom of the hill lies the village.

The bench by the tree offers a peaceful resting place. A crudely written sign framed behind dusty glass, hangs on the trunk of the tree.

The sign addresses the one who reads it. "Sit quietly in this place. Do not think or speak worldly thoughts. On one side of you is death and the other is life. The mosque is in the middle. Contemplate this." When the *mu'ezzin* calls the prayer, we enter the mosque.

Sheikh Akbaba taught the eight principles of the Naqshibandi path, to be aware of your breath, watch over your steps, the internal mystical journey, solitude in the crowd, recollection, restraining your thoughts, observing your thoughts, and concentration upon God.

Swimming In The Bosphorus

Later that week Nuri and I accompanied Tosun Baba when he visited Munevir Hanim, an elderly Mevlevi, who had introduced him to Muzaffer Efendi in 1972. She lives in an old *yali*, a villa on the edge of the Bosphorus, on the Asian side of Istanbul, whose interior takes you back to the last century. Tosun Baba and Nuri strip to their underwear and plunge into the cold sea.

A swim in the Bosphorus becomes a fitting birthday gift for a twelve-year old boy from New York City.

The Quiet Man

My father was a quiet man, and his father before him was also a quiet man. It is not surprising that I am a quiet man. I am comfortable in this skin and because I meditated for long hours in my youth it is not difficult to be alone, although not pleasant to be lonely. There is a difference. Aloneness is fed by solitary activity, art, music, and poetry. Loneliness is fed by awareness that something indefinable is lacking. Meditative solitude requires an inner happiness not necessarily nourished by another human being. I have experienced both.

Hilda's Picture

Hilda Charlton spent eighteen years in the East and studied with many yogis. In the early 1970s she held meditations in

New York and attracted a number of young people who were drawn to the gurus and meditation practices.

Once when we met in her Upper West Side apartment she showed me a picture of Master Khutumi, one of the ancient masters whose picture she hung on a wall and kept covered with a cloth. As she unfurled the cloth a golden light entered the room. I was struck with a feeling of awe.

Ahmet Badawi only went outside with a covering over his face, because his *nur* was so strong.

House Made Of *Zikr*

It is a Picasso grey Istanbul winter day. Black dust is embedded in the lines of my hands and when I make ablutions to pray, that same dust is mixed with the moisture coming from my nose. Dust is a cloud over this city, layered with a black powder emerging from the coal stoves heating the houses.

I am at the Jerrapasha Mosque in Aksaray for Friday prayers. The men of the crowded mosque are now departing. Some walk to the leather door holding their shoes high above their heads so as not to touch anyone with them. I see Raik Baba, a Rifai sheikh who is a friend. I often sat in his tiny tailor shop repeating *zikr* along with some elderly men of the neighborhood.

He is going to lead a *zikr* across the street in a four-hundred-year-old Ottoman building that is held together by the breath of the repetition of the Name of Allah. I walk with him up the rickety stairs to the *majlis* room. There are holes in the wooden walls and the floors not only creak but sink from the weight of men praying.

Nureddin Jerrahi, the *pir* of the Halveti Order of dervishes in Karagumruk, was born in an upstairs room of this house. We pray in the "room of gathering," in this wooden structure that outlasted the body of the *pir* by some three hundred and fifty years. His memory is reborn with every breath of praise that permeates the walls each Friday during the "gathering of the people."

My son Nuri is with me. We came from Egypt where he attends The American University in Cairo. I am a Professor of Practice, teaching Visual Communications in the Journalism Department. He is in the stage of becoming.

The *zikr* is powerful. Raik Baba has a strong, husky voice and charismatic personality. About twenty men are seated in a circle swaying as the repetition reaches a crescendo. I am aware that the floor is also swaying. *Ya Hayy, Ya Hayy, Ya Hayy*. The Names of Allah soak into the wooden walls creating a sacred space. Many of the men still wear their coats, as the room temperature is similar to the outside of the thin-glassed rattling windows.

After the *zikr* a simple lunch of soup and vegetables is served. Drink lots of tea while Raik Baba gives a dervish lesson. The *adhan's* voice breaks into the room. We stand in several lines and pray. As we are leaving I ask Raik Baba; "Can we start a collection to refortify the house." He plunges his finger into one of the supporting beams. Sawdust pours out. "The house stands only because of the breath of the *zikr*."

Within a year the government procures the entire block intending to build a hospital on the land. All the houses, including Pir Nureddin's, are razed. I manage to salvage a small wooden board from the house of the Pir. The hospital is never built and a parking lot sits there instead.

A Library On Fire

A sheikh used to say, "The believer should say to himself, 'There are only three days. Yesterday and what was in it has already passed while tomorrow is a hope that you may perhaps not obtain. Only the present exists. If you are among the people of tomorrow then the Lord of Tomorrow will bring you tomorrow's nourishment. Before tomorrow there is a day and a night in which many persons will lose their lives. You may perhaps be one of them.'"

In Africa an old person dying is "a library on fire." On the Friday before he passed, Sheikh Muzaffer wrapped a scarf around his head to keep out the February cold, and walked the short distance from his bookshop in Sahaflar Caddesi, past the crowded stalls in the covered bazaar, down a small street to the mosque tucked in between two larger buildings. He was the *imam* for Friday prayers and his presence drew so many men that one could only go into *sajda* by touching your palms to the back of the man in front of you. During the *khutbah* Muzaffer Efendi paused and said, "You won't understand this, but I do. My neck has been cut by a sword." The next week he was dead.

I was in the *tekke* in Istanbul two weeks before. Sheikh Muzaffer was filled with energy and joy and looked fine. He wore a new brown suit and was smiling. That evening the *zikr* was especially powerful and had the smell of honey. Many of us were weeping and felt as though the hairs on our arms were standing on end.

Several days later I returned to New York. On the day of our arrival the news came that the sheikh had died. Tosun Baba, Gul Baba, Salik Baba and I were on the first plane to Istanbul.

The night before, Baji Sultan, Efendi's wife called Safer Baba who was sick in bed. "Efendi was praying, he was in *sajda* and didn't get up." Kemal Baba was called and they raced to Efendi's house. Baji Sultan's brother Tevik was already there. Efendi was gone. Safer Baba lay down on the floor next to his sheikh's body. If only there was a way to transfer his breath to the sheikh. He lay there for some time and then they took Muzaffer Efendi to the *tekke* in Karagumruk and washed his body.

When we arrived he was in a plain wooden box in the old section of the *tekke* in the "Hall of Gathering," near Pir Nureddin Jerrahi.

The lid was removed, and for a moment we gazed at the peaceful face of our sheikh.

A green cloth was wrapped around the box. We took turns carrying him down the back streets of Karagumruk to the Fatih Mosque. It was Friday. At one point a flock of birds flew above us and it seemed as though Efendi in all his stature, his *taj*, the golden turban of the sheikh, resting on the coffin, was leading these hundreds of people.

We left him outside, entered the mosque and joined the thousands who were there for *Jum'a* prayer. Prayers were later made outside and then we carried him back to the *tekke* where he was going to be buried. By now the word was out. The streets leading to Karagumruk were mobbed. Traffic was stopped. People stood on bridges, peered from apartment windows, and hung from balconies to see the Jerrahi sheikh of Istanbul. Many of his dervishes from America and other parts of the world converged on the city to honor the one who had filled their hearts with love and knowledge. To some he was a bookseller, to others an *imam*, to us he was a Sufi sheikh who opened doors of understanding and perception and poured in love.

I helped some of the Istanbul dervishes dig the grave. We removed his body from the box and lowered it into the earth. Wood was placed around it, the hole was filled with earth, and cement was poured. We stood by the grave for a long time making *zikr.* It was an amazing experience repeating the Name of Allah on top of the fresh grave of your sheikh, feeling his *baraka*, and being part of an end and another beginning.

May Allah be pleased with him and give him a house next to the house of the Prophet Mohammed.

Frozen Images

Cairo, 1994

Roxbury, 1955

My father in New York, age 30

My mother, Montreal, age 27
Left: Learning the sema in Konya, 1973

1958 Roxbury Memorial High School Basketball team

Above: With Leonard Cohen, New York City, 1969
Below: Nezih Uzel in his house in Uskudar, Turkey, 1998.

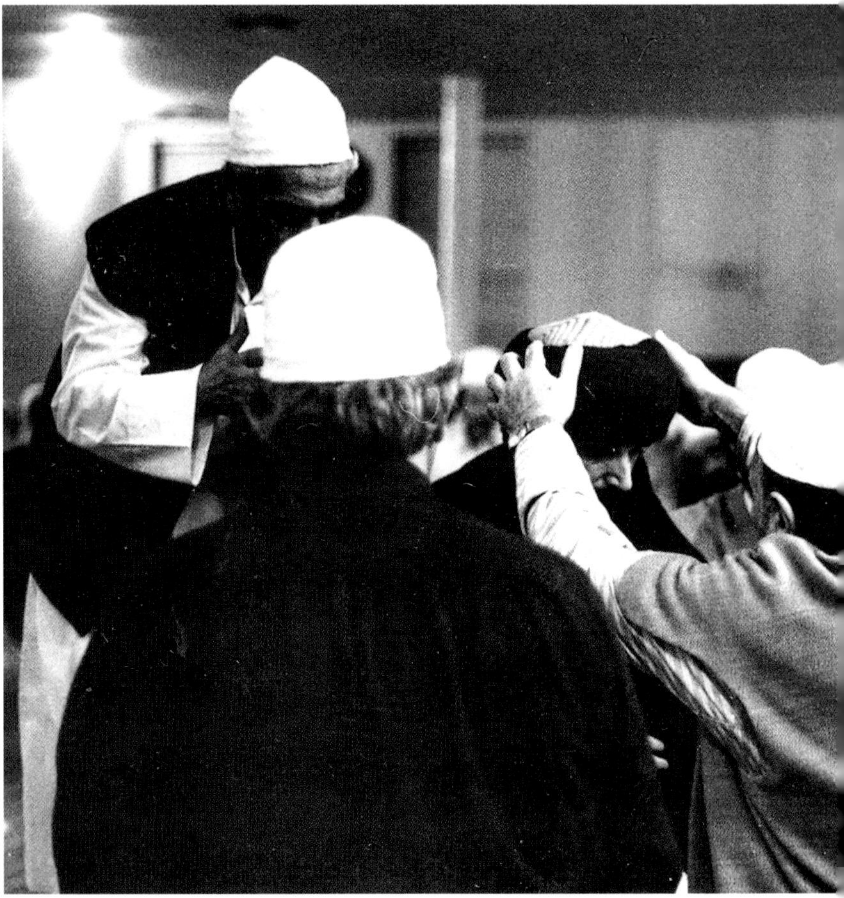

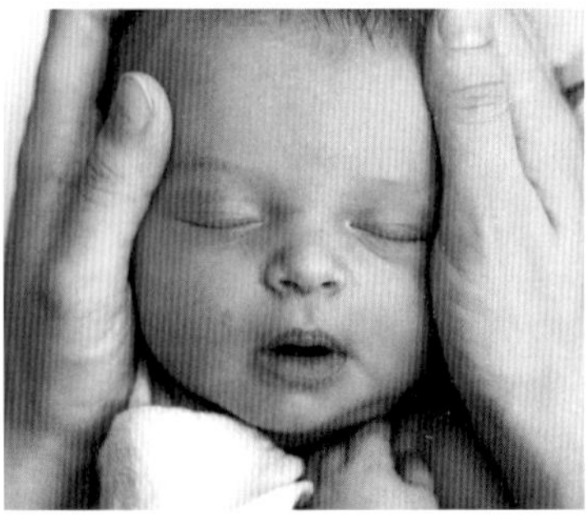

Sheikh Muzaffer al-Halveti al-Jerrahi initiating me as his khalifa, 1981.

Alia Rose.

My grandmother, Montreal, age 103.

Swami Muktananda at Big Indian, NY.

Paintings by Shems Friedlander

Above, Manscape, acrylic on canvas, 2013
Below: Reading Rumi (detail),acrylic on canvas, 2012

Right: Man as Macrocosm (detail) acrylic on canvas, 2011

Above, Man Who Dreamed He Was a Bird, acrylic on canvas, 2013
Below: Dervishes, watercolor, 2009
Right: The Calligraphic Man, acrylic on canvas (detail), 2013

Left: With Sheikh Muzaffer in his bookshop at Sahaflar Caddesi, Istanbul.
Above: With Sheikh Khateeb, Tanta, Egypt, 1980

Mawlid of Omar ibn al-Farid, Cairo, 1999

Above: Nuri playing bendir at the Jerrahi tekke, Istanbul on his twelfth birthday.
Below: Gurdjieff preparing a meal in Paris.
Right: Willem Nyland, Brewster, NY. 1963

Above, With Hassan Gai Eaton, London.
Below: The house of Pir Nureddin Jerrahi in Aksaray.
Left: Sheikh Muzaffer with Nuri in NY.

Above: Raik Baba and Manissa Dede doing zikr in Raik Baba's tailor shop in Aksaray.
Below: Nezih Uzel and Kani Karaca in Konya, 1973.

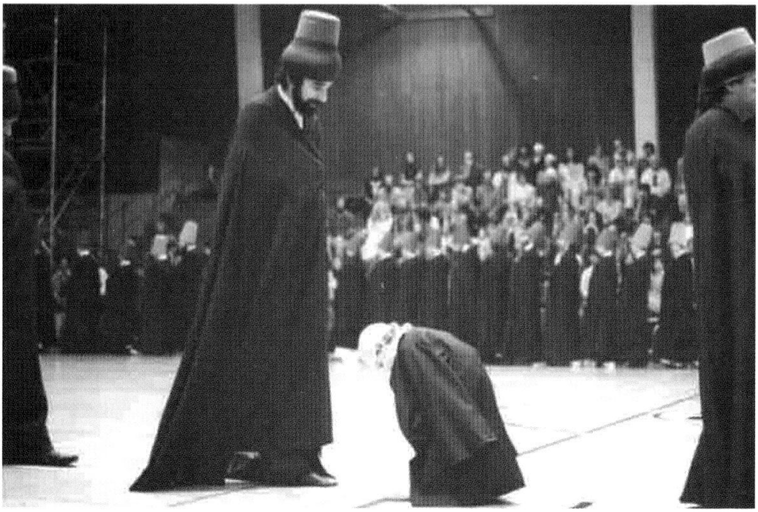

Above, Nuri age 4 bowing to me in the Mevlevi sema, San Francisco, 1982.
Below: Hazrat Inayat Khan, Chistia murshid.

Sheikh Safer Effendi in Madinah.

Above, A gathering with Sheikh Suleyman Dede, Konya.
Below: With Willem Nyland, constructing The Music Room at the Barn in Brewster, NY, in the winter of 1962.

Above, Mevlevi Sheikh Suleyman Dede turns alongside his son Jalaluddin at the Halveti Jerrahi tekke in Istanbul.
Below: Sheikh Fehmi, Madinah
Right: Early photo of Sheikh Safer Efendi.

A Night Of Sorrow And Tears

That night of "sorrow and tears," Tosun Baba, myself, and a few other American dervishes joined Safer Efendi in a small upstairs room at the Istanbul *tekke* and took hand with him.

Safer Efendi asked us to speak to the people at the Masjid al-Farah in New York. It was left to me to give the talk. Many of them were attached to the person of Sheikh Muzaffer and did not understand the necessity of taking hand with the new sheikh. This often happens when a sheikh dies.

I likened it to a train travelling in the direction you needed to go and before the destination it was necessary for the engineer to leave the train and travel another road, an invisible road. One does not trail the engineer, one stays on the train as long as its destination remains true.

It was a clear analogy, yet some stayed and others separated, creating a tear in the *tarikat* that eventually is mended by the sheikh.

Heart To Heart

Friends in New York used to ask why I had a spiritual teacher who lived in another country and spoke a language that I did not speak. When I departed from Sheikh Muzaffer in New York or in Istanbul I felt as though an icicle of knowledge had been placed in my heart, and only the warmth of my heart could melt the icicle.

I knew this Sufi knowledge was permeating my being, like the scent at the Prophet's Mosque in Madinah, because I would say things that I did not know and do things that I did not know how to do.

I am with Safer Baba in Istanbul, having dinner at his house before midnight coffee with Muzaffer Efendi at the street café. We are warming ourselves with tea and spiritual conversation. He relates a deep, profound, philosophical story.

The next day I am with Tosun Baba in Beyazit. I tell him of the conversation with Safer Baba.

"That is impossible. It is too deep. You do not speak Turkish and he does not speak English."

"We spoke *qalb ve qalb*, (heart to heart)."

Later, Tosun Baba mentions this to Safer Baba. "Yes I said that, he understood correctly."

"But you do not speak the same language."

"We speak *qalb ve qalb*, and we understand one another."

Treasure Maps

Like everything in this life the spiritual teachers who journeyed from the East to boost our inner lives were just as quickly taken from us. How else would we believe that this life is temporary, save by the taking of those we love?

The eighties witnessed the physical disappearance of Suleyman Dede, Sheikh Muzaffer, and Sheikh Muhammad Khateeb in 1985. Omraan Mikhael Aivanhov, Guru Bawa and Sheikh Fehmi followed them quickly in 1986. Trungpa Rimpoche in 1987 and Habib Omar in 1988.

They carried treasure maps across the oceans of the world, and taught us how to tune into the celestial sounds in our bodies that were temples of God. To meditate, move with consciousness, repeat the Names of Allah for they were a key to happiness and paradise. We tuned in and temporarily dropped out of the consumer race. When we returned to society, replenished, we found it occupied by those who worshipped greed, power, and gold.

Society had chosen to dance with the animals inside the cage of themselves. The pig in them ate unlawfully, the fox cheated, the monkey only wanted to have fun, the peacock wished style and the wolf was angry. Could the wolf be replaced with compassion, and the peacock with humbleness?

We continued to climb Struggle Mountain.

It Is Not An Easy Work

When the first man was complete, he was told to look over his right shoulder. There were three lights. He asked the first light its name and where it resided.

"I am Intelligence," it answered, "and I live in your head."

He asked the second light the same question.

"I am Conscience, and I reside in your eyes."

He looked at the third light and had to shield his eyes from the glow. "Who are you and where do you live," he asked.

The light answered, "I am Compassion, and I live in your heart."

On the other side of the Prophet Adam stood three darknesses. He forced himself to ask the first darkness its name.

"I am Arrogance and live in your head."

"That is where Intelligence lives."

"Only until I enter, then there is no room for Intelligence," said the darkness.

"And who are you," he asked turning to the second darkness.

"My name is Insatiable Ambition, and I reside in your eyes."

"But that is where Conscience lives," replied Adam.

"Not when I am there," uttered Ambition.

"And you," he asked the third darkness. "Who are you?"

"I am known as Envy, and I occupy space in your heart."

"Compassion is in my heart," said Adam.

"When I enter your heart," whispered Envy with a smile, "Compassion departs."

Can Arrogance be substituted with Purity and Sincerity, Tyranny with Justice, and love of the World with the love of God? This is what Sufism is about. It is not an easy work.

We were faced with the nineties, the decade of personal and political greed. The seeds of the economic crash of the entire world, as well as the Arab Spring, had been planted.

In a hundred years there will be all new people.

"We're only a pawn in their game," wrote Bob Dylan.

Misuse Of The Gift

A man came to the sultan with tattered clothes. He was asked, "How can you come to the sultan looking like this?" He said, "This is the way I am. I am not ashamed of this, but if after seeing the sultan and leaving the palace, I still had these clothes then I would be sad."

Man comes to Allah with the tattered clothes of his sins and leaves clean. Everything good in this world is a gift of Allah, and everything that we call bad or evil is the misuse of that gift.

The Cadi's Gift

Safer Baba peeled several oranges and placed the sections on a white plate in the center of the table, next to the red-ochre tea. A smell of clean air came from the Bosphorus. The billowing clouds moved slowly in a pale blue sky. We were sitting in the garden of his family home in Uskudar. Moments before we had lifted ourselves from the noon prayer.

His voice had a serious timbre as he began to speak about healing. "If there is illness recite *Sura an Nas* and *Sura al Falaq* then blow breath over the body. Breathe *Hu* on the hands and pass them over the face." Then he repeated a prayer.

"O Allah! Lord of the people, remover of trouble. Please heal this patient for You are the Healer. None brings about healing but You, a healing that will leave behind no ailment."

"The Prophet Mohammed's wife Aisha related that before he slept the Prophet would recite *Sura al Ikhlas*, *Sura al Falaq* and *Sura an Nas* then blow on his palms and pass them over his face and the parts of his body that his hands could reach."

Sometimes Safer Baba would just turn to me saying one word, "story."

"The *cadi* of Egypt sent the Prophet Mohammed a gift of a servant, honey and a doctor. The Prophet kept the first two and returned the third. He sent the doctor back along with a message, "I come from a people who eat only when hungry and don't overeat."

The oranges and tea were nearly gone when Safer Baba said, "Black love can kill. Many have died from too much love. If you have a tremendous love for someone it can turn him or her away so it is best to hold back a little. Anytime you love anyone more than Allah, you turn them into an idol."

Folded Prayers

I am in Muzaffer Efendi's bookshop. The wood stove is fired up and crackling. He is hunched over the old wooden desk folding paper, on which he had written Qur'anic verses, into triangular packets for recently born children or sick people to wear pinned to their clothing. Sacred origami.

Words That Heal

The quince trees were laden with fruit on a brisk day in October. A one-armed white bearded man in a blue coat was selling bird feed. He was surrounded by hundreds of pigeons. We were walking in the courtyard in front of the Beyazit Mosque when Safer Baba turned to me and said, "story."

"The grandfather of Sheikh Fahreddin Efendi visited a *pasha* in his palace. A friend of the *pasha* summoned him because the *pasha's* son was very sick. Many doctors treated the boy and had given him various medicines, but he did not recover. The sheikh said, "Bring the boy here, I want to see him."

The *pasha* asked, "What will you do?"

The sheikh answered, "I will read a prayer over him."

The *pasha* laughed and said, "The time for saying prayers has passed, we must give him medicine."

The sheikh asked, "Do you not believe in prayer?"

The *pasha* said, "I believe, but now there are many medicines. If we use prayer instead of medicine, the people will laugh. It is now important that the boy takes medicine."

To this the sheikh said, "You became a *pasha* without becoming a real man. You are still a donkey, and the son of a donkey." And he called him by many other derogatory names. Hearing this the *pasha* began to sweat and turned red.

The sheikh suddenly changed. He became quiet, peaceful, and gentle. He no longer looked like a man who had just spoken those angry words. He was sweet and kind. The sheikh looked surprised and asked the *pasha* if he was sick. "You spoke terrible words to me, of course I became sick," said the *pasha*.

The sheikh said, "Yes, I am a human being and spoke a few angry words to you and you became sick. If I speak the word of Allah to that little boy, why do you think it will not affect him and heal him? Is not the word of Allah more powerful than the word of man?"

The *pasha* wept. He said, "Excuse me, I did not understand, nothing could have been clearer than the example that you have presented to me."

The sheikh read a prayer and the boy recovered from his illness."

The Silent Conversation

Halveti Sheikh Mohamed Khateeb lived around the corner from the mosque that houses the tomb of Pir Ahmet Badawi in Tanta, Egypt. I first met him with Hussein, one of his *mureeds* who grew up in this small city whose focal point is the mosque and the annual *mawlid* for the *pir* that draws several hundred thousand people. I sat with him on a number of occasions and once after an *umrah* brought New York Sheikh Tosun Bayrak to bask in his wisdom.

Hussein and I drove the two hours from Cairo to visit the sheikh. We had just arrived from *umrah* and wanted to see him. It was March of 1983. Egypt was in summer. We mounted the three flights to his flat and were warmly greeted by a woman in *hijab* who ushered us into a small sitting room. Physically this short man with a huge nose and poor eyesight propped up by two canes is not the image one would have of a Sufi master. But within minutes I feel I am with the most beautiful being in the world, as if he was pure gold and the rest of us an alloy.

The endless glass of Arabian tea arrived. We drank, talked and breathed in the moment. *Allah Hu Akbar, Allah Hu Akbar*, the call to the *maghreb* prayer enters the simply decorated room. I tell Hussein that I need to make *wudu*. He gets up to show me the toilet and washroom. Sheikh Khateeb asks where we are going. He insists that he be the one to accompany me to the inner part of the house. He says, "Who knows when I may get the chance to serve Shems again."

There is a dry taste in my mouth, as if I swallowed desert sand. I hasten from the toilet and make the fastest *wudu* in history for this octogenarian sheikh, perched before me on two canes is holding a hand towel and waiting for me to face him. In one gesture I understand the essence of Sufism.

Slowly the sheikh drags himself back to the sitting room. He asks Hussein, a *hafiz* of the Qur'an to lead the prayer. I am standing behind Hussein with the sheikh to my right. *Allah Hu Akbar*.

I quickly put my thumbs to my ear lobes in the first position of prayer while standing. Sheikh Khateeb seems to be struggling. He raises his hands to his ears several times and then drops them again. After about five or six attempts during which he is uttering, *Ah, Ah, Ah,* he finally softly says *Allah Hu Akbar* and we both follow the *imam* in our movements.

Arabian tea and additional sweets are served. I ask Sheikh Khateeb: "I couldn't help but notice that you raised your hands so many times before beginning the prayer. As if there was some difficulty."

"Yes Shems. When you stand in prayer you are about to speak to Allah. In order to do that you must break through the whole world."

Sheikh Khateeb answered questions by raising himself to a high interior level, mentally wandering about in a meditative state where he saw things, and after several minutes descending with an answer.

Sheikh Mohammed Khateeb left this world in March of 1985 in Tanta, Egypt. His love was far reaching. Although he never met my son Nuri, he saw him in a vision and loved and prayed for him.

I am writing about Sheikh Khateeb from a small room in Istanbul that looks out onto the Marmara Sea. The maid interrupts me and says the room has a smell of beautiful perfume. I hadn't used any, nevertheless she insists there is a sweet scent in the room. Perhaps it is because I am thinking so deeply about this great sheikh.

Fragrance

Forty years after the Battle of Uhud it was decided to move the graves of the martyrs to higher ground, as floods were washing away the earth in the lower areas. The bodies of the martyrs were uncovered and carefully transported to a higher elevation. Each martyr still wore his bloodstained battle clothes and each body looked exactly as it had when buried. There was no sign of decomposition. There was a sweet odor.

When I stood at the edge of the martyrs' unmarked graves at Badr a perfume permeated the air. The pure scent of roses comes in wafts to some who are near the tomb of the Prophet Mohammed in Madinah. Sayyidina Hamza's desert burial place is surrounded by a beautiful scent, and the tomb of Sayyidina Hussein in Cairo bears a scent that remained on my clothes for several days. These are the ones who loved the Prophet and loved the Message he revealed. The *wali'ullah* is like the cumin seed. For his fragrance to be released he must be crushed.

Dream

At 6:30 a.m. on Friday April 11th, 1986 I had a dream of Sheikh Muzaffer Efendi. I was in Istanbul. Nuri was with me and seemed a few years older. We were walking around a mosque or *tekke*. Safer Baba saw us in the crowd and guided us through the courtyards and passageways. A large glass case rested on the floor off to the side of a main room. Safer Baba signaled not to go near because Nuri was so young. A glow came from the case. I thought Efendi was there and wanted to go near but waited.

Nuri's mother came from the crowd. I had purchased some books and wanted to give them to her but they were too heavy for her to carry. She was going to take Nuri for a while.

I approached the glass case and peered inside. I saw the *taj* of Efendi and what appeared to be a life mask of his head. His *jubba* was lying horizontally in the case and covered his body. Efendi's head faced the side. As I sat there an eye slowly rolled open. I felt as though I was in *jezbeh* and repeated, *Allah Hu Akbar, Allah Hu Akbar*. A crowd formed around the case. Efendi's head moved upwards. His face was colorful and he had the white stubble of a beard.

He smiled at me with that charming look of his and said, "Shemsi Baba." I said, "*As salamu aleykum Efendi.*" He rolled his body into a seated position and leaned against a corner of the case. I felt his face so close to mine.

Honey In My Throat

I sit with the taste of desert sand in my mouth, amidst black boulders historied by revelation and cracked open by time and heat. If I see the bones of Joseph, will I be washed by the tears of Jacob?

Safer Baba and I are walking the grey streets of Madinah surrounded by thousands of Muslims making their way to the Mosque of the Prophet for *fajr* prayer. It is three months after Nuri's birth. This is my first *hajj*, and my first time in the City of Light. It is like moving through a film. I clutch the edge of Safer Baba's *jellaba* so as not to be swallowed by the crowd. We gently nudge our way to the raised platform, built by the Ottomans, behind the tomb of the Prophet. A gentle *adhan* is chanted and hundreds of thousands of people, unknown to one another but with a common belief of peace and love, bow toward Makkah.

After the collective prayer Safer Baba continues to perform a number of *reka'at*. I don't know how many to do so I just follow him. I am stunned by a waft of rose scent entering my chest as I bow down in *sajdah*. The scent moves within my body like a zephyr. I continue the movements of prayer only now tears flow uncontrollably from my eyes. Safer Baba is also weeping. My heart may burst but I pray that this flood of tears may wash the blackness in me and leave space for me to fill it with the Name of Allah. There is honey in my throat and rose scent in my heart. After some time Safer Baba stops praying. We embrace one another on the tear-stained carpet then silently walk the streets of Madinah.

The pre-dawn greyness has been replaced by clear light. In Muzaffer Efendi's room Safer Baba and I relate the morning experience. The sheikh said, "The Prophet sometimes chooses to reveal himself to his lovers."

The Ant's *Hajj*

We are having coffee with Muzaffer Efendi in an outdoor Madinah café. A street sweeper is doing his job and the mild wind is sending dust into our faces.

"We are breathing this dust," said Efendi. The sweeper calmly looked up and said to the sheikh, "The dust of Madinah is worth more than gold from anywhere else."

The *alim* can be anywhere at any time.

After forty prayers in Madinah we boarded an old bus driven by Pervaz, an Iranian working in Saudi, to Makkah where we would perform *Hajj*.

Arrangements had been made for us to occupy an old school. There was a section for the men and a women's section. We slept on mattresses laid out on the floor like a row of soldiers. When we weren't at the Ka'bah or performing the necessary obligations of *Hajj*, we all gathered under the moon in the schoolyard and listened to Muzaffer Efendi talk about *Hajj*, Sufism, and Islam, between sips of hot tea and deep breaths of Makkan air. Tosun Baba is translating.

"An ant decided to go to Makkah and make *Hajj*. Others said, 'You will never arrive, the journey is too far.'

The ant replied, 'Then I will die on the road to Allah.'

Isn't this the state of all men? We are all going to the Mercy of Allah, whether we know it or not.

"The companions of the Prophet came to him and said, 'We are your brothers.'

"No, you are my companions. There will be a time that people who have never seen me, eaten a meal with me, walked with me, prayed next to me, fought with me, breathed the same air, or touched me, will love me more than you. They are my brothers."
We are those people.

The House Made Of Breath

It is 1984. I am in Santa Fe, New Mexico with Egyptian architect Hassan Fathy. We are there for the inauguration of Dar al Islam, a dream Islamic community that Steve Durkee, now Shazilli Sheikh Nurideen has established. I am writing an article for Geo Magazine on the mud-brick mosque that Fathy designed and built in Abiquiu. My friend Walter Chappell is taking photographs. Walter knew the Hopi Indian chief who lived in the village on the top of the mountain. We drive the dusty road to the chief's house. The Indians admire Fathy because he built the first mud-brick structure in North America using domes and vaults, that had no need for wooden beams to roof his structures. The Hopis build with mud brick but use wood for the roof supports. We are served tea. I asked the chief about a building we saw on the way up the dirt road to the village.

"I noticed a mud-brick house dried and crumbled to the ground."

The chief inhaled smoke from his pipe before answering. I glance at his tanned, strong, worker's hands. He spoke slowly. Sweet incense burned in the corner of the room.

"The people moved from this house. Soon after the walls dried and the house fell to the ground like crumbled bread. The moisture from the breath of those who dwell in the house keeps the house alive. It is the breath of man that is important. A dried out heart will also crumble like dust."

In Arabic calligraphy above the entrance to a *tekke* in Istanbul are the words "*Zikr Allah* Satisfies Hearts."

The Egyptian Violin

His violin was now silent, leaning on a pillow at the edge of a long couch in his Cairo apartment. The large, square window framed the dome of the mosque across the street. The aroma of emptiness crept into the room of silence. A silence that breeds the solitude of death. Age had melted his thoughts.

Journalist Abdallah Schleifer describes Hassan Fathy's room during his last days. "Hassan Bey was very weak but did not appear to be in pain. At his bedside was the book, *An Introduction to Sufi Doctrine*, by Titus Burkhardt, and a copy of *The Ninety-Nine Names of Allah,* by Shems Friedlander, a practical guide for those who sought the Divine Presence."

Eyes Taped Shut

O father perhaps you are only sleeping in my head. How less confused was the imagination of your youth. You lie on the hospital bed that has witnessed a thousand dreams of dying people. Your eyes are taped shut to prevent the liquid in them from becoming crumbled earth. No sight is allowed to break through those eyes of dust. The Bird of Life flies behind a distant cloud but has not yet disappeared.

King In A Patched Robe

Several years earlier I am in Raik Baba's tailor shop. He tailored me a suit from heavy Turkish wool to keep out the harshness of Istanbul's winter. Photographs of dervish sheikhs, including his father, hang on one wall of the tiny shop, alongside several calligraphies of Sufi sayings, and *hadiths* of the Prophet Mohammed.

Raik Baba is mending a pair of old trousers that belong to Manisa Dede, a Rifai dervish from the Kasimpasha *tekke*. The aged dervish sits quietly, invoking a *zikr* and showing us how he moves his tongue as part of the control of sound. His face shone, his eyes squeezed to light filled slits as he breathed *ya Hayy* in a manner familiar to the Rifai, Halveti and Qadiri dervishes. I was sitting next to this old, poor, man who in a moment transformed himself into a "king in a patched robe."

Raik Baba and I join in a short sweet *zikr* that lasts for about ten minutes and leaves the room with a smell of roses and the color of light.

Muffled Prayers

Nuri was in my arms when I stood in line to greet the Dalai Lama after his talk at the Cathedral of St. John the Divine in upper Manhattan. The Dalai Lama looked over to me and asked: "Is this your son?"

"Yes."

"Give him to me."

I felt the importance of the moment and handed Nuri to him. The Dalai Lama cradles Nuri in his arms while speaking muffled prayers into his ear, and after some time looks up and says to me, "Now you can have him."

The Toy Alligator

Sheikh Muzaffer is bouncing Nuri on his knee in front of a packed living room in the house of Haydar and Feriha on 82nd Street in New York City. Nuri is three or four. He had just shown an astonished Muzaffer Efendi a plastic green mechanical toy of a small alligator that is trailed and eaten by a larger alligator. Muzaffer Efendi was talking about the relationship of the mureed to the sheikh. He interrupted his talk and lifted Nuri off his knee proclaiming, "This is my dervish."

Mevlevis In America

Rumi said, "I am neither from the East nor the West, No boundaries exist in my breast."

For over 700 years men in black cloaks turned toward Allah in continual remembrance of their creator. When the seed of love is planted in the heart of a believer, only Allah knows where it will bear fruit. In September 1975 Suleyman Hayati Dede, the Mevlevi sheikh from Konya, in Anatolian Turkey, returned to his town after the second of five trips to America. His *mureeds* gathered at his house to share food and precious talk. I sat among them in Dede's small visiting room in a house planted at the edge of the Konya cemetery. Dede, then 70 and white bearded, began to speak to us. After a few minutes he stopped in mid-sentence and called for his son Jalaluddin who was preparing tea in the kitchen.

Keeping his son close to him Dede stated in a loud voice, "I have planted a seed in America my son, and one day you will pour water on it." Jalaluddin was taken aback. It seemed an impossible task for one who felt unprepared in both language and training. But one always feels unprepared for such a mission.

With the sweet pacing of patience Suleyman Dede trained his son in the Mevlevi way. It was only much later in life, as a grown man, that Jalaluddin, who had been born in the shadow of Mevlana's green dome, began to taste the flavor of the nourishment and learning that his father buried in his heart. Suleyman Dede knew a recipe for Mevlevi knowledge and slowly cooked it into the mind, body and heart of his son. Daily, father and son sat knee to knee, and while breathing the Konya air Dede filled his son's ear with the Name of Allah, his body with the meaning of prayer, and his heart with the connection of the inner meaning of the Name. He planted in him the habit of goodness. Only later would Jalaluddin fathom what was happening at that time. No one understood this. Dede once told me as we sat together at the Jerrahi Tekke in Istanbul: "Shems, I am preparing a feast of Mevlana for America."

The night before Jalaluddin was to go into the army he and his father were at the Jerrahi *tekke* in Karagumruk. Jalaluddin whirled wearing his dervish clothes and Suleyman Dede turned slowly, his head bent toward his heart and his right hand holding the lapel of his jacket. I was in the first circle of Jerrahi dervishes and along with Muzaffer Efendi loudly proclaimed the Name of Allah as we circled the two Mevlevis.

Three years later, the father embraced his son and put him on a plane to America. With no language and little money, Jalaluddin arrived at the community of Claymont in Maryland where he would teach the Mevlevi *sema*. Claymont was directed by Pierre Elliot, a student of Gurdjieff and friend of John Bennett who established this Gurdjieff-oriented community just prior to his death. Bennett had created Sherborne House, The Institute for the Comparative Study of History, Philosophy, and the Sciences, a Gurdjieff-oriented center outside of London.

Bennett awoke early one morning, went to the kitchen and prepared a soup for the entire community. Then he slipped back into bed and quietly left this world. His students ate the soup for lunch.

I met with John Bennett many times. In Istanbul we attended the Uzbek Tekke with Nezih Uzel, and in London we met and were arranging the publication of Gurdjieff's third series, *Life is Real Only Then, When I Am*.

The next year Suleyman Dede was invited to Claymont and sat on the sheikh's red post as Jalaluddin directed the *sema*. I was present at this *sema* that officially introduced the Mevlevi order to America. Jalaluddin Loras began to pour water onto the seed that his father had planted.

The following year Jalaluddin moved to San Francisco. His father had announced him as his successor and made him sheikh of the Mevlevis in America.

On January 19th, 1985 as the winter sun set in Konya, the family of Suleyman Dede gathered in his room. Several weeks prior I was in Istanbul and asked Muzaffer Efendi for permission to go to Konya and visit Dede who was ill and dying. "Go, it is good to see a person who is dying. You can learn from this."

I boarded the overnight train to Konya from Haydarpasha in Istanbul and arrived in early morning. First I visited Mevlana and then Suleyman Dede. We sat together in his bedroom. He had a dry hacking cough and there was a chill in the house. He looked at me, held my hand in his, and said, "If we do not strive for inner perfection, we will remain what we are now, talking animals. The world has never been without teachers. Each age has its teachers. Jesus, Buddha, Mohammed were some of the great ones, but there are always *qutbs*, special beings who take care of the world. The perfect man, the complete man, lies within each of us."

When I was departing he insisted that he leave his bed and walk me to the door. I photographed him standing at the door to his Konya house. Dede made it through that time but now he sat on the edge of his bed and spoke sparingly. *Yasin* was being read. With a weak voice Dede asked for his son Jalaluddin's dervish hat. As he gently fingered the wool, a smile appeared on his face; his soft eyes, which had seen the Holy Ka'bah in Makkah, closed and he slid from this life.

May your good deeds be a witness for you Dede and may Allah be pleased with you.

American Dervishes

In 1981 Jalaluddin Loras son of Sheikh Suleyman Loras of Konya is training Californians in the Mevlevi Turn. His father had made him the Sheikh in America and Jalaluddin, who was one of the best *semazen* of Konya, was sharing his Mevlevi knowledge with the west. A nail with a smooth rounded head is sunk into a meter square slab of wood, salted, and then the *semazen* places the nail between his big toe and next digit. He slowly begins to turn as Jalaluddin observes and makes subtle corrections. Right palm up to receive the energy from above that travels through the body and descends through the left palm facing down. Perhaps it is western pressure; perhaps an idea of unity, but for the first time, Jalaluddin introduces women *semazens* turning alongside men in the *sema*.

Jalaluddin has trained the Californians to sew the black cloaks, *tennures*, and vests. Dervish slippers and *sikkes*, the tall honey-colored hats worn by the *semazens* arrive from Konya. The tall hats represent the tombstone; the *tennure* is one's shroud and the black cloak the world. At a certain point the *semazen* leaves the world, drops his cloak, and begins to turn towards his heart quietly repeating *Allah*. The musicians practice compositions of 17th century Mevlevi music. This music is made neither for listening or applause, but for participation.

On the night of the *sema* Jalaluddin represented The Mevlevi and Salik Baba and I wore the *taj* of the Halveti order. Wali Ali and Shabda represented the Sufi group established by Sufi Sam Lewis. The Turners were all Californians taught by Sheikh Jalaluddin Loras, the son of a sheikh, and a baker and boxer in his youth.

A black cloak and t*ennure* was made for Nuri and at age three and a half he was the youngest to participate in a Mevlevi *sema*. He followed me in the Sultan Veled Walk and bowed at all the correct moments.

The Mud Of Paradise

Muzaffer Efendi deeply inhales the smoke from his cigarette. He pauses for a moment and follows the trail of smoke as it lingers in his lungs. The Koska café is not crowded at 1 a.m. The dervishes occupy a long table facing the street. I am sitting between Safer Baba and Kemal Baba. We are drinking black, bitter Turkish coffee. Everyone is smoking except me. Of course during the extent of the night I must reluctantly breathe into my body enough second hand smoke to tempt Cancer.

Muzaffer Efendi is eating a dessert of *kaymak*, a thick sweet cream that the Turks often serve alongside other sweets. "I love *kaymak*," says Muzaffer Efendi. "For me it is the most wonderful food on earth. But it is the mud of Paradise." The sheikh continues to talk about Paradise.

"A small circle had gathered around the Prophet Mohammed. When he concluded his short discourse the group dispersed. Referring to a certain man who was among those who walked away the Prophet said that that man would go to Paradise.

"The companions of the Prophet wanted to know why the man merited such praise, so they followed him for an entire day and also observed his actions at night. He prayed, ate, slept, did all the ordinary things that they also did. The companions went to the Prophet and asked about this man wanting to know why he was singled out as a future resident of Paradise.

"The Prophet Mohammed said, 'Before he goes to sleep each night he forgives anyone who wronged him in any way.'"

Observe Four Things

A man approached the Prophet and asked for an injunction, and for it to be brief.

He said, "When you stand up to pray perform your prayer as if it were your last.
"Do not say anything you will have to make excuses for tomorrow, and resolve to give up all hopes of what men possess.
"Observe four things," the Prophet Mohammed told him, "the guarding of a trust, truthfulness in speech, good conduct and moderation in the taking of food, including eating, drinking, and living."

The Harmonic Rope

The sugarless bitter tea was hot. The call to *isha* prayer reverberates from *minaret* to *minaret*, creating a harmonic rope that fastens the night to prayer. Safer Baba gives his back to the quince tree in his garden above the Bosphorus and says to me, "After night prayer we sit quietly and review our day, how we were, how we treated people, good or not good, an impartial review that can help us the next day."

The Bridge

Sheikh Muzaffer Efendi is giving a *sohbet* at the Masjid al-Farah in New York during one of several trips that he made to America. His words and thoughts are capably translated and interpreted by Sheikh Tosun Bayrak, Efendi's designated *khalifa* in the U.S.

Safer Baba is next to me along with the thirty dervishes that accompanied the sheikh from Istanbul. Muzaffer Efendi is a master storyteller and weaves Sufi lessons into every sentence. The hundred or so Americans seated cross-legged on the grey-carpeted floor were grasping at the hem of his wisdom.

"We pass from the womb to the bridge (life). Here we experience pain, sorrow, we strive to own and possess things, but this bridge is a dream. Some pass quickly on the bridge. The slow ones take eighty years and are pushed and shoved on that bridge until one day they come to the end. On the other end is a frontier where you will be asked for a passport.

"Who put you on that bridge? Why have you not looked for Him? We have not located the one who can give us the needed passport. Faith is the passport. If you have the passport of Faith the guard on the bridge will say that there is a stamp missing. The stamp of the Prophet Mohammed is missing.

"The passport is made complete when three things are known; the reason for being here, who brought you here, where you are going, and has the signature and blessing of the Messenger of your Creator.

"It is also necessary that you have performed what has been asked. The officials at the other end of the bridge are prepared to bid you welcome. You are then shown to a distant place that will be your eternal abode, but cannot travel there just yet. For now you will be a guest in a large light-filled room and from there you can see the place you will soon reside.

"The one without a passport is grabbed by his coat and reminded of who he thought were his many friends, but is shown that he is now alone. That man sought what he thought were the fruits of this world, and had no time to find his Creator or listen to the Prophet. His fame and fortune are gone.

"These are not stories. As sure as we are here we will be there. One enters this world with pain and can only leave by death."

Muzaffer Efendi paused to drink some tea and light another cigarette. He looked out at us, saw that we were still awake, anxiously listening, and continued his talk.

"A man came to the Prophet to learn the Qur'an. While learning the *sura* of the Earthquake he reached the words, 'Whoever will have done the smallest particle of good will see it on the Day of Judgement, and whoever will have done the smallest particle of evil will also see that.'

"The man said, 'This will suffice me,' and returned home. The Prophet said, 'This man returned being one who has acquired the understanding of religion.'"

The night was getting old, but Efendi seemed to want us to consume as much knowledge as we were able. Like Egyptian bread that must be eaten immediately before dust settles on it, the sheikh wished to share his knowledge before departing for Istanbul. "Allah gave to each of His creation a protection. Every animal has a way to protect itself from danger. The porcupine has quills, the skunk a scent, the snake can inject poison, the gazelle is swift, the lion has a fierceness and strength, the chameleon can change color, birds have talons and wings, and to man He gave the *zikr Allah*.

"To each of His creation Allah gave knowledge. The tiger does not know the knowledge of the bee and what the snake knows the zebra does not know. To man He gave the knowledge of how to know Him.

"'I was a hidden treasure and wished to be known, so I created the world in order to be known.' In this world only man can know Him. He has taught man His Names so that through invocation he can have knowledge of Him.

"Through *zikr Allah* man can enter the *malakut*, the spiritual world, the unseen world, and slowly leave the *mulk*, the world of choice."

New York Stories

I designed the country house in Lebanon Springs, New York with my friend the architect Hadi Clements. Actually I revealed spatial needs and Hadi came up with the concept of juxtaposed square rooms attaching themselves to a core octagonal room with a high ceiling. The octagon and the triangle worked together to geometrically marry various spaces. The design evolved and we made changes as the building was constructed. The initial influence of blending the house, like a Japanese Tea House tucked into the woods, came from the Egyptian architect Hassan Fathy who I met when he was designing and constructing Dar al Islam in Abiquiu, New Mexico. I wanted a house of tranquility, and a place for Nuri to experience the outdoors, so I chose a three-acre site that backed onto 50 acres of undeveloped woods.

Nuri and I would drive upstate from Manhattan on weekends and help with the construction. We stayed in a large house in front of our unfinished one that belonged to my friends Arif and Elizabeth. Nine months after construction began, after the last shingle was placed on the roof and the last tile secured on a back wall of the octagonal room (tiled because a Fisher Grandma Bear woodstove was to sit in front of it), Nuri and I stepped back from the outdoor deck and viewed our house nestled in the edge of the woods. The house was a short drive to the Abode of the Message, Pir Vilayat Khan's Sufi community where I attended meditations, retreats, and Sufi workshops, and Nuri hung out with Daniel and Ramiel, the children of Arif and Elizabeth.

I bought Nuri a bow. On weekends we practiced archery, and became masters of starting fires in the wood stove that staved off the winter cold. Snow was the norm in winter. A skin of snow on the land brought frigid beauty, except for the time we were caught in a storm, and drove into a pit at the fringe of the land. I could barely see the front of the car through the falling snow as I backed out of the driveway. Like a wound in the earth appearing from nowhere, a huge froth-covered mouth swallows the back end of the Honda into its jaws. Nuri later told me that when he saw we were descending he jumped to the opposite side of the back seat to try and balance the car. We had decided to be intrepid and attempt the journey back to New York, but the snow fell with the speed of a sprinter and our decision proved futile. Nuri couldn't walk in the deep drifts that were up to my waist. I carried him on my shoulders through the fresh snow.

Electricity vanished, so we used candles and kept "Grandma" heated to remain warm and cook soup. I told Nuri stories of Mustapha the Carpenter, who could make anything, and one day made a flying rocking chair. We would climb onto the chair with Kaleb the Camel and fly to distant places such as Egypt, where we saw the Pyramids. We trekked the mountains of Afghanistan, landed in the Himalayas and traveled to other intriguing and mysterious locations. We danced with dervishes in Anatolia, drank hot tea from glasses that fit into the palm of our hand and invoked the Names of Allah in *zikr* circles in the deserts and mountains of Arabia. Wherever we landed Kaleb the Camel was there to provide land transportation. I made the stories up in the moment, and continued to tell them as bedtime entertainment for several years in New York.

Days later the car was towed out of the hole by using a clever arrangement of pulleys and ropes. The snow was melting, and we headed back to 84th Street.

Hailstones as big as golf balls once bounced off the wooden deck and one dark June night, we witnessed a thousand and one fireflies paint a coruscating sky in the woods behind our house. Only the male firefly lights up to indicate his whereabouts to the female.

When You Hear Hoofbeats Think Of A Zebra

In November of 1998 I was invited by Irex Promedia to give several graphic design workshops in Bosnia. A short leave was requested from the American University in Cairo where I had been teaching visual communications for four years. James Napoli, a colleague from AUC, was in charge of the journalism program for Irex in Bosnia, and was aware of the necessity of teaching an accessible form of redesign, to the post-war struggling newspapers and magazines in Sarajevo and Banja Luka.

Jim and his Bosnian assistant Alena meet me at the airport on the 12th, and after dropping my satchels at a small, but clean hostel, we immediately get started on the first of four information packed days of design workshops attended by the editors and art directors of such publications as *Dani Magazine*, the newspapers *Oslobodenje* and *Vecernje Novine*.

The scent of war is still in the air. Blue helmeted United Nations forces pace the streets, and are perched in tanks at several intersections. Buildings are bullet ridden; some half collapsed to the ground. It is emotionally and physically cold.

The problems I hear from all participants are lack of money, computers, printers, and advertisers who don't fulfill payment contracts.

We analyzed each publication. I teach them how to use a twelve-part grid to create clear pages that have continuity. Their publications are crowded and cluttered. They are, for the most part self-taught, hard working and interested. Bombed out buildings are their offices and studios. Often they work with no heat, and sometimes no electricity. War thoughts and experiences are shared.

"I sat through university classes, the steam coming from my nose and mouth, freezing for there was no heat. I wore sweaters and three coats, my fingers were numb and I lost my kidneys." -Amila

It is November sixteenth. Ahmed, who is assigned to me, drives the winding, turgid, mountain roads to Banya Luka. I think to myself, as we pass small farms with broken walls and uprooted trees, how the terrain so resembles Turkey. But each farm is either without a man, or houses a man propped up by a hand-made wooden crutch that has replaced the leg he lost in the recent war. Banya Luka was razed. All sixteen of its mosques were torn to the ground by the Serbs, and replaced by small parks.

"I cannot remember my teenage years in Banya Luka. They were dark. There was no electricity for years, and no candles. We made light by taking a glass half full of water and any oil, even cooking oil. On this we floated a cork then took a shoelace wrapped in wax and lit it as it floated in the glass." –Selma

I give several graphic design workshops at the Soros Media Center. Sasha from the Reporter Magazine places the publishing programs and files that I brought into all the computers. Basically I repeat the Sarajevo sessions and give four days of workshops to editors and designers in Banja Luka.

We surround the general design work with an attempt to solve each of the publication's problems.

"We had to walk ten kilometers for water. Sarajevo had no food, water or electricity for years. The people starved. After they walked so far for a little water a sniper would shoot them through the window of their own house." –Senad

I give them assignments to redesign the existing cluttered pages of their magazines and newspapers and replace them with clean, accessible stories. I move from computer to computer giving individual comment about their work and offering some alternatives to adjust their designs when necessary. I leave them some articles I had written on typography and copyright.

"My youth was replaced by war. How can I have religion after what I have seen? A banana was a dream." – Leyla

It is the afternoon of the nineteenth. We drive the SUV over the mountains and return to Sarajevo. Men with missing limbs dot the landscape and wave us past their small thatch roofed houses.

Samira, one of the designers for *Suijet* magazine was reluctant to speak of the war. She left her house every day to work at a humanitarian organization.

"I was always aware of snipers."

She moved quickly along one of the main streets renamed "the street of running" by the Bosnians. Almost every building exhibited the pockmarks of gunfire that the citizens called "roses."

"Snipers were everywhere. I would even race, bent over, across a street, with a newspaper above my head."

Dr. Hasanovic Mevludin from Tuzla was waiting for me at the hostel in Sarajevo when I arrived. I had never met him but he knew me through my Bosnian friend Enver who told him where I would be. Years before he had read my book *When You Hear Hoofbeats Think of a Zebra*, and was moved to find a Sufi sheikh.

We squeeze into his small car and drive the snakelike road to Visogovic to meet the sheikh of his sheikh. The downstairs room of the modest cottage is crowded with circles of Bosnian dervishes. They seat me in a place of honor after Mevludin introduces me as a *khalifa* of a Turkish sheikh of the Halveti Order.

Hajj Hafiz is an 89-year-old Naqshibendi sheikh. He has a short cotton-white beard. His body is thin and frail. His eyes are filled with a light that casts a soft glow in the direction he is looking. His hands are large, as if he had worked long hours in the fields when he was young. He speaks softly but with authority.

"Allah has put Light everywhere in this world. There are some who would like to extinguish this Light. If they succeed in one place, Allah makes the Light appear in another place.

"Allah gives His Light and the knowledge that is not from books to whomever He wishes. He gave this Light to the Prophets. To many other *alim*, He has given a little. For centuries there have been men who studied the books and lived a good life and they have been given a little Light.

"Before Noah there had never been anything like a boat. Noah built this ark from the direction of Allah. He used wooden nails and as he inserted each peg with a mallet he said the name of one of Allah's prophets. With the last nail he said the name of Mohammed, PBUH. Mohammed was the last prophet. With him came the completion of religion. If any prophets who had come before came again, they would teach according to Islam. Although Mohammed was the last prophet there have been many *alim*, who have Light and came after him."

Sheikh Hajji Hafiz drinks tea with us and then slowly turns and goes to his bedroom. On Thursday nights he leads a small circle of men in *zikr*. A gathering of around two hundred men and women attend his Monday night *zikr* in a local mosque.

After leaving the sheikh's house we go to the house of one of his *mureeds*, an *imam* who heals using verses of the Qur'an. He feeds us and serves tea. There are a number of men who were at the sheikh's house and they are anxious to know how Sufism is presented in the West.

They have suffered through the recent war yet are not broken spiritually. They are strong. It seems that Islam in pre-war Bosnia was not well practiced. During the war many mosques were torn down. This was not a civil war. This was a war against people of different religions who had been peacefully living together.

Mevludin told me of his sheikh who was also a *mureed* of Hajj Hafiz. He spread Islam during the war although it was dangerous.

Sheikh Mehmet was thirty-seven when he stepped on a mine, toppled to the earth, rolled over and hit another mine that also exploded. He came from the Serbian side of the Drina River where he had a small mosque filled with the energy and blessings of repeated *zikr*. He had many *mureeds* extending to the other side of the Drina and one night when the fighting was at its peak, he was advised to take his family and flee.

He departed for Vienna with no possessions. Some time later he visited Bosnia and decided to return and live there with his wife and two daughters. He started the Sufi brigade and was its commanding officer. They lived according to the Qur'an. Two years after he formed the brigade, on May 2, 1994, he stepped on the mine. Just before dying he spoke the Name of Allah. His *mureeds* carried his body high during the funeral and one of his young daughters still sees him in dreams and describes his actions. She describes the way his hands look when he rolls his prayer beads.

Two women in the village were seers and when asked whether Sheikh Mehmet died in pain, they answer that at the moment of death he was in front of the gathering and died as he raised his hands and said *Allahhu Akbar*.

Roses In The Desert

December 15, 1986, Pages from a Journal

It is more than a year since the passing of Sheikh Muzaffer. I arrive in Makkah via NewYork-Riyadh-Jeddah. When we crossed the line of *hejaz* the pilot announced that those who were making *umrah* should put on *ihram*.

Hussein and I make *umrah*. It is 11:30 p.m. This was the first time that either of us kissed the Black Stone in the corner of the Ka'bah, at every circumambulation.

During the *sai* (the walking and running between the two mountains Safa and Marwa), we spoke of the prayer of Sheikh Khateeb.

Ya Allah, my sins cannot harm You,
and Your forgiveness can take nothing from You.
Please forgive that which cannot harm You,
and give that which takes nothing from You.

Sunday, December 20, Madinah

In the al-Bay'ah district of Madinah, down winding dirt streets the span of a tall man's outstretched arms, near the house of the late Mahmud Khan, behind a green door with the Arabic number 4 whitewashed on the door jamb, is an old Naqshibandi *tekke*.

On the outside of the door is a wide courtyard open to the sky, part of which has an arboretum with crawling vines suitable to shade the desert sun. The scent of jasmine floats in the air. Walls are lined with tea utensils, and a refrigerator stands on the southwest corner of the yard. A small kitchen is beside it. Down a mud brick corridor is the place for ablution.

Hassan is from Turkey. He has lived in Madinah for over twenty years, and at sixty insists that if his sons want to see him they must come here, for he fears not dying in Madinah. He lives with his wife in a small flat around the corner from the late Mahmud Khan's house. We climb the tall stone steps and enter a room carpeted and pillowed for comfort, that is about two meters square. It is here, on the Oriental carpet, that Hassan and I drink soup and tea and make *zikr Allah*. We listen to a tape from Konya of Naqshibandi dervishes. At times we are touched to tears and once Hassan loudly cries out with the tears of a child. The love of the Prophet is so deep one cries tears of joy and separation.

Madinah, the Illuminated City, is like this.

In March of 1988 this entire area is razed to make room for the mosque's expansion. Mud to mud.

After *asr* prayer I once again meet the old Syrian dervish Sheikh Hussein, who I met two years before with Tosun Baba. He made a prayer for me and for my son Nuri and then kissed my hand. I kissed his heart.

Later that night I accompany Mostafa al-Badawi to the blind Sheikh Ibrahim's house for Qur'an reading. Sheikh Ibrahim is from Tanta, Egypt and knew Sheikh Khateeb. Tea was served and later Mostafa takes me to a large open field, walled in, but with no markers, where Sayyidina Hamza is buried. It is very late and no one else is here. As I approach the iron gate that encloses the area,

I smell roses in the desert. Each of the three times I've gone to the place of Sayyidina Hamza, the scent of roses has been present.

Monday night, December 21, Madinah
Hassan collects me after night prayer at the raised platform behind the Prophet. As we depart the mosque by Bab al-Salaam, the Door of Peace, several men are discreetly signaled and they hasten to follow. Sheikh Suleyman from Cairo is outside. He greets me warmly as do the others after Hassan makes a remark in Arabic. We walk under the new expressway, pass a municipal building and enter the small dirt streets of the Qeeba District. Down Safer ibn Abdul Aziz Street, a few turns later and we enter an apartment building that is next door to a barbershop. An elevator takes us, a few at a time, to the fifth floor.

Our shoes are left at the door and we enter a small, carpeted room decorated by Arabic calligraphy on the walls. One by one bearded men enter the room. Each man is given a white robe and a white hat. The robes are slipped on over our clothes. The sheikh sits with about thirty men against the four walls. The Qur'an is read. Each man reads one *juz*. In this manner, thirty men can read the entire Qur'an. The quicker readers help the slow readers. In about an hour the Qur'an is read. Those who cannot read recite *sura Ikhlas*.

The *silsila* of the Naqshibandi Order is recited. The lights are then turned off. Out of the silent darkness the Name of Allah is spoken. The *zikr Allah* begins. Various recitations are mentioned and chanted by the men. The *tawhid, la illa ha illa Allah,* and the Name Allah is repeated thousands of times both aloud and *qalbit* (from the heart with a heavy breath). The darkness offers anonymity and no one gets caught up in personalities. The sheikh leads the *zikr* and sets the verbal pace. As my eyes grow accustomed to the darkness, the white robed men take on an ethereal look, the look of angels. For indeed, there is an angelic feeling here. Hearts and breath merge with the Name of Allah, the proclamation that there is no reality but Allah, and that the Blessed Prophet Mohammed is His Messenger. In this darkness I hear the weeping of spiritual warriors. Ibn Arabi said, "Some tears of men have a healing quality."

After the *zikr*, lights are again turned on. A large white cloth is placed on the floor and a meal is presented to all. The sheikh serves everyone himself. Huge platters of rice and chicken are brought in from an unseen kitchen prepared by anonymous cooks.

Before we depart the sheikh again tells me how welcome I am and repeats the *Fatiha* several times for the *shuyukh* and the people of the way.

I like this sheikh. He has a gentle but firm manner. His *zikr* is soft and sweet, yet strong. And he serves his *mureeds*.

A sheikh was asked, "What happens if you continue to do *zikr* and it doesn't reach your heart?"

"Keep doing it. Sometimes *zikr Allah* doesn't take effect on the heart until fifteen minutes before you die."

Thursday night, December 24, Madinah

Shadhilli-Kaderi Sheikh Fehmi died in Konya in late Ramadan, 1986. He never wanted to leave Madinah for fear of dying elsewhere, but went to Turkey for family business and took his last breath near the tomb of Mevlana Jalaluddin Rumi. May Allah be pleased with this loving sheikh who, for twenty-five years led *zikrs* long into the Madinah nights.

I walked into the historic section of Madinah, not far from the Mosque of Omar and came to the green door of Sheikh Fehmi's *tekke*. Abdul Hamid, the current sheikh recognized me and said, *Masha'Allah*.

We sat awhile in the dimly lit carpeted room, and then the seven of us who were there, piled into two cars and drove to another part of Madinah. Having spent so much time in Turkey and other countries, where I only knew a smattering of the language, I was used to being stuffed into cars in the middle of the night and transported to secret *zikr* circles in remote areas.

The house was large with an even larger garden. Sheikh Gemal from Cairo was there and introduced me to a number of men who were already seated in the large room. Some of them I recognized from the mosque. The group quickly swelled to over a hundred, and among them walked Abdullah Farag, known as the *Praiser of the Prophet*, because of his vast knowledge of poetry and his golden voice that now only voiced poems and songs praising the Prophet Mohammed. When Sheikh Gemal began to introduce me, Abdullah Farag interrupted, "I know Shems." A wonderful evening of singing *ilahis* (songs praising Allah and the Prophet Mohammed) was followed by a *zikr* that went deep into the night. When Abdullah Farag makes *zikr Allah* it feels as if your heart will burst and the walls of the house will fall.

After the *zikr*, in true Arabian style, there was a feast. Lamb was served on huge metal trays surrounded by mountains of rice cooked with raisins and Arab spices. The skull of the lamb sat in the center of one of the trays as we all ate with our right hands from the abundant platters. A large man in a white *thobe*, his red-checked *ghutra* around his shoulders, plucked the eye from the skull and popped it into his mouth. A delicacy, I am told. Blond Arabian coffee flowed accompanying trays containing hills of sweets.

The days unfurled and a week later Hussein and I stop to pray at the new Quba Mosque on our way to making another *umrah* in Makkah. It is a beautifully designed mosque and was still under the final bits of construction and decoration. Hassan Celebi, the master calligrapher from Istanbul, was brought to design the writing on the inner dome and the ceilings. The oversize calligraphies are drawn by the master on huge sheets of tracing paper and then transferred to the ceiling and walls where they are "painted in" by the calligrapher's apprentices.

Hussein was speaking to the Egyptian foreman in charge of the construction. When Hussein called me over to introduce me, the man said, "I know him." "But how?" asked a surprised Hussein. "I saw Shems the other night at the *zikr*." We embraced.

An Angel At The Prophet's Mosque

Madinah, Ramadan, 2010

We are unrolling streams of plastic at the Prophet's mosque in Madinah as a surface to place food for the thousands who have come for the last ten days of Ramadan. I am next to the place of the Prophet drinking *zam zam* water from a small metal bowl whose inside inscription is the *tawhid*.

Sheikh Zaki Yamani, the former Saudi Oil Minister and a lover of the Prophet, is perched on a chair at the edge of the wall next to the Prophet.

We eat some dates together, then Mohammed Adaaqqaq and his brother, Madinah historians, serve the ones who have gathered near the Prophet.

A twelve-year-old wearing a *kamis* in the syle of the Afghans, is serving the men seated knee to knee on the carpet. He has authority, dignity, presence, and beauty, and does not appear to be much like the rest of us. He is like an angel who has come for a few minutes to share the grace of Mohammed.

The call to prayer reverberates through the mosque and bounces off the walls, embracing each person. Men scramble to form straight lines in the overcrowded area next to the Prophet. Everyone wants to pray here. After the *maghreb* prayer I glance to see the boy again. He has disappeared.

Seventy

On my seventieth birthday at a family dinner in an Istanbul restaurant, I was asked to say a few words.

"When you see older men, their backs arched, it is not from age, but from carrying our sons on our shoulders so they can see further than us."

On a facade of the Chartres Cathedral outside of Paris there is a frieze of New Testament Prophets standing on the shoulders of Old Testament Prophets so they can see further than those that came before them.

The Sultan Of Food

A sheikh was invited to a grand feast at the sultan's table. There were many guests, but the sheikh, appreciated for his knowledge of Islam, was placed close to the sultan.

Twenty-six kinds of food were served. Lamb, chicken and rice placed on golden trays, formed mountains of nourishment for the guests. Fish and a variety of vegetables were on other serving trays in the center of the table. Non-alcoholic drinks of every color and taste were poured from huge glass containers. Everyone ate to his or her fill. The sheikh said *Bismillah*, to himself, as he ate moderately. Soon he stopped eating. The sultan looked over to him and asked if he was pleased with the food as he ate so little. "I have filled my stomach. There is room for no more," said the sheikh. The sultan accepted this and the feast continued. After some time the tables were cleared and Arabian coffee and tea were served, along with a mountain range of *baklava*.

The sheikh slowly began to eat the *baklava*. He ate several of the honeyed pastries, until finally the sultan interrupted him and said, "You said you were full. That there was no room for more, yet you continuously consume the *baklava*."

"My dear Sultan," said the sheikh, "If you came to the door of a room crowded with people sitting knee to knee and shoulder to shoulder, and there was no space for any one else in the room, everyone would move a little this way and a little that way and make a place for you O Sultan. *Baklava* is the sultan of food so everything in my stomach moves a little so that the sultan may enter.

The Sound Of A Saw In The Hearts Of Men

I knew the *tekke* of Sheikh Fehmi was somewhere behind the Mosque of Omar in Madinah. I had been there the year before, but was taken in moonlight, and couldn't remember the way through the small winding streets. I was determined to locate the building and wandered the desert streets with their mud-brick houses searching for a way in. I recalled the Buddhist phrase: "The way in is the way out and the way out is the way in."

Whenever I saw a man on the street and assumed he was from Madinah, I approached and asked, "Do you know Sheikh Fehmi?" Perhaps there were ten questions and ten apologies. "Was the sheikh not to be found?" The sun baked the streets and anyone on them. Finally I spot a Turkish man.

"Yes, down this street and behind the green door. But they do not meet until after night prayer."

I thank him, mark the place with my mind, enter the mosque through Bab Salaam, and wait for the sunset prayer.

The green door on the ground floor opened to the *tekke* of Sheikh Fehmi. I remove my shoes and enter the *majlis* room. It is a bare walled rectangular room. Men wearing *jellabas* are sitting against all four walls. I join them.

Sheikh Fehmi enters and sits in a corner of the room. He is in his eighties, with a closely cropped white beard. His back is bent from osteoporosis. There is the glimmer in his eyes of one who has continually repeated the Name of Allah.

The sheikh glances down the row of men on my side of the room. When he sees me he reaches into the inner pocket of his white vest and pulls out a wad of papers and cards held together by a rubber band. From this packet he draws out a thin green disk with the *tughra* of Pir Nureddin Jerrahi, that I gave him the previous year.

The *zikr* begins. Sheikh Fehmi enters the center of the room and repeats *la illaha illa Allah* numerous times. We all repeat the phrase acknowledging that there is no god but God. The sheikh chooses another man to lead the *zikr* and returns to his place. After several minutes he signals that I should enter the center and lead the *zikr*. I start slowly, increasing the speed and tempo until the Halveti *zikr* is like a saw roaring its sound into the hearts of the men who are now swaying in place.

Sheikh Hussein from Syria is present and weeps each time the Name of Allah is sounded. I step before each man and as the *zikr* continues the energy in the room nourishes every heart. After almost half an hour Sheikh Fehmi concludes the *zikr* and I return to my place. He gives a short discourse and answers questions as we all drink Arabian tea.

My Egyptian friend Hussein and I walk back to our hotel. A sliver of moon peeks from behind one of the *minarets* of the Prophet's Mosque. As we pass the *minaret* Hussein says, "You know, I saw a remarkable thing tonight."

"I was with you all night, why didn't I see this?"

"The remarkable thing was that you, an American from New York City, whose parents came from Russia, were leading a group of men from not just the Arab World, but from the entire Muslim World, in a *zikr* in Madinah, the City of Illumination."

A Cage Of My Body

There was frost outside in February of 1999. The trees in the garden of the Uskudar house were bare. They were breathing internally, preparing for April. Safer Efendi would not see the flowers of spring.

He died on the birthday of Pir Nureddin Jerrahi. He was taken to the *dergah*, his frail body washed and wrapped in seven and a half yards of white cloth that had previously been washed in *zam zam* water. Dervishes packed ice against him and pointed several fans toward him so as to keep the body cool. He felt no cold. His body was placed on the floor of the sheikh's *sohbet* room upstairs for the night. His last words before dying were, "I am going on a voyage."

During his final two days on the earth he lay quietly in bed dressed in his white *tennure* and his *kamer*, the dervish belt tied at his waist, and his white Jerrahi hat on his head. He lay like a bride in waiting, sensing he would soon be called. No more heart attacks, no more liquid filling his lungs, no more hospitals, no more sweet and sour things, no more pain. He was about to sprout wings and join the ones he loved who had preceded him to their Lord. "Going to Allah," he used to say.

The generals of Hazreti Pir can never be replaced. Someone else will sit on the blue post of the *asitane* sheikh, squirm beneath their skin in inadequacy and continue the *zikr*.

Years ago when his body was still healthy, we sat in the garden of his home facing the Bosphorus, and he told me that the *khalifeler* of Hazreti Pir were like soldiers waiting to be called into battle. Our duty now was to prepare and know that not everyone is called.

When Muzaffer Efendi passed in 1985 Safer Baba was called as the sheikh of the *asitane dergah* in Karagumruk. He had been groomed for this since childhood having been raised in the laps of sheikhs. He had little formal schooling but knew the ways of the *tariqa* and never dreamed as he served Fahreddin Efendi with the love of his heart that he would sit on the blue post of the Halveti Jerrahi dervishes. His goodness was his simplicity. His imitation of the manner of the Prophet Mohammed, and his unending kindness and love towards others, fashioned the wings he now adorned. He had the humbleness of Fahreddin Efendi. Once when asked what he did, he answered: "I teach what I know, and learn what I don't know." His body was almost useless. It had become translucent. Soon he would not require it for anything.

Then between breaths, lips moist with the name of Allah, he slipped past us to his freedom. February is the cruelest month.

Mevlana wrote:

I am a bird of the heavenly garden.
I belong not to the earthly sphere.
They have made for two or three days,
A cage of my body.

Ashtavakra said: "Look upon friends, possessions, wealth, mansions, wives, gifts and other good fortunes as a dream or a magic show, lasting only three or five days."

Push Gently

It is around 2:00 a.m. in Makkah. I am in a short line hugging the wall of the Ka'bah waiting my turn to kiss the Black Stone. A sparse crowd is circumambulating the "House of Allah." I knew I would get to kiss the stone, and wait patiently as people shove to the front from the right side in an anxious attempt to avoid the line.

After a while of not advancing, the tall Sudanese man behind me, he appeared even taller than he was for his turban was wrapped high in Sudanese style, spoke to me. He was impressive. "You must push."

"We are at the door to the House of Allah. I fear what might happen to me if I push someone and he fell and hurt himself."
"Yes, but you must push gently or you will never arrive."

Origin Of The Turban

One day the Angel of Death appeared to a poor elderly man travelling between two towns in the desert. The old man was taken aback and began weeping.
"Why do you weep?"
"My *jellaba* is ragged. If I go with you now many days, perhaps months may pass before my body is discovered, it will be decomposed and have the odor of death. Some poor traveller will have to bury it and my *jellaba* will shred in his hands. Let me reach the town I am going to, obtain a new *jellaba,* and I will return in three days to this spot where you may visit me again."

The Angel of Death agreed, and the old man continued his journey. The old man honored his promise. He went, returned, and the Angel of Death carried him away.

Several weeks later some desert tribesmen came across the body. His *jellaba* had been tattered by the sand and sun, but wound about his head they found a strong, clean, white cloth, and they buried him in that. Since then, men of the desert have carried their shrouds wrapped about their heads, but such a long time has passed, that today few Arabs understand why they wear a turban, and few still even wear the turban.

The Prophet's Cloak

In Fatih, an historic district in Istanbul, there is a small mosque with a special wing where the *hirka* of the Prophet that was given to Uwayys Karani is displayed. Barish, a soft-spoken Turkish man in his thirties is in charge of the wing where people come in droves during Ramadan, when the *hirka* is exhibited publicly. Barish is the 59th grandson of the brother of Uwayys Karani whose family has protected the cloak of the Prophet for nearly 800 years. I met him at the Jerrahi *tekke* in Karagumruk. We became friends and he invited me to the mosque at any time. I went with my wife Hatice and saw the cloak close-up in a private viewing. It was stretched out on a slightly slanted platform that was under glass and acclimatized for preservation. One is awe stricken to be so close to a garment worn by the Prophet Mohammed. The white cloak had the most detailed pattern woven into it and seemed not to be of an earthly nature. Barish told us that "masters of fabric" had examined it and the conclusion was that this cloth was not only sacred but did not originate on the earth. I thought of other cloth that must have been otherworldly. The untattered shirt of Joseph, who was thrown into a well by his brothers, and the clothes of Abraham after he emerged from the fire, must have also been brought by the angel Gabriel.

There are worldly clothes that have been made sacred by the permeation of spiritual energy that remains in the natural fabric. When one is in a high spiritual state, such as may occur during *zikr*, fragments of energy emerge from the body and enter the clothes one wears. Worn later, they can be a reminder of a state of remembrance. That is why the same clothes or woolen shawl are often worn in meditation. The Halveti dervishes wear a particular vest during *zikr*. The room where one meditates, prays, and repeats the Name of Allah, takes on a presence that is built up by these practices.

In earlier days, after a particularly spiritual *sema,* when *semazens* embraced the state of *wajd* and *jezbeh*, the Mevlevi sheikh would have all the *tennures* and cloaks worn in the *sema* placed on the floor of the *semahane*. They were then cut into small pieces and given to the *semazens* and musicians as "fragments of *baraka*." The fragments gathered from several *sema* ceremonies would be sewn and patched to make a cloak referred to as *morrakka* which was worn as a blessed garment.

Mind Thieves

Bob Cato's room was stuffed with memories that he could no longer approach. Years before he was the creative director of Columbia Records, where he brought a visual magic to the design of record album covers, and befriended many of the label's stars.

Now he just sits and stares past the orange chair in the corner, his own collages hanging helplessly on the wall, into the sea of his memories which cling to the edge of the inside of his skull, and slip and slide about just enough to confuse him. "It's enough to break glass," he says.

"I'm a Quaker, we think differently. I'm married, where is she? It's been weeks." His voice shakes as he speaks. Along with his words tears squeeze out from the corners of his brown eyes, and make their way down the rivers of wrinkles that come with a 74-year-old face. "This is not right. Why am I here? I'm not Picasso, but I am an artist."

I suggest he keep a journal, collect new words and pictures, add to the collages that he has always loved. He used to glue images on paper, cut them, arrange them, make them conform to a thought or memory of the father he can barely remember, or a joke on de Kooning, an homage to Van Gogh, those fields he'll never see again. What of the Florentine lessons?

"I'm a Quaker. I think a lot about suicide. I wish I could do it."

Tears flow. "I don't have the guts, but I think of it." He stares at the black covered sketchbook that offers no inspiration. "My wife is young. Do you know her? She hasn't been here in days, maybe weeks. Perhaps she has a boyfriend. Tell me. I would rather sit here alone," he stressed the word alone, "with the agony of truth than with the agony of absence."

He kept apologizing for his state. Was he keeping me? I'm happy you are here. I would be sitting here alone. Where are my friends? When I had entered the unlocked door to his room he stared at me with eyes of doubt and said, "Help me, give me a name."

The house on 57th Street just off First Avenue once belonged to Greta Garbo. Now it was a design studio where Bob and I had churned out record album cover designs, books, the typography for movie credits and any other graphic design jobs that came our way. The studio was upstairs, joined to the living room by a circular metal staircase. I imagined Garbo silently climbing these iron stairs to her quiet bedroom. We always had music. Dylan singing about Hollis Brown who lived on the outside of town, The Band, Johnny Cash, Sly and the Family Stone. Lena Horne would come over with Geoffrey Holder to shoot her latest album cover. Flowers for Barbra Streisand, dancing with Janice Joplin, lamenting with Leonard Cohen; Bob was always there with his generous smile and sound advice, always the gentleman from Cuba. The Quaker.

"I am a Quaker. I was brought up different. We care and we have insight. I'm glad I don't have children to go through this with me." Of course he did have children, grown now, two sons who come to visit every week. I wonder if in this state he remembers his sweet daughter, plucked from life in youth, an implosion of the head that left her lifeless within moments. But that was long ago.

Time seems to have been erased. There is lucidity of thought that is mixed into a thick soup of events that cannot be extricated from the past. The new impressions are confined to this tiny room. Not as bright as Van Gogh's in Arles. The single bed, the dull orange chair, a desk, photos and collages, some books by James Joyce and a sketchbook with a black cover and his signature scrawled on the front. Impressions stop here. A room, yes, but no match for the cyan-walled room in Arles which looked out at the sunrise of the south of France with its rows of twisted grapevines, blue-armed farmers and elegant cypresses reaching toward a mare's tail sky.

His was a faded room, buried among the greys of New York City. Impressions stopped there. They stop. I look into his face and wonder how long a man can live without impressions. "Tell me your name." I do. "Oh," he sighs with recognition and leans over to hug me. "It is the beard that threw me," he says, but I know it is dementia. The mind-killer of the healthy. "I sit here. I can't have an intellectual conversation with anyone. I'm a Quaker. Where is she? Can't she just poke her head in the door and say, I love you, I'm late. A letter goes a long way. Just a word, I am alone."

He stares at the faded orange chair and for the tenth time admits his thoughts on suicide. "I can end this. If I had a gun." He turns his hand into a pistol, checks the bullets and puts it to his head. "It will end. I have to believe that it would end, or I couldn't do it. I force myself to believe that it would end. Guns were made to end things."

When I leave he stands and hugs me. I kiss his cheek and hold his hand. Waiting at the elevator I see him walk in and out of his room to catch a last glimpse of me before I evaporate into a memory that no longer exists. We wave at the air. He touches his heart. A good feeling seems to transcend the long hall. It had to weave itself through a corridor lined with wheelchairs and motionless people frozen in their illness, waiting....

Will someone erase the day my uncle took his 12-year-old

nephew to a Yankee game at Fenway Park in Boston? We saw Joe DiMaggio, who hit safely in 56 consecutive games and married a movie queen, slide into home plate to score a run on a sacrifice fly, and Ted Williams, "the Splendid Splinter," a Korean War pilot and the last man to hit over .400 in a season, send a ball spinning 500 feet in the air, over the green fence, and into the rail-yards of Boston's Back Bay. Could I protect this memory from the mind thieves?

He forced himself to stay awake into the early hours of the day with the hope of glimpsing the thief of his mind. Sometimes he sat there in his orange chair while tears the size of eggs pushed their way out of the corners of his eyes, slid down his face, onto his chest and down his legs, forming a pool at the edge of his iron bed, and continued under the door of his room out into the putty grey corridor and as the salt from his tears touched each frozen man or woman they miraculously were healed and rose from their prison chairs and did a slow dance along the halls of the hospital. But these were only thought pictures pasted together with wishes, for nothing short of God's grace could unlock the minds and limbs of the patients frozen in time.

Every person's life is his own. As he sat there day after day after long day, until the days glued themselves into one continuous revolution, his friends and lovers would occasionally break from their routines in the mill of nonsense and think of him from the distance of their lives, not knowing that each thought was a tiny light, a star which entered his lonely room and sparkled for a brief moment. He went on like this, the ink stains on his fingers now erased, no longer the badge of a working artist. "I am not Picasso, but I am an artist, why am I here?" He had his voice but where, where are his thoughts. "I am a Quaker, I can't kill myself." Although his aged mother released the burden of an old, sick woman, from her loved ones by ingesting mail-order hemlock.

Thoughts came and fled. Where were the connections? How could he re-paste the puzzle of his life even to know that he had lived? Was he always like this? If so, then how did he know so much? He was like a man searching for his sunken name. Dancing upon the Sea of Forgetfulness, never reaching any shore, he saw himself walk upon a sacred river bubbling with scenes of his life.

It was his birthday. He didn't know it. We told him. We came with two kinds of cake, candles and love and took him to a small city park, near the nursing home, that had a waterfall on one wall. A lanky George Plimpton walked passed us on 79th street. Where had his youth gone? Where has mine gone? Bob ate cake and laughed. Then like a child walked with his little steps over to the wall and let the water flow through his open hand. The sun reflected colors in the water.

He was in his studio making a collage, mixing colors with water, homage to the writer James Joyce or perhaps to his father who was now a distant memory in someone else's mind. That day he made two watercolors, a collage, and wrote a secret poem. One watercolor showed streaks of different colors braided together and interwoven like the long flaxen hair of an early lover that had been touched by sunlight. When he finished he drew a horizontal line across the bottom of the page, titled it "Prayer Carpet" and signed his last name beneath the line, much in the manner of Paul Klee. He loved the painters, their style and wit, the way they make circles of color look like fruit. Cezanne's fruit. He was happy that he was also called an artist. He did not know that rainy Tuesday that his mind, like de Kooning's before him, would slip onto a blank canvas as he stood before it, brushes fanned between his fingers and no colors. No colors. Not even the caked cerulean blues and yellow ochre wedged beneath his fingernails.

When Renoir's fingers became gnarled from arthritis he taped long-handled brushes to his wrists and continued to paint. Van

Gogh placed a circle of candles on the brim of his straw hat to see the night landscape.

What could he do? His mind had slid into a world of little content, into a world of discontent. The bread of dreams would never satisfy his appetite. He briefly travelled further back to when he was a protégé of the Russian designer Alexey Brodovitch who taught him about white space on a page and how to crop a photograph and position it on the landscape of a layout. He always knew that words were art, but now Brodovitch taught him that stems and serifs, shapes of letters positive and negative, descenders, beards and loops all were limbs of the art of typography.

The water felt good between his fingers. He smiled, ate some apple cake, and blew out the candle that we all agreed represented his life. One thin faded red candle that we insisted he blow out. No one would help. He had to summon his own breath to snuff 74 years in a moment.

It wasn't that his mind was gone, just memories. He still had impressions, saw colors, heard sounds, and touched hot and cold things but somehow in the shuffle his desire vanished. His heart had no diseases. No jealousy or arrogance, no false pride, yet sobriety was decreasing. If only wishes had wings. That night he slept with that thought. He dreamt he was on a hunt for memories. There were a number of venerers in the winter forest, yet he was alone. He arched his bow and found his quiver empty of arrows.

Now he tries not to sleep for he heard somewhere that saints do not sleep so they can see their souls depart from their bodies. He just sits...and waits....

Sailing To Byzantium

Sheikh Necmeddin sits cross-legged on a divan covered with a floral-patterned cloth in the Uzbek *tekke*. A small dark-colored skullcap covers the top of his head and a black woolen *haydariya*, the style of vest worn by Ali, the fourth rightful *caliph*, is worn over a white, collarless, unkempt shirt.

Behind him, a plate decorated with Turkish patterns is nailed onto the wall. A small, green cloth is behind the plate. Next to the cloth is a calligraphy of a *Bismillah*, mounted on an *ebru* painting drawn on water and written in *thuluth*, by Neclet Okugay who grew a black rose in his garden after Ataturk closed the *tekkes*.

In an open green cupboard built into the wall to his left are dervish artifacts. Two *neys*, some photographs, another decorative plate, prayer beads in the shape of teardrops, and some old wooden inlaid boxes. On a tea-stained sheet of paper leaning against a pencil drawing of a grey-bearded Sufi, someone had scribbled a few lines from *Sailing To Byzantium*, by William Butler Yeats. Near this page was a dried red rose whose scent had long since returned to the rose seller. By his right arm on a low table sit two *nargiles*. In his left hand Sheikh Necmeddin holds the smoking part of the *nargile* that snakes back to its home in the glass apparatus in the rear. He seems to breathe in the smoke. His eyes reveal that he is either in deep thought, or silently invoking the name of Allah. His mustache is mostly white now, and his beard is a stubble of several days growth. He is present to the moment and looks out into a part of the room that I cannot see.

The smell of burning tobacco has long permeated the divan, the chairs, his clothes. A hint of apple is in the tobacco and offers the room sweetness, like the incense burning in an invisible corner.

The sheikh turns his head slowly and addresses one of his *mureeds*. "If you are somewhere, you are everywhere, and if you are everywhere you are nowhere." As he speaks smoke leaves his mouth creating a cloud around the words and holds them in the air a little longer so those in the room can exchange them for thoughts. He resumes the art of smoking.

The second *nargile*, the one that rests on the front of the table, is also being smoked, as the tobacco lit by burning coals indicates. The rope end of this *nargile* loops over the glass neck and forms the Arabic word *Hu* (He), then weaves its way toward an unknown smoker. On the far end of the wall hangs a Turkish *kilim* from the Lake Van district, and beside it a calendar indicating the times of the five daily prayers. In the corner of the wooden floor of the Ottoman room is a prayer carpet from Erzerum, whose central image is an alcove in a mosque pointing toward Makkah.

Perhaps the sheikh is thinking of the train ride to Konya, where he will go tomorrow and visit the tomb of Mevlana Jalaluddin Rumi. Tonight, he will cook...all night, food for a hundred people. He will put *baraka* in the food, recite the phrase of unity, breathe the attributes of the Lord into the food, and write the name Allah on the ground meat and the soup with a wooden spoon. After the train departs from Haydarpasha station and journeys toward Anatolia, he will distribute the food to the other passengers.

First a kitchen, then a *tekke*, all the sheikhs know this. The blessing of food is to feed others.

But now he inhales the smoke cooled by water in the glass bowl, or perhaps he is breathing in the name of Allah...only he knows.

The photograph is about ten inches square and is surrounded by a forty-year-old black mat stained by old coffee. A thin brown frame, beveled at its edges, creates a boundary, but the Naqshibandi sheikh has long ago departed for a space with no boundaries.

On this night the Uzbek *tekke* in Uskudar is crowded. Nezih Uzel and Kudsi Erguner have organized a music evening that will begin after we all eat the special rice cooked by Sheikh Necmeddin's elderly widow.

The building is on its last legs and it is still years before Ahmet

Ertegun, the music producer and owner of Atlantic Records in New York, will supply enough funds to renovate the structure. Ertugun was a relative of Sheikh Necmeddin.

Nezih is now the focal point of the *tekke,* bringing musicians and dervishes together every Sunday night for *zikr* and dervish music. Kudsi is the son and grandson of two great Turkish *ney* players. He will later become an important musician, composer and archivist in his own right. During a long pause in the music a *zikr* would begin by a circle of men seated on the carpeted floor. Nezih has brought me here many times so I am familiar with the musicians and the dervishes who come from different Sufi orders.

The Rifai Rose

On a winter Friday in Istanbul I followed the cobblestone street that bent toward a three-hundred-year-old wooden house. Hanging from the side of the structure was a tiny green *minaret* whose color had been scraped by age. A single bare light bulb hung from its roof and the enclosure itself was large enough for only one man, the *mu'ezzin,* who long ago, when the dervishes were legal in Turkey, sounded the call to prayer from this little balcony.

I walked down a dimly lit corridor, up a flight of stone stairs and was taken to a small, carpeted section separated from the main room by a low wooden railing. The overflow of men had just begun their prayer and I joined the line. When the prayer concluded the *imam* of the *tekke* spoke for fifteen minutes and read aloud the lineage of the order beginning with its founder Ahmed Rifai.

The main floor of the *tekke* tilted, and from the slanted ceiling many bell-like glass jars were hanging from brass chains. These used to be oil lamps but now some of them had electric bulbs. The wooden walls were painted green with brown trim.

About seventy-five men sat around the walls of the room forming a square while another eight men sat in two rows dividing the room into thirds. Sheikh Moyneddin sat in the center of the back row. He was in his eighties and hadn't shaved for several days. He seemed to control the energies flowing through his body. At first he looked like a sick old man who needed help in getting up and going to his knees to sit in the dervish manner, but once the ceremony began he took on a great presence and seemed to have the strength of a man forty years his junior. I was asked to participate in the *zikr* and was led to a place in the front. During one of the more gentle practices of swaying and repeating *bismillah* one of the men began to shake his head violently, to and fro, in an uncontrolled manner, and soon his hat was flung from his head as he jumped around the room on his knees, and loudly proclaimed the name of God.

All the dervishes wore either white or green skullcaps or had on woolen astrakhan hats that were kept on during the entire ceremony.

Directly in front of the sheikh stood ten glass bottles filled with water and several pieces of under-clothing. This was for ill people in the community who, after the *zikr* vibrations had permeated the bottles, would be given the water to drink and the clothes to wear.

The women were behind wooden grates and could not be seen, although they were able to view the ceremony through the small apertures or venetian blinds.

The practices began slowly and gently as the men performed many *zikrs* standing, kneeling or in motion. Very soon the *zikr* picked up in intensity and one understood why the Rifai are known as the Howling Dervishes. Theirs was a heavy howling *zikr* during which some dervishes would revolve in place and shout *Allah, Allah*. Some jumped about the room on their knees frantically swaying their heads from right to left and crying *ya Hayy* or *Allah,* while others slapped the floor.

All this built to a crescendo of silence when the *Rifai Rose* was brought into the room. Two men carried a large brass container full of burning coals and placed it in the center of the room. A long-handled iron implement shaped like a child's shovel was heated until it was white hot. There was a murmur and movement among the men.

The old sheikh removed his jacket, rolled his sleeves to the elbows, and bent his head to remove his false teeth that he placed in the palm of one of his dervishes. He then slowly walked to the container of coals and picked up the white-hot iron by the handle. The tension and vibrations built as some of the dervishes began to jump in place shouting *Allah, Allah* or *ya Hayy*. Others began to repeat *Hayy, Hayy, Hayy* or *Hu, Hu* as the sheikh walked around the center of the circle. Directly in front of me he touched the hot iron to the palm of his left hand. He did this several times and it left no mark on his hand, nor did he show any ill effects or even a change in countenance or posture. For several minutes he walked among the men licking the hot iron as if it were a child's lollipop. The coals were removed from the room and the sheikh then began a circle of dervishes who repeated *ya Hayy* in a deep howling sound that came only from the breath. As the dervishes moved around the room continuing their repetition the sheikh slapped the top of his hand and shouted commands of position and physically moved some men to different positions in the circle according to their various vibrations. The men turned toward their hearts, holding hands, and repeating the name of God as their left foot touched the floor and the circle wove a fine light around the sheikh who stood in the middle controlling the kinetic energy. During one phase of the *zikr* I felt the *jezbeh*, the gentle wind of paradise that seemed to make music as it touched the heart of each man and caused the hair on one's body to stand on end.

When the circle of men stopped, everyone fell to their knees and listened to the sheikh who pronounced a long prayer. When he finished the *zikr* ceremony was over, all stood, to begin late afternoon prayers.

Old Age Is Not For Sissies

Hassan Gai Eaton is a tall, slender man in his early eighties, with slicked-back salt-and-pepper hair, who has written extensively and brilliantly about Islam and the West. We first met in 1990 in Washington D.C. when he was visiting his son Leo, an independent filmmaker. He had a deep understanding of Islam and Sufism and, in his British manner, had the gift of expressing this knowledge. We liked one another from the first meeting. I traveled to London at least once a year, and we met for talks and milk-tea. His collection of pipes was vast but now he smokes cigarettes that he rubs with a piece of clove to give the tobacco a pleasant odor while burning. These days he wonders why no one he sees on the street or in the supermarket was around when he was born. He often quotes the American actress Bette Davis who said, "Old age is not for sissies."

It is a typical grey British Sunday morning. I am interviewing Gai in his cottage just outside of London for a documentary film I am making called *The Circles of Remembrance*. The room is chilly. Gai wraps an orange scarf around his neck.

"*Zikr* which is basically mention of God's Name is in fact the way we remember Him. We may mention Him aloud, which of course Muslims do constantly, or mention Him silently in our minds or in our hearts. Now why remember God? In the first place it is a matter of keeping in contact with the Real, for *Allah* is *al-Haqq,* which is normally translated as the Truth but can also be translated as the Real.

"To some extent in our earthly lives we are in a kind of dream. Not the kind of dream in the sense of something less real than what is before us, above us, below us, and after us. And if we ignore that something, whatever you choose to call it God or Reality, we are quite simply out of touch with Reality. The common phrase that would describe this state is insanity. In that sense anyone who forgets *Allah*, forgets Reality constantly in his or her life is effectively insane. They are out of touch with Reality.

"Beyond that, there is the methodical remembering, inward mentioning if you like, and that is *zikr*. It can take many different forms. In Sufi practice it takes a fairly precise form varying according to the *tariqa*. In the ordinary life of a Muslim it plays a very important role. Not least when we are busy. Not least when we are troubled. Because in a sense this world is a prison, and many people in fact feel imprisoned. The cause of many neuroses and various mental problems in the modern world, a sense of claustrophobia, is a result of this imprisonment.

The remembrance of God, the reassertion of what is Real is an escape. If you are in prison what's wrong with seeking a way to escape if you possibly can?

We have that way to escape, through the remembrance of Reality, the remembrance of God."

Hassan Gai Eaton passed at the age of eighty-eight, on a balmy day, in April 2010, surrounded by family and friends in a hospital in London, England. The world is less for his no longer being here.

What Is In The Glass Is Not The Sea

Muzaffer Efendi is giving a *sohbet* to a circle of listeners. I am sitting next to Safer Baba drinking the endless glass of unsweetened tea. We have just finished the night prayer.

"The dervish is even closer than a brother. *As salamu aleykum* means peace be upon you. For the dervish it also means peace upon everyone, even those not present and that you affirm you are ready to do anything to help your fellow dervish if he is in need or trouble. To be a dervish implies closeness. Being together and helping. When a Muslim enters a room he places his hand on his heart and says *As salamu aleykum,* may the peace of Allah be upon you all. The hand on his heart symbolizes that the five pillars of Islam are in his heart and no harm can come to anyone in the room from him. It is an old thought that you are a Christian, Jew, or Muslim. Now what is important is that we are all brothers. If you are a Muslim you must accept all men. If you don't you are not a Muslim."

Sheikh Muzaffer looks at me and then toward Tosun Baba. "When you return to New York you and Tosun should see each other. The dervish is closer than a brother. Even before you come together there will be a third, and then another and another.

Tosun Baba began a *dergah* in Spring Valley, New York, by feeding people and it soon grew into a mosque and today is one of the most important communities of Sufism in the West.

The next night several of us are having dinner at Baha's house. They are a Bektashi family. Muzaffer Efendi never misses an opportunity to share his knowledge. "You begin every meal with *Bismillah* and end with a prayer repeating God's Name. When you eat and think of God it puts *nur* into the food. You are then nourished to continue praying and saying His Name. It is the job of the sheikh to lead people to God. They will be led according to how open they are. The sheikh is not God, but a sheikh can be close to God. If you fill a glass with water from the sea, what is in the glass is not the sea, yet it is the sea. This is how the sheikh can be to God.

"Jesus came when medicine was at its height. All cures were known, but no one could bring a dead man to life. Allah gave Jesus this power, showing that Allah is greater than man.

"In the time of Moses magic was at its height. Allah gave Moses a power of magic so great that it amazed the pharaoh.

"In the time of Mohammed, literature was at its peak. There were men who were great poets and could recite a thousand verses. Allah sent the Koran through Mohammed and no poet could match its content. Allah provides through His messengers whatever is needed on the planet at a certain time."

Tears Of Blood

January 1976, Istanbul.

Nezih and I are up the entire night with a few friends listening to dervish music and talking. I plunge into a deep sleep at six in the morning and have a dream of Willem Nyland. It is in a wooded area in the country and many people are present. The air smells of oncoming snow. He asks me to clean his glasses. They are very thick. I breathe vapor on the lenses and clean them with cotton. I keep cleaning and cleaning. He asks me if they are ready. "Soon." I had to clean them perfectly so he could see because he was blind. A horse and rider appear on the path. "I was told to make certain that he is okay." I ran up to him grabbing the reins and say, "I'll lead you to the house."

I am at the tekke of Sheikh Muzaffer. *Ah Teslimiyet* is written in *thuluth* and hanging on one of the walls. There are two red drops coming from the letters. Zulfu is sitting next to me and explains. "*Teslimiyet* means the submission and from the letters come drops of blood. The submission to *Allah* is so difficult that you can cry tears of blood."

A large spoon decorated with Arabic calligraphy hangs on an opposite wall. The dervish feeds many people.

Horns Of Light

When Moses came down from the mountain his skin radiated such light that the people could not look upon him. When he finished speaking he covered his face with a veil. The light coming from him was so great it looked as if he had horns of light. This is why Michelangelo mistakenly painted Moses with horns. The horns of light are the horns of understanding. Gurdjieff makes this reference in the chapter on Impartial Mentation in *All and Everything*.

In the caves at Lascaux in France, the animals painted on the walls had varying lengths of horns. These horns and antlers represented the degree of understanding that a person obtained.

Enlightenment In The Kitchen

January 1977 Istanbul. Pages from a Journal.

I am in the *tekke* in the daytime with my brothers Kemal Baba and Safer Baba. Sami and a few other dervishes later join us. It is a joyous day preparing for *ashura*, the pudding that the Prophet Noah made upon sighting land. I wash huge pots with Kemal Baba, cook grains for Noah's Pudding, stirring them with huge wooden spoons and oars. Kemal Baba was working on one pot me on another; it looked like we were rowing a boat. We broke for tea, to pray and then back to work.

Two sheep were slaughtered as sacrifice, skinned, decapitated and, their bodies dripping blood, were hung from iron hooks in the ceiling. We continued to row our grains. The liver was cooked and we eat it with rice, bread and yoghurt.

My heart is at home working, praying, eating with these men. No task is menial. We clean the huge old pots, wash the floor, help a brother, all brings a warm glow to my heart. I am free here. Perhaps here, as so simple a being, Allah will see me.

How the complexities of man bind him. I look for enlightenment in the cosmos and it is here in the kitchen of the *tekke*. There is uselessness in words when one can read the heart. Life is real only when I Am.

January 1977 Istanbul

I spend two hours in a small, clean Turkish *hammam* and then go to Efendi's bookshop in Sahaflar Caddesi. There are many questions, answers, tea, and discourse on *zikr*. Sheikh Muzaffer gives me practices to do. After the trip to Bursa Efendi and Safer Baba now call me Shems Baba.

"There are seven *azkar. Zikr jahri* is recited aloud. *Khafi* is a silent *zikr. Ruhi* is the *zikr* of the spirit. *Sirr* is the secret *zikr. Sirrusirr* is the *zikr* of the secret of the secret. The *jahri zikr* is said with the tongue making a sound and the hearts' response is a *zikr.* There is response of the heart to the *zikr* with no sound. *Zikr ruh* is not said with the tongue but with one's entire being. *Zikr sirr* is living every moment, every action with God. Whatever you do, pray, eat, walk, and use the toilet, you are conscious of God. This is the secret *zikr.*"

The *shaitan* approached Prophet Jesus and beckoned him to repeat the Name of God aloud. Jesus was confused, why would the devil want him to say the Name of God, this is not his work. Jesus was always in *zikr sirr* and the devil was trying to bring him to a lower place by repeating the Name of God aloud.

A Taste Of Honey

Tosun Baba and I are visiting the old *tekkes* in Istanbul. It is a brisk February afternoon in 1977. One of the *tekkes* we saw was a beautiful, old, run down Bektashi *tekke.* Over the door of a Saadi *tekke* in Arabic calligraphy the phrase, "*Zikr Allah* Satisfies Hearts," was written.

Later in the afternoon we visit Kadiri Sheikh Nazmi Efendi at his home in Eyup. He often comes to the Jerrahi *tekke.* He is eighty, stern of stature, with a good heart and has been a sheikh for over fifty years, since Ataturk sealed the *tekkes* of Turkey. "Only now I have this taste of honey in the back of my throat when I am repeating the Name of *Allah* and I want to live."

He told stories of when he was a young man. "My sheikh only had a few *kurush* on the night that many dervishes were coming to the *tekke*. I sat by the window until noon not knowing where money would come from so we could feed the brotherhood that night. The women in the kitchen complained that there was no food to cook. Finally I tied the *kurush* in a cloth and took it to the grave of my *Pir* and said, 'These people come tonight to see you, so do something, they are not coming to see me,' and I threw the little money on the grave and returned home.

Within an hour someone came and said something was sold and he wished to give the money to the *tekke*.

"A Halveti sheikh had a Kadiri wife and a young daughter who was dying of tuberculosis. The sickness was so bad this one day that the wife said to her husband, 'Do something, go for a doctor.' Just as the man went out the door the daughter died and the woman went to the window to tell her husband. She pushed her fingers deep into the wood frame and cried, 'O Abdul Kadir Gilani, please give me back my child.' She turned and saw the girl move her arms. She called her husband who came as the girl asked what had happened. The mother answered, 'You died but now you are alive.' The girl said that a bird came and carried her high into the sky and another bird, a white one came and said to the bird that it must let her go. The bird said it could not, and the white bird said that it asked permission and was told that she was to return."

Nazmi Efendi was respected in the *dergah* for his manner of *zikr*. On Monday night we were in the *zikr* line together. He taught me to be aware of the tip of my tongue touching the roof of my mouth each time the letter *lam* is repeated in *la illaha illa Allah*.

When we leave I kiss his hand, look into his eyes, touch my heart, point to his, and say *qalbit*. He is moved and does a *zikr* movement telling me to keep doing *zikr*. I feel a heart connection with him. When Muzaffer Efendi passed, it was Nazmi Efendi who insisted that Safer Efendi sit on the blue post immediately.

A Box Of One's Actions

Februaries in Istanbul are cold and damp. The wood-burning and coal stoves leave black dust in the lines of my hands that never seem to wash away. A stove, as well as the breath of the dervishes repeating the Names of Allah, warms the *sohbet* room at the Jerrahi *tekke*. Sheikh Muzaffer is talking between drags of his cigarette. "Flying and walking on water are miracles but a mosquito can fly. What is important is to find a direction. You can say bread, bread all day but it will not satisfy your hunger. For that you must eat the bread. We say Allah, Allah and it is like saying bread unless we put our entire being into the repetition. The bread of Allah goes to the heart and is then directed to the seven centers. It is important to ask for bread so we say Allah, Allah even without our entire beings, for we could possibly be fed."

A question comes from the crowd. "How can I know God?" Sheikh Muzaffer adjusts himself in his chair and says, "Read the Book of Yourself, the Book of Man. You have eyes to see. Eyelids allow you to sleep, and eyelashes keep out dust. When you work your eyebrows prevent the salt from your perspiration from entering your eyes and eventually blinding you. There is a nose above your mouth so you can smell whether the food you take is good or bad. There are two rows of hard teeth to enclose your tongue and allow you to think before you speak. Teeth in the front of your mouth bite, and teeth in the back chew. In addition Allah has placed two lips around your teeth to further ensure that your words are protected. From two small holes in the sides of your head you can hear sounds from both near and far. Do you think of the One who gave this gift to you? This is only the outside; there is also an inside that contains blood and sperm and a system for digesting food.

"When you look at a sculpture you think of the sculptor. When you think of the sculptor do you think of the One who created the sculptor? The traces of Allah are all around us. If you see tracks in the desert do you not think that a camel was there? The traces of man reveal the presence of Allah.

"The coffin is a box of one's actions. Read yourself and find Truth. When you find Truth you will find the Creator. Read the map of your body and seek Allah in yourself. His power and gifts are endless. His essence has been reflected in man's heart.

"Five times a day when you stand up to pray you are in the presence of Allah. Allah says that around your neck He has hung a book where everything you have done is written, even the smallest of deeds. During morning and noon prayers you account for your actions to Allah. When you read your Book at afternoon, sunset, and night prayers you will feel shame and fear and bow. Allah will tell you to get up and read your Book.

When you turn the page you will see even more horrible things that you have done and you will throw yourself upon your face in *sajda* and three times you will say, 'Ya Allah have mercy upon me.'

"You will be told to rise and read your Book. You will get up, turn the pages, see even more of your actions and again you will throw yourself upon your face and seek Allah's mercy. Finally you will sit.

This is all like the beginning of grammar school. We are talking about just a drop of knowledge."

The Grace Of A Champion

Early in the nineties the Saudi Arabian Embassy in Washington, D.C., sponsored the exhibit, *Saudi Arabia, Yesterday, Today, and Tomorrow.*

I had designed a brochure, Islamic calendar, and a series of postcards for the event. At the opening dinner my table was next to the one with Muhammad Ali.

"Can you sign this for my son Nuri, champ?"
He picked up the pen, and began showing signs of the Parkinson's disease, that had slipped into his body between rounds. His hand was shaking.
"Champ, it's okay, I'll just tell him that I met you."
"No," his hand quivering, the letters shaky, "This is for Nuri."

He was no longer in the body of the warrior, who stood victorious over the flattened form of Sonny Liston, prostrate on the canvas, like a painting frozen in time.

Alif, Dal, Mim

In the *Fihi Ma Fihi* Rumi tells us that when bread is wrapped in the tablecloth it is the inanimate thing that it is called, but in the human body it becomes the spirit of life. It becomes transmuted in the body.

In all things in life there is the *zahir* which is perceived by our external senses, and the *batin*, that which is hidden. The *zikr* can be pronounced by our tongues and heard by our ears; that is the *zahir*. The *batin*, the hidden meaning of *zikr* is within each of us.

Zikr Allah is a bridge to Allah and regulates breath. Harmonious rhythm of the breath provides health to the body. There are benefits within man that are unavailable because he lives an imaginary and inharmonious life. Allah has placed His signs in the horizons. He has presented us with an allusion, a hint as to how to live. We have changed the allusion into an illusion and live our life in fantasy, in imagination.

We have been given clues as to how to live. The Prophet Mohammed was sent as a guide, a warner, and an example. In Arabic within the name of the Prophet Adam, is a secret as to how to live. The *alif* represents man standing in prayer. The *dal* represents man seated in prayer, and the *mim* represents man in *sajda* (bowing).

The Ninety-Nine Names of Allah are symbolically written on the palms of our hands that begin every action, work and greeting. In the Arabic language each letter takes on a different form when it appears in the beginning, middle and end of a word, just as man is in a different form in the beginning, middle, and end of his life.

The Day The Music Stopped

In 1956 Ali Nezih Uzel graduated from Galatasaray High School in Istanbul. He was intelligent and had a gift of conversation. His school friends thought he would become a diplomat. Instead he came to the *tekke* and entered the world of the dervish. In December of that year he made his first journey to Konya...and life changed.

He studied calligraphy with Ustad Refi Jevad, music with Sadettin Heper and Ulve Erguner, illumination with Suheyl Unver and *ebru* with Aktar Mustafa. He studied Ottoman art and learned Sufism from the *tekkes* and the sheikhs.

With his lifelong friend, the musician and composer, Kudsi Erguner, Nezih gave concerts and organized Mevlevi ceremonies that were seen from Cairo to California.

We met in 1970 when the Mevlevi came to the Brooklyn Academy of Music in New York, became fast friends and whenever I traveled to Istanbul I stayed at his home in Uskudar. He opened the gates to the Turkish dervish orders for me and many other seekers. He had a mane of auburn hair, bushy mustache and thick fingers that seemed to be made to play the *bendir*.

Once we were walking across the old wooden Galata Bridge in Istanbul after midnight. It was cold, windy, and snow was streaking across our faces. Nezih stopped and was looking toward the Suleymaniye Mosque.

"It is cold," I said, "let's keep moving, what are you looking at?"

"It is not important what I look at," he said, "what is important is who is looking."

Speaking of Mevlevi music he once remarked; "This is not music for listening, this is music for participation."

It is almost forty years since that night and I can't recall a conversation with Nezih when I didn't learn something.

Nezih Uzel had been invited by the sheikhs of Istanbul to the *Station of Alhamdulillah*. He lived his life moving in and out of this place. We do not know if he was shown the Secret Path before the road closed before him. Perhaps the music guided him.

Music was in his heart, his eyes, his ears, his voice and hands. At times one felt while listening to him play the *bendir* and chant a loving phrase to the Prophet Mohammed that he became music. It surrounded him and permeated him.

"He was a secret treasure that was difficult to explain or to open because he protected himself by opposites," said Kudsi Erguner. He played music weekly at Turkish Radio and Television and during the night he entered the *zikr* circles of various *tekkes* and enhanced their repetition with his music. He was at home in the *tekkes* of the Mevlevi, the Naqshibandi, the Kadiri and Halveti dervishes.

After the doctors took all the toes of his right foot two years ago because of diabetes, he said to me; "My whole life I am trying to understand what it is to be a dervish. Now I am beginning to learn."

When I saw him a few weeks before he died he confided in me; "The game is over for me, I am now living in overtime."

The pale yellow walls of his living room are covered with old Turkish carpets, various musical instruments, Arabic calligraphy, some photographs of the Whirling Dervishes that I had taken in Konya and Cairo, and a faded oil painting of his father in a military uniform.

We sat together, ate lunch, he played some music and attempted to collect the air from his room, where the Name of Allah had been repeated so many times, before the time came when he could not breathe any longer. We spoke of life, time and age. How we did not know our youth was on loan to be replaced by age, like our bodies on loan to be replaced by Death.

The Bird of Life was soon to leave the musical cage of his body. In the end he left his beloved books, his *bendirs*, his friends, all of his cherished instruments, the *haydariyya* (dervish vest), the one that hung on the wall by his bed, that Sheikh Necmeddin wore for years and gave him when he died. He even left his baritone voice that used to sing the Names of Allah and praise the Prophet Mohammed.

Our mutual friend Murat, owner of the Kanat restaurant in Uskudar, on the Asian side of Istanbul, where Nezih had eaten as many meals as his mother had once cooked for him, called me with the news. I was on the next plane from Cairo to Istanbul. It was May, 2012 just before the Ramadan he would not see.

As we lowered his body into the earth we repeated *zikr Allah* for a long time. Then his friends, his students, the ears of his music, left him to read the Book that Allah hung around his neck in which everything he did was written; even the smallest deed.

"Shems, we are losing our references," said Kudsi Erguner later that night when we gathered in Nezih's apartment, recited Koran verses and sang *ilahis* to the Prophet Mohammed. I recited a poem by Hafiz.

When Hafiz's coffin comes by,
It will be all right
To follow behind.
Although he is a captive of sin,
He is on his way to the Garden.

I'll Organize It For You

The Angel Gabriel and the *shaitan* were walking. The *shaitan* noted a shimmering light coming from between the fingers of Gabriel's closed hand.

"What do you have?"

"It is a present from Allah."

"Let me see."

"No, it is a gift that Allah gave to me."

"Well, open your hand."

Gabriel did and a bright light was in the palm of his hand.

"What is that?"

"It is the Truth."

"Give it here, I'll organize it for you."

My Mother's Secret

I believe for most of her life my mother carried a secret within her breast. Perhaps it disappeared when the cancer ate her or the heart attack shot into her chest like an AK47 or when the diabeties began to shut out the light in her eyes. I am not certain.

On my birth certificate there is a question for my mother. "How many children were born to you before this one?" In the small ballot box to the left of the question someone wrote the number one.

This is the mystery. No one in my family had ever indicated that I had an older sibling. Officially stamped government forms don't lie...or perhaps she didn't understand the question.

One Of The Final Lessons

Sheikh Muzaffer's tiny bookshop in the Sahaflar Caddessi at the edge of the Grand Bazaar was the place where many *sohbets* were held and even more Sufi stories told.

The tea boy had just brought seven glasses of Turkish tea on a small metal tray and distributed them to those present. Our overcoats were not sufficient to keep us warm. Muzaffer Efendi began to speak as we sipped the hot tea, not knowing that this would be one of his last "bookshop talks."

"*Zikr Allah* is the greatest prayer. To love your wife is a prayer, it makes a heart feel good. The prayer of money is to help the poor. To help humanity is prayer. As long as you have faith in your heart, whatever you do is prayer. Prayer of the body is to prostrate before Allah. Prayer of the ear is to hear and listen only to the Truth and act accordingly.

"One comes to this world pure, but if you revolt against the Creator then you leave less pure than when you arrived.

"Never think that you are higher than those you address or those who address you.

"When you are in the presence of a sheikh you feel peace in your heart. When you follow what he tells you the Truth can be reached. Before you ask your question he will answer your question. If you find such a sheikh you will be fortunate.

"The one who does not have mercy and compassion for his family will not have it for others. The one who does not have compassion toward others, will not be shown compassion by others."

'Allah Hu Akbar, Allah Hu Akbar.'

The call to *maghreb* prayer from the Beyazit Mosque begins the harmonic overtones of several *mu'ezzins* chanting the *adhan* and punctuates the sheikh's talk.

City Of The Dead

It is the tail end of the nineties in Cairo. I am in the City of the Dead, where squatters, the poor, addicts, and dealers live among the desert tombs and narrow passageways that create a trail for life among the dead.

Shadi abdel Salam's film, *The Mummy*, perhaps the best Egyptian film ever made, depicts the robbing of graves by villagers who live above and below the surface of the ochre desert.

You can hear the call to prayer, the merging of the sacred and the profane. I am walking in the City of the Dead, to pray in an old Sufi mosque and *tekke* nestled among the sand-covered tombs. Old women dressed in black sit on stone steps in front of broken wooden doors.

The keeper of the mosque recognizes one of my friends and opens the door. The vast space inside smells of faded roses.

In the center sits the large sarcophagus of Mohammed al-Wafaa the founding sheikh. At the extremity of one wall are small cell-like rooms where dervishes once sat in *khalwa*. They fasted and listened to the sound of the *zikr* as it wove its way into their hearts.

You can hear the Name of Allah in the air that seems to have been stopped by time.

The Tree Of Paradise

Safer Efendi is talking to a circle of dervishes in the Istanbul *tekke*. "Generosity is a tree of Paradise. It locks the gates to Hell. Stinginess is a tree of Hell whose branches have reached this world.

"The Prophet Mohammed was in the Ka'bah and saw a person crying profusely and begging for forgiveness. 'What is it that makes you suffer so much,' he asked.

"O Messenger of Allah, I am such a sinner and fear that I will not

know the Mercy of Allah."
"Depend on it, for Allah will forgive."
"I fear my sin is too large."
"What is it?"
"Whenever someone asks something of me it is as if a fiery spear comes near my heart."

The Prophet stepped back and said, "Cry, cry, for even if your tears are like rivers and green trees grow by their sides, I fear you are far from the Mercy of Allah."

Arrival In Cairo

September 6, 1994

After a long night and part of a day on TWA, Nuri and I arrive in the desert city of Cairo. The city of history and mystery. The American University in Cairo's representative whisks us and our many bags through customs control, and places the luggage on his faded blue pick-up truck. He will meet us at our new home in El Maadi.

Our flat is across the street from Nuri's new school, the Cairo American College. My friend Abdallah Schleifer, Director of the Adham Center for Television Journalism at AUC, picks us up at the airport and we travel with him.

The view from the airport is the color of sand. We pass mud-brick houses and an area where craftsmen make and sell pottery. Their large pots line the side of the road in front of their kilns. The desert seems to swallow the city with its color and dust. We pass the City of the Dead, a burial city, with roofless houses and mosques, all of which appear to be underground. This is what Cairo must have looked like a thousand years ago.

Maadi is an oasis. It is tree-lined and quiet. Our apartment is large, allowing Nuri and I to have our own rooms and a large living room. The luggage arrives. We unpack our New York history, strategically place a few *kilims* from Turkey and Iran, pray and then enter a long sleep.

September 7th

Nuri's school is large and spread out like a university. A far cry from the stone row-house buildings in New York City where kids crowd classrooms and fly up and down stairwells. CAC has a swimming pool, tennis courts, soccer field, full size track, a theatre and the cleanest buildings one can imagine. We get photographed, receive ID cards and talk with the registrar.

These are days of exploring. We take the metro to Saadat Station and have a meeting at AUC. In these early days there are few decent restaurants in Cairo and most people rely on the large hotels for dining out. We have a mediocre lunch at the Hilton and return by subway to Maadi. We are both jetlagged. Nuri re-enters the long sleep he began yesterday.

My friend Hussein telephones from Jeddah. There are no cell phones. Immediate problems seem to be the antiquated phone system and the water pressure in the apartment. It is September and still summer hot. I am apprehensive of the move from New York, a city I am comfortable in and know so well. Cairo is new, I have few friends, and don't speak the language. Nuri has left all his friends in New York, and will have to cultivate new ones among the Egyptians and foreigners living in Cairo.

Two weeks later, the twenty-seven boxes containing our books and clothes arrive.

September 8th

Nuri, Abdallah and I go to *Jum'a* prayer at the Sultan Hassan Mosque. Now I know why I am here. This mosque, with its simplicity and grandeur is a spiritual experience surpassing even the Chartres Cathedral outside of Paris. Abdallah takes us through the mazes of

Khan Al Khalili, the grand bazaar of Cairo. We stop at the spice man, the metal shop and the man who makes *sebha*. In each shop we are served tea and share conversation. We stop at Abdallah's house on Champollion Street and later have dinner at a Japanese Restaurant.

Flocks of Egyptians enjoy the warm night by hanging out on the bridges and staring at the Nile River.

The night continues when we hail a taxi to Maadi.

Early Conversations With Nuri

I feel as though I blinked twice after Nuri's birth and we are in Cairo. My thoughts go to 1986. Nuri accompanied me to Florida where I was overseeing a photo shoot for American Health Magazine. He is also taking swimming lessons every day from a coach who prepares young swimmers for the Olympics. Nuri is learning the basic strokes. We had a lot of time to ourselves and often sat and talked.

I asked Nuri, "Does everybody have a heart?"

"Sure, if they didn't have a heart they wouldn't have a brain. Because the heart and the brain are connected. We have little extension cords inside our body."

"How do you know this?"

"My mind told me."

In an open car with the wind blowing, Nuri asks,"Dad what is wind?"

"Wind is air moving."

"Do we need it?"

"We need air to breathe so we can live."

"We don't. But if we didn't have air we wouldn't need our noses. We would look different. You wouldn't look the way you do and I wouldn't look the way I do, but you would still be my dad."

"Dad, we have more than one life. The soul is the same but the

parents are different and it is the same God. Am I right Dad?"
"Almost, Allah has prepared another more beautiful world where those who believe in Him go. We don't have different parents, but you are right, it is the same God. Did someone tell you all this?
"No."
"How do you know this?"
"My brain told me."
"Alhamdulillah."

Nuri has a book of riddles.
"What has ears but cannot hear?"
"The music composer Beethoven."

"Dad, do you know what I don't like?"
"No, what?"
"I don't like it when my mind thinks about things that I don't want it to. I really don't like that."

In Lebanon Springs, NY, Nuri watched a caterpillar he contained in a glass jar become a pupa and then a butterfly.
"There is a long word which describes what happened."
"I know Dad, transformation."
"Well, you're correct but I was thinking of metamorphosis."
"What does that mean?"
"When something makes a complete change over to another being in the same lifetime, and very seldom does that happen."
"I know another time. When a boy becomes a man, that is a complete transformation."

Upon giving Nuri some earth to taste that the Prophet Mohammed walked upon in Madinah:
"Dad, when I ate this earth I could smell roses in my heart."

Is It A Dream?

I watched a Turkish calligrapher as he wrote the entire Qur'an with honey. After he finished writing the final *sura* he ate the book and became enlightened.

Eyes Wide Shut

Dreams can be elusive. In the eighties I was the art director for American Health magazine. Our offices were on 5th Avenue and 13th Street, close to Greenwich Village. In those days there were few computers and as one editor observed, "art directors are editors with tilted desks," refering to the drawing boards we used to design pages.

An article on dreams had to be designed. I read the article and for days walked around thinking about how to illustrate the story. I thought of personal dreams and dreams in general.

They floated, sometimes appearing in thoughts the next day. Dreams were not contained, they travelled beyond barriers. Dreams could inform, relate messages, and sometimes are nothing more than a movie based on the events of my day.

I phoned an illustrator and we spoke about how to create the visuals. We decided on a man sleeping on a pillow in the clouds, surrounded by glittering stars. The clouds would weave themselves beyond the main part of the illustration, go behind the headline type and even float off the page. Like a dream within a dream.

Shakespeare wrote a play within a play in "Hamlet," and the Prado Museum in Madrid once placed a mirror in front of a large painting by Velasquez, thus creating another dimension for the many people depicted on the canvas. There are stories within stories in the "Thousand and One Nights."

The most important thing I learned about dreams was that I could see another world with my eyes shut. A world that had trees, people, buildings, cars and was clearly visible. I had always thought my eyes had to be open in order to see.

The Black Box

As a senior lecturer and later Professor of Practice at The American University in Cairo I wrote two monodramas. "Dream Water Does Not Quench Thirst" (a title taken from one of Rumi's teachings), was about a woman waiting for a phone call from a man. It was performed at the Howard Theatre at AUC, a small space with a completely black interior.

Nuri was at the first performance and said; "It was weird watching a woman walking about the stage talking about your books, paintings and ideas about life and art." The director Peter Brook once said; "A man walks across an empty space, and someone else watches him. This is theatre."

Gurdjieff used to sit at the Cafe de la Paix in Paris and watch the "street movie" as he drank Turkish coffee.

Yara, a young actress friend of Nuri's in Cairo was complaining about the lack of work. I said that I would write something for her to perform. I had no idea what made me say this or what to write. One night thoughts stirred my sleep and I woke with a thousand ideas racing through my mind. I grabbed a pencil and on a hundred scraps of paper tried to keep up with the pace of the pencil as it scribbled my thoughts. Seize the moment.

In the morning I put it all together, fed it to my computer, and had the first draft of "Dream Water Does Not Quench Thirst."

I have always been interested in Arabic calligraphy, with its bird and wing-like shapes, its elegant lines and diacritical marks, so I began writing about calligraphy and its relationship to man. Each of the 28 letters changed shape according to its position in a word.

Just as man goes through physical changes at different stages of his life. Revelations of the Prophet Mohammed were first written on camel bones and palm leaves.

"The Calligrapher's Daughter" was performed at the Howard Theatre in May of 2008. The one-person play with a number of student actors in supporting roles caught the imagination of the students, faculty and the art crowd of Cairo.

Sometimes one is surrounded in one's culture and tradition to the degree that it can no longer be seen and when presented by an impartial observer becomes revealing.

The Secret Sema

Rumi said that the outward of a thing is its illusion and the inward of a thing its reality. The *Gharib Sema,* known to the Mevlevis as the *Secret Sema*, is rarely performed since the closing of the *tekkes* in Turkey by Kemal Ataturk. This special *sema* only begins after the regular *sema* has concluded. Some of the older Mevlevi *dedes* felt the *sema* did not complete a deep inner fulfillment. When the sound of bare feet turning on smooth wood has ceased, when the *ney* has become silent and the last *Hu* no longer reverberates in the Hall of Celestial Sounds, when the doors are locked to all but the *semazens*, and the lights dimmed, the *Gharib Sema* begins.

The scent of incense floats through the *semahan*e as the Mevlevis file onto the floor and one by one begin a slow, meditative turn. They turn wearing *sikke,* the tall honey-colored hat, and *khirqa*, the black cloak that wraps around their body. Their arms are not spread wing-like as before, but held as the sheikh and as Mevlana did before them. The right hand holding the top of the *khirqa*, opened slightly, and the left holding the *khirqa* at the waist. This is the real *sema* of Mevlana.

They turn toward their hearts, slowly, eighteen times, the same amount every *semazen* turns each morning in the *tekke* or in their home. The white of their shirt collars and the highlight of their faces are revealed by the soft light of candles, as they turn in the mysterious space, contained by no boundaries.

No music is played, and the only sound is the Name of Allah that is breathed out by each Mevlevi as he slowly turns, for it is the breath that is a bridge between man and God.

The moment reminds one of the *zikr* known as *walad al qalb* (Child of the Heart), when the heart of the dervish, with tongue still and lips sealed, begins to repeat "Allah, Allah."

Not all is told to everyone. The Prophet Mohammed told Ali a secret regarding the *miraj*. Upon hearing the blessed words he kissed the palm of the Prophet's right hand and his right knee. This is why dervishes do the same to their sheikh.

Withdraw Into The Protection Of Allah

There are things hidden and things revealed. Generally we see only the surface of things. The ear of a deaf person looks exactly like the hearing ear. So we know that hearing is hidden in the ear. The music is not in the piano and the taste is not in the apple. The taste of the apple appears when the person and the apple come together.

The Mevlevi in their *zikr* do what appears as a turning dance. But in fact as they turn toward their heart they subvocally repeat the Name of Allah. Something happens, an experience within them that is hidden from the viewer. Dervish music is not for listening, it is for participation.

The totality of one's experiences is in the world inside and the world outside. One has to know when it is time to withdraw into the protection of the *zikr*. The illness of "spiritual amnesia" can be cured by *zikr Allah*.

The greatest gift of Allah is faith. Faith is a cloak that is always larger than its wearer. A cloak that never shrinks, but one that the wearer must grow into. The process of fitting the Cloak of Faith is Life. For those who can read, Allah has revealed His secrets in the Qur'an. For those who can see with the eyes of the heart, Allah has placed His treasures within His creation.

The world is invisible to the ones whose eyes are closed. When the eyes of the heart are opened the hidden treasures of Allah are revealed.

A Village Painted White

In the late 1960s I had a small flat in Mijas, a tiny mountain village in the South of Spain. It was mostly used as a summer retreat where I spent time in meditation and *zikr*. All the buildings in Mijas were painted white. The sunlight bounced from wall to wall forcing dwellers to seek shaded areas or daylight dreams during the noon hours. There were few foreigners in those days.

During March of 1969 amnesty was granted for political dissenters from the time of Franco. When the civil war broke out in 1936 Manuel Cortes was the Republican mayor of Mijas and went into hiding in a tiny room behind a stairwell in his house. On the day of the amnesty he opened the false wall and, as if in a dream, walked the sunlit streets of Mijas for the first time in over thirty years. I joined the villagers who paraded to a cafe where he had his first black expresso in three decades under a burning yellow sun.

Time seemed to have stopped here, or at least slowed down to a crawl.

On the 8th of September, 1972, after sitting in *zikr* for several hours in the whiteness of Mijas, Barbara wrote this poem:

We sat in the semi-darkness
And you spun zikr *around us.*
Soon there was no cool stucco wall
No staccato voices
No impatient horns.
There was only you
Erect, regal, devout
Who had become that ancient sheikh
(whose holy name you wear silently)
Sitting on the doorstep of a mud house
In a Persian sunset
Too much in tune with Him
To feel your devoted student, this Rachel who I am.
You spun zikr *until*
It became heavier than air
Until it was all we breathed
Until there was nothing but you and I and God.
Just that–nothing and everything.

A House Filled With *Barakah*

The house on 84th Street was a center for spiritual energy during the seventies. Pir Vilayat Khan stayed there when he was in New York. Ram Dass visited. Swami Atmananda arrived from India, stayed for weeks and performed *pujas* every day in what was to become Nuri's room. Kudsi Erguner with a cloth bag of *neys* found his way there at dawn during a blinding snow-storm. Sheikh Muzaffer and the dervishes from Konya and Istanbul made *zikr.* The Mevlevis came and played dervish music. John Lennon and Yoko Ono ate vegetarian dinners and Jack Nicholson visited Ellen Burstyn after she won the Academy Award in the living room.

Walter Chappell lived there for a while and artists and musicians frequented the house and drank Turkish tea from bottomless glasses.

The house was filled with *barakah*. I lived under its double skylight for twenty years.

The Secret Of Work

Brewster, NY, Sunday April 26, 1963

We are gathered in the old barn at Gage Hill. It is dusk and a thankful fatigue has occupied our bodies. The Gurdjieff group was working the land, building doors, and constructing the new Music Room above the barn. I am twenty-three years old, one of the youngest in the group and building a house that I will live in, one that is not friable.

Mr. Nyland begins to speak as we drink coffee from our floral designed metal cups. "I would like to talk a little about physical work.

"You have a certain rhythm that you know. For one-half hour slow this rhythm down intentionally, and try to be present. At the end of this time speed up your rhythm as fast as you can. You will see how it will help you if you work in this way. Relax during this time and do not look for a result. If you look for a result you become tense. You must relax and work in a rhythm that you direct. If something directs it then you will be there. If you work this way you will be more *Awake* and it can help you tomorrow. It is storing in the bank of yourself. This is the Secret of Work.

"Work this way and if you find yourself asleep become active and direct your rhythm. If you are seated, change your position. This is *Work-to-be-Awake*. It helps you see how quickly you are taken by something else. At this moment change your rhythm."

Krishnamurti said, "To be still after tilling and sowing is to give birth to creation."

Food For Thought

There was a butcher in a small village who one day was called elsewhere. A young man came to replace him.

Before killing the sheep it was necessary to wet the knife and then sharpen it on a stone. Each day this man would spit on the knife and then sharpen the blade.

Outside the shop sat an old man of another religion. As the man sharpened his knife the old man would look at him and shake his head as if to say, "You are doing it wrong."

Finally the young man was agitated to the point of approaching the old man and told him to stop disturbing him, after all how would he know if he was doing it right or wrong.

The old man looked at him and said, "I watched the man before you. Prior to killing the animal he would sit quietly with the knife in his hand, close his eyes, and begin to sway gently. Very soon tears came to his eyes and fell on the blade of the knife. It was with these tears that he sharpened the knife."

Nuri and I are with Nezih at the Uzbek *tekke* in Uskudar. It is Ramadan. We have returned from a nearby hillside stable where they are selling sheep for sacrifice. A sheep was chosen that we brought to the *tekke* to be slaughtered and the meat distributed to those at the *tekke* and the poor.

Nuri is given a sharp knife and we hold the sheep to the ground. He says, *Bismillah*, and draws the knife across the sheep's neck. A butcher is present and he masterfully cuts the skin and blows air forming a pocket between the skin and flesh. Then he strips the skin off and hangs the carcass on a hook that has been placed on a metal fence. The blood flows into a hole in the earth. Within five minutes the bleating sheep has disappeared. It only exists as food.

I am left with an empty feeling in my chest and the cold realization that what exists one minute may not exist in the next.

One Ramadan in Cairo I perform the ritual of slaughtering a sheep. We are in the garden of a friend's villa in Maadi. I purchased the sheep so the meat could be distributed to the needy.

I am given a large knife whose blade is razor sharp. The sheep is held to the ground. I do not let the animal see the blade. The ground is muddy but I kneel to get a better balance and draw the blade across the neck after saying, *"Bismillah."* I am not confident in killing, yet I have hired killers all my life to provide me with food. It takes two passes with the knife (not a good thing) to sever the jugular.

The Egyptian butcher takes over and diminishes the animal into a memory. The meat is cut, bagged in portions, and given to the poor. We keep some bones and a little meat to make soup.

Dans Le Noir

I am blind. There is no light. The world is black. Ten minutes before I could see. When Hatice, Sara, and I entered Dans Le Noir in London, the restaurant that is basically run by blind people and simulates an experience of eating a meal as though you are blind, the lights were dimmed but clear. We are asked to leave any jewelry or shiny objects in small lockers in the entranceway. We are shown the menu and choose one of the four possibilities for a meal. I have chosen the "surprise meal" with the restriction that there is no pork. Then we are led along a dark corridor, our right hand on the shoulder of the person in front of us, into a room whose size and shape is undetermined because of the pitch-blackness of the space. A blind waiter leads us to a table.

I feel for the back of the chair, ease myself into the seat and use my hands to locate the edge of the table and find a comfort zone. The waiter takes our drink order. No hot drinks are served. We order sparkling water and lose track of the waiter's voice but become aware that the room is filled with people in conversation, but have no idea how many are in the room or how close to my elbow sits a stranger.

The blind waiter returns with our drinks and the first course that he says is being placed on the table. My hands gently feel for the glass and the utensils and the plate of salad. I spear some salad and sip water as my eyes seem to adjust to the darkness but no shapes or colors or light is revealed. I think of my friend Ismail who is a blind *hafiz*, and the way he uses his fingers to locate food or tell him the plate is empty. I emulate my memory of sharing meals with him.

We exchange some conversation but each of us becomes more internally aware as the meal continues. I try to define what I am eating. Some tastes are easier than others. During the main course I think I am eating chicken but find out later it was crocodile meat. The bottle of water is on the table. I have to locate the rim of the glass to pour a refill. The taste of the food is more acute than usual and I am aware of the act of eating.

I think of the silent meal in Frejus at the *ashram* of Le Maitre. I remember the day in the studio on 84th street when I wore an eye mask to block out all light and images to experience blindness. Although I knew the space well, moments became acute and tentative, tastes more evident, my hearing sharper and there was a focus on myself as a being gliding and stumbling through space.

My fingers tell me that the plate is empty. The waiter removes the plates and places dessert on the table. Sharing is a bit difficult so we each stay with what we ordered. After some time the waiter arrives and we stand and trail him through the darkness in the same manner as we arrived. The constant echo of talking guests fills the still undefined space.

We are led back to the entrance of the restaurant, collect our shiny objects and pay the bill in the light that reveals faces, bodies and objects.

Two years later, in December of 2013, I am being checked by a retina specialist in London for what had been diagnosed as the beginning of cataracts by an eye doctor in Cairo. Scans reveal that along with the cataracts I have a degenerative eye problem that is a form of macular dystrophy and as I grow older I will see less clear.

This Too Shall Pass

With the gaining of years you recognize something about age that could never be understood when you were young. Those blessed with the experience of seniority in life have age behind us, and can look at things differently.

A small mirror is nailed to a wall in a corridor next to my bedroom. Thirty years ago I wrote on its surface, "This Too Shall Pass." When you look in the mirror, along with your reflection you also see this phrase. For all these years it has been a reminder to me.

The Prophet's companion Omar asked someone to remind him every day that there is death. The man did it for many years, then one day Omar said, "I no longer need you for this task."

"But it has been good for me to remind you that there is death, because I also reminded myself at the same time."

"Now I don't need you because Allah has put grey in my beard and I'm reminded every day that death exists."

Reflecting, one sees life in a different way but realizes, regarding age, that you are not different. I am as I was at thirty. My being is not older, except perhaps wiser in some way, but not older. My body is older.

As I walked by the mirror recently, I took a step back, looked again and thought, "How did I get into that old guy's body?"

Why I Stayed In Cairo

Maadi is linked to the Corniche by a flyover. Traffic was creeping toward the Nile and came to a full stop on the up-grade. I wondered what was happening when I spotted a man in his early twenties hop out of the back seat of an old black taxi and run forward. A man in a wheelchair was struggling to push him-self to the crest of the hill. The young man ran behind him, grabbed the arms of the wheelchair and pushed it to the top of the hill. He then ran back to the taxi and the traffic began to flow.

Islamic architecture and the people of Cairo keep me here.

Some Rooms Are For Solitude

I built a room that requires people.
Some rooms are for solitude.
I have one of those too, in Cairo,
But here in Istanbul there is a need for people,
To sit on the long divans
Covered with Ottoman cloth,
To talk and drink a thousand glasses of tea
And gaze at the Marmara Sea.
To sit in circles
And graze in the garden,
Where no time exists.

A Mawlid In Cairo

It is the mid-nineties. Yasin Tuhamy, the renowned Egyptian singer, is leading a *zikr* at the *Mawlid* of Omar Ibn al-Farid in the Muqattem Hills above Cairo. The narrow, winding, dirt streets leading to the mosque are occupied by a swelling festive crowd. Pointed, colorful party hats, toy flutes and sweet drinks are sold from makeshift stands along the streets. Hundreds of people have gathered in the open space outside the tomb of the Egyptian Sufi "sultan of love." Tuhamy is wearing a grey *gallabiyya*. His head is wrapped in a white turban as he bellows out a chant to the undisciplined *zikr* lines.

I climb a pole near the center and photograph the chaotic *zikr*. No one in the photograph will experience the moment in the same way as it is recorded by the camera.

Abdallah and Nuri are on the side, swaying with the crowd. Dozens of men, women, and children, the lovers of Omar Ibn al-Farid, climb trees and rooftops to get a clear view. The energy of the *zikr* is contagious. Everyone sways and sings with Tuhamy. They are mostly illiterate but know the words of every song and poem sung in praise of the Prophet Mohammed.

During the *zikr* problems and anxieties are forgotten. Some music and sounds are healing.

The Sound Is Made By The Breath

Kudsi Erguner has arrived in Cairo to give a concert of Sufi Music at the Manial Palace. His current CD, "Islam Blues," is a mix of Sufi Music and Jazz. We meet at Fishawi, the oldest tea-house in Cairo tucked into the winding maze of alleys in the Khan al-Khalili. The smell of tobacco coming from the *shisha* smoked by the patrons permeates the summer air. The smoke is inhaled deeply from the long rope-like apparatus attached to a glass bell jar filled with water. Large mirrors hang on the peeling walls reflecting the alley and alluding to a Cairo history peopled by men wearing *gallabiyyas* and women in *hijab*.

We talk of spirituality hidden within music. Our English conversation mixes with the Arabic of the Fishawi crowd and interrupted by the waiter bringing pots of tea and small bowls filled with white sugar. The smokers and tea drinkers appear to have stepped out of the pages of a Naguib Mahfouz novel.

"The *ney* is more than an instrument, an empty reed with seven holes. It is one of the oldest and simplest instruments in music. Jalaluddin Rumi had a deep understanding and feeling for the *ney*.

"The *ney* player breathes into the *ney* and gives it life. Without breath the human is dead. When I am asked if there is sacred music, Sufi music, deep music, I answer no, but there is sacred understanding, sacred listening, a sacred way of thinking that transforms everything into a higher understanding.

"Sound helps to remember something one shouldn't forget. We invoke the Name of Allah because we want to be with Him without distraction. For the Sufi tradition music has never been entertainment but has always been a deep meditation that reminds us of a state of being before coming to this world.

"The sound that is made by the breath of the *ney* player, comes through the *zikr* of *Hu*. Each time you play the *ney* you must be with Him, not with yourself. Like in any action of your life, but more when you play the *ney*. In your hand is a *ney*, empty inside, and completed by your breath. You must become like the *ney*, completely empty and fulfilled by another inspiration which is manifested through your breath. The real goal is transformation which can come when there is intention."

The essence of the conversation finds itself in the film I directed on *zikr Allah* called "The Circles of Remembrance."

One Thousand Times A Day

I saw Sheikh Hajji Hussein from Syria another time in the Prophet's Mosque in Madinah. His face shone as he asked me to repeat "*Allahumma Salli 'ala Sayyidina Mohammed,*" one thousand times each day. He said that he would also repeat the phrase. If you repeat this phrase you are written as "a lover of the Prophet."

After *Maghreb* he prayed for us at the Prophet's house, then gathered a cloth wrapped around his shoes and said: I have to pray *Isha* in Makkah and disappeared into the crowd.

The Power of the Pir

Fahreddin Efendi decided to change the sarcophagus of Pir Nuriddin Jerrahi because it was very old and the wood was deteriorating. At this time Safer Baba and Kemal Baba were working in the Istanbul shipyard. It was just after the Second World War. As it was difficult in those days to obtain wood and nails, Fahreddin Efendi asked Safer Baba to arrange the building of the structure at the shipyard. When Ali, a dervish who made *tesbih*, and also worked at the shipyard saw the almost completed sarcophagus he fell to his knees and wept. He was so moved that such a work was being done in a place where ferry boats were being constructed. Another man joked about coffins being made at the shipyard. Some see, and some do not.

When it was finished and painted with the green shipyard paint they brought it to the *tekke*. The old sarcophagus was broken and the pieces placed inside the new one. At this point some wood shavings from the new coffin fell on the open dirt. Kemal Baba carefully placed his hand inside to remove them.

At this moment a storm began in Istanbul. It was so great that parts of roofs were blown off buildings. Safer Baba was concerned. The women of the *tekke* were screaming not to touch the earth. Fahreddin Efendi said to continue. They did and completed the work in the midst of the howling wind.

It is said never to move the dirt or sarcophagus of a *Pir*.

Bob Dylan Unknown

Nina Simone is singing in the background.
"I had a mother who could pray.
I had a mother who could pray,
And if I die and my soul be lost,
If I die and my soul be lost,
Nobody's fault but my own,
Cause I had a mother who could pray."

At sixty-eight I married a woman who didn't know who Bob Dylan was but knew how to pray. I was sent a reminder.

Hatice had an effect on my spiritual life. She was in the same *tariqa* and went to Madinah each year during the last ten days of Ramadan.

Relationships had always been difficult for me. I was better at courtship than I was at marriage. We were introduced at a dinner in Istanbul at the home of mutual friends. There was an attraction, and as she was the mother of one of the young dervishes at the *tekke* who also attended the dinner, it was easy to make contact.

She had also been previously married so we entered a relationship that offered us a comfortable wisdom based on the experience of how to be with another person. I had been alone for a long time, living in Cairo and not knowing many people outside of the university.

She was intrepid with a bold and stylish manner that did not reveal her hidden spirituality. We shared an internal expression of understanding. Hatice lived an observant, orderly life and brought a balance into my life. I no longer had the need for control. I am now more confident in myself and in who I am so I could release the need for being in charge.

In our years together she has blossomed into a unique jewelry designer, a photographer, and an interior designer whose work has found its way into the pages of magazines. And best of all she brought Omer and Sara into my life.

But always she prays. Whether she has had a good day or a bad day, whether the bedroom is hot or chilled by winter, whether in Cairo or Istanbul, before the first light of day she awakens to the call to Morning Prayer.

The Paradox

Sheikh Muzaffer Efendi added a cigarette to the chain of them he was smoking, filled his lungs, and turned to the small, midnight circle of dervishes who sat before him at the Koska Café in Istanbul.

"We begin our *zikr* slowly and each word can be understood. Soon all that is heard is a heavy breath but the *zikr* goes on in our hearts. Philosophy is finished. Now is the time for love. God wants love.

"We spend the health of our youth to gain wealth, and the wealth of our old age to attempt to buy back our health."

The Invisible Library of Knowledge

There is a mild stirring to discover, translate and digitize the hand-written books in Arabic that are secreted in libraries, both private and public, throughout the world.

Sheikh Ali Jum'a is sitting in his office in Cairo, surrounded by beautiful painted calligraphies by Ahmed Moustafa. He turns to me and says, "Here is the shock. Only one percent of all knowledge that exists in manuscript form is available to us."

This statement stuns me. Where are the books that Mimar Sinan read, that Avicinna read, that Abdul Qadir Gilani read, that

Mevlana Jalaluddin Rumi studied. Shams threw his books into a well and brought them up dry. What were those books?

For years Farid Gouvernour has tried to awaken the Arab world to the untapped treasures that are in the libraries of Persia, India, Cairo, Istanbul, Bukhara, Mali and numerous other lesser-known locations. This process is beginning on a small scale. Instead of the Arab nations spending their wealth on weapons to destroy one another they could be searching for and digitizing the treasures of medicine, architecture, and science that lie beneath the skin of their culture.

Astride a Sleeping Donkey

Rumi used the events of everyday life, the fragrance of fruit and flowers, the sound of thunder and snow, to reveal a way for man to wake from his somnambulistic jouney through life. He revealed to others how he experienced the world through his senses.

Rumi showed us how we can learn ten thousand things from one thing. Water is shapeless and takes the shape of the vessel in which it is contained. If it is poured out of the vessel it evaporates and returns to its source. It is the same with the soul of a person. When breath no longer exists in the body, the soul departs and returns to its source.

We are stranded in the midst of life astride a sleeping donkey, at work in the mill of nonsense, doing everything that is urgent and little that is important, leading lives of quiet desperation until we reach the grave. Awake, awake my beloved, how you sleep.

Tears and Joy of Tahrir

It is late January, 2011. Most of Europe and Northeast America are buried in snow suffering from a chill factor below zero. The earth in Japan was about to crack and cause a tsunami that would take the lives of thousands and turn homes and villages into matchsticks.

Cairo was ablaze with revolution. In the center of the city, swelled with a million Egyptians, there was a cloud of hope. But it also rained live bullets, rubber bullets and canisters of tear gas with the imprint, "Made in America." There were martyrs after intrusions by murderers. Some of the people retaliated with Molotov cocktails but most expressed an unarmed defiance. Many were swathed in bloodied bandages. When the call to prayer was heard, thousands lined up to pray in the square, their heads to the ground, resting on newspapers whose headlines declared revolution. They prayed for peace and freedom.

Christians formed a human ring around the praying Muslims to protect them from the onslaught of security police. Then they all returned to the grief, pain, suffering and joy of Tahrir Square.

It began to rain. One man turned to me and said; "We thought our children would not amount to much, and now we are grateful to them, they are a generation that did what we could not."

President Mubarak, encouraged by the army, abdicated. The square filled with a euphoria that breeds naivety.

As I walk the desolate streets of Garden City, the area surrounding Tahrir Square, I feel as if I am in a war zone. An eerie emptiness fills the air. Stagnant water builds up on the streets, broken glass, burned out buildings, the graffiti walls of the downtown campus of The American University in Cairo, streets blocked by walls of huge stones and a lingering smell of tear gas mixes with street food to form a new city landscape replacing the historic architecture of the past two centuries.

A momentary joy that woke the entire Middle East and could

change the balance of power in the world was beginning to fade.

Tanks crawled along the street in front of my house in Maadi preceeded by the thunderous sound of metal on asphalt. I fashioned a weapon from a metal closet pole and a large kitchen knife that I held together with silver duct tape.

Fortunately soldiers were stationed across from my my house. Large men who wore black balaclavas, desert camouflage uniforms, and were heavily armed. In the late night and early morning I brought them hot tea.

The Muslim Brotherhood with Mohammed Morsi as president, was elected to govern and proved inept. Patience was thin. The people of Egypt spoke again. Morsi was ousted and replaced by the military and a promise of better days. Three years have gone by since Mubarak and his sons were jailed. They were greedy but not facinorous like Saddam Hussein's sons. The city remains under a cloud of despondancy and awaits better times.

Libya's Hard Road to Freedom

We exhibited images in "Libya: The Road to Freedom," in The Photographic Gallery at The American University in Cairo. I wrote an article merging the photographs with the events for the *Cairo Review*.

Death is at the end of every street. Mohamed Messara whispers this in my ear as he points to a photograph he took in the Libyan desert that bleeds dust and belches hot air as bullets fly, many bullets, as the photo of a rebel fighter in the battle to free the city of Sirte shows. Myriad empty shells, a carpet thrown over the dust and mud of the road.

Before leaving his hotel room Amr Abdallah recites the *shahada*, bearing witness that Allah is One and Mohammed is the Prophet of Allah.

Hussein, a soldier with the opposition kneels under the weight of a necklace of oversize bullets glittering under the Libyan sun, a golden necklace fanned over his chest. Amr Abdallah stands facing him. His weapon is a small black plastic box. It shoots pictures. Bullets fly around him. He steadies his hand and shoots the picture. I'm standing before it at The Photographic Gallery at The American University in Cairo.

It hangs on an Indian-yellow wall among 51 others in the exhibit, "Libya: The Road to Freedom," photographs taken by Amr Abdallah (Reuters) and Mohamed Messara (European Pressphoto Agency).

They always worried about snipers. Gaddafi loyalists who picked them out of the landscape of a broken city and squeezed triggers on weapons that poured out death like a hard rain falling on the desert floor.

Both men had been shot. Abdallah in the fleshy part of the shoulder and Messara whose bullet-proof vest protected him from death, but did not stop metal from piercing his shoulder just under the neck. The next day he returned to the scene of combat. Adrenaline rushing. Like a junkie who can't stop using, he goes back to the streets and alleyways, his cameras slung over his shoulders. The right one was still aching from the wound.

Gaddafi had promised to search out the dissidents in every house, every street, every alley. *Zanga zanga*.

The driver looked like a teenager. Many of the opposition soldiers in their jeans and tee-shirt uniforms were. The truck he was driving swerved in an attempt to avoid the onslaught of pro-Gaddafi bullets against metal. The truck overturned. A rebel soldier ran to the car, pulled the dead, barefoot driver from the wreck, cradled him in his arms as if nurturing a child and ran into the street that was a river of dirty water. A soldier was on his heels. A rifleman covered their escape. No one even glanced at Messara, crouching before them, bracing his camera for a steady shot. The

New York Times ran the picture the next day.

Messara saw the woman, a Gaddafi supporter with the colors of the Libyan flag painted on her face. Red was in the shape of a heart. She was shouting, cursing the opposition. She was shouting for the attention of United Nations Secretary-General Ban Ki-moon as he left the Arab League headquarters on his way to Tahrir Square. She held a large photo of Muammar Gaddafi in her left hand. Messara clicked the frame while she was in mid-sentence.

I turned a corner in the pristine gallery and faced a photograph of a dead Gaddafi placed above another one of his dead son.

"*Man antom,*" who are you? Gaddafi had interrupted a speech to the thousands of Libyans crowding the streets of Tripoli and Benghazi. Incredulous, how could you do this to him, he was a king in a colonel's uniform worn to show that he was for the people; he was the King of Kings. But in the end he was dragged through the streets, his face a bloodied mask of pain and poison, stripped of the decency of clothing, his bare chest stained with his own blood, begging for his life to the surrounding dogs of war who showed no mercy. A despot's end. Perhaps a bullet in the head from his own gold pistol. Empty of life, of pain, of the 40 years of oppressing the Libyan people, he lies on a plastic sheet inside a storage freezer, motionless in Mohamed Messara's graphic image.

I leave Gaddafi laying there and pass an opposition soldier, a man with one leg and crutches, peering down a long empty desert road, the futility of war. What was he thinking? Was there an end to this road? Is this Freedom Road or the Road to Hell? Abdallah caught this frame just as the man passed him.

Allah will know them by the imprint of their hands and foreheads on the desert sand. They fought for liberation and they prayed. A line of rebel soldiers, as straight as the teeth in a comb, their weapons placed before them. This was at the western entrance of Ajdabiyah. Amr Abdallah was there.

I stopped before an oversize photograph of a Libyan man whose sunglasses reflected the coffins of men who had been killed after Friday prayers in Benghazi. Amr Abdallah framed the picture in his lens.

The sniper's bullets were heard and felt on the streets of Sirte. Rebels in makeshift uniforms, black tee shirts and camouflage pants, take cover behind parked cars and pick-up trucks pockmarked by bullets. Mohamed Messara crouched behind a broken car as he shot this photo.

The treeless road to freedom. New governments. New hopes. But it will be difficult to get the people to agree. Difficult to get them to turn in their weapons.

Oil brought Gaddafi wealth and a desire for absolute power. Secret stashes of gold, paper money, real estate in foreign countries, but he used his money not to help the world but to pay for and incite the anger that created events of pain in the world. Now he is dragged like a dog through the dusty streets of his youth. The road to freedom is a hard road.

The Arab Seasons of grief and hope. People wandering the surface of normality in the Middle-East. It has been ten months. Not much change besides the ousting of unconscionable old leaders.

The acceptance of oppression is a difficult habit to break. The payment is dear.

Perverted Religious Morality

The most deadly of the three hotel attacks on November 9, 2005 was at the Radisson SAS Hotel in the Jordanian capital of Amman–a hotel often frequented by foreign diplomats and business people, as well as Jordanians.

An Iraqi "husband and wife team" entered the Philadelphia Ballroom where a Palestinian-Jordanian wedding party with 900 guests was underway. The woman was unable to detonate her belt – her partner admonished her and told her to get out of the room. As soon as she had left the ballroom, the Al Qaeda suicide bomber jumped on a dining room table and blew himself up killing 38 people. His partner was arrested.

The couple had been married just before leaving Iraq on their mission because according to *shari'a* a woman should only travel in the company of a man if he is either a close blood relative or her husband. So in order not to violate a technicality so-to-speak of religious law, this "married" couple were then sent on their way to murder men, women and children at a wedding party.

That totally misplaced or perverted sense of religious morality sums up and reveals the mind-set of Islamist terrorists – "Islamist" not Islamic, for terrorism in Islamic law, the killing of innocent people, is the worst of all crimes.

The Secret Heart

I met Sheikh 'Ali Jum'a shortly after arriving in Cairo. We climbed endless stairs in a dimly lit corridor of dust and age. Sheikh 'Ali twisted the key into a nondescript door and we entered one of the three small apartments in a *baladi* district of Cairo where he housed his library of over thirty thousand books. The smell of old books emerged from the wall-to-wall cases. Dusty windows allowed filtered light and the bare electric bulbs that hung from the ceiling added the rest. As a lover of books I felt as though I had entered a bejeweled palace.

Mosques that bespoke history dotted the landscape of old Cairo. Sheikh 'Ali became the Imam of the Sultan Hassan mosque whose interior revealed secrets of man's relation to his Creator.

Not far from the *mihrab* was a small room off the main prayer area that Sheikh 'Ali used as a place to meet questioners after the *jum'a* prayer. The room was bare, hadn't been painted in a century, and had a hole in the wall open to the outside that let in the dust of the desert.

It is not allowed to alter any mosque without endless documents of permission from obscure authorities that take ages to secure. This was not part of the prayer area so I decided to make a proper *majlis* room for Sheikh 'Ali. Workmen from the university arrived to clean and paint the room. Someone provided a large Turkish carpet and a carpenter friend built a long low couch. I shopped for cloth with an Islamic pattern to cover the cushions. Randa Fahmy, world renowned for her interior design and traditional Islamic lamps, gave us several and I had electricians wire and hang them. We framed and glassed in the hole in the wall to make a window. All this was done at night.

Within a week we had renovated the space.

Every Friday thousands of Muslims in Cairo hear the call to prayer and make their way to Sultan Hassan, a fourteenth-century mosque located in the heart of the old city, to pray and listen to the *khutba* of Sheikh 'Ali Jum'a. As one enters the courtyard of the mosque, framed by four enormous vaulted halls, one is struck by the simplicity, beauty, and scale of the structure. It arouses the feeling of man and his Creator.

Sheikh 'Ali climbs the stairs of the *minbar*, faces the congregation, and begins his talk. He invokes the Name of Allah with such intensity that men weep, for it has been said that when you hear the Name of Allah you should weep, and if you do not weep, you should weep because you do not. After the prayer almost the entire congregation remains to hear the lesson that Sheikh 'Ali presents. As he speaks, his soft eyes penetrate, his voice rings with strength and quivers with emotion. He is the embodiment of intelligence and light.

It was after a Friday prayer, in the *majlis* room, on a hot Cairo evening that Sheikh 'Ali began to speak of the heart.

"There are words in the Arabic language that speak about the level of the heart as physical or metaphysical: the heart *(al-qalb)*, the sensitive heart *(al-fouad)*, the essence *(al-lubb)*, and the intellect *(al-aql)*. The word *al-qalb* also refers to the physical entity, the pump that pumps blood, the cessation of which separates life and death. But as to this other heart – meaning the inside of a thing, its truth, its central core, and its essence – there are five levels that Sufis speak about regarding this matter. They have spoken of the heart, the spirit, the secret, the hidden, and the most hidden.

"These five levels are like circles within circles, each circle higher and narrower than the one before. Meaning that if there are one thousand human beings at the level of the heart, at the level of the spirit there are eight hundred, at the level of the secret six hundred, the hidden two hundred, at the level of the most hidden one hundred – and what is beyond this fewer than one hundred. These levels form a pyramidal shape.

"The heart is a level among the levels, and not a piece of flesh. But there is a relation of sorts between the heart as a piece of flesh and the heart as a level. This relation is not perceived or sensed. It is not possible to touch, see, or experience it through the five senses. And yet, we feel the level of the heart near the breast, below it and to the left. We feel it in a place lower than or under the part of the body that is the physical heart.

"The way leading to the heart is remembrance, repetition of the Names of Allah *(zikr)* and contemplation *(fikr)*. Just as a human being feels that thinking takes place in the head and does not feel that his hand is thinking, so he feels near the heart the unveiling of the secrets and lights in the five realms.

"There are five realms which the human being experiences. The world of *al-mulk*, this is the visible world experienced by the five senses; the world of *al-malakut*, this comprises the creatures and creation that man cannot see and cannot arrive at through his five senses, like the angels, jinn, hell, and heaven. Together; *al-mulk* and *al-malakut* are the world, which is what is other than Allah.

"Beyond this are three worlds at the divine level; the world of beauty, the world of majesty, and that of completeness. They are also referred to as 'what is above the throne' and is what is meant by His saying *"Al-Rahman ala al'arsh istawa."* What is above the throne is Allah in His Beauty, Completeness, and Splendor. What is beneath the throne is what is referred to as the carpet. There is a throne and there is a carpet.

"The five levels – the heart, spirit, secret, hidden, and most hidden – are levels among the levels of lights and secrets in the world of *mulk* and *malakut,* the world beneath the throne, and through which man ascends to the positions of the throne.

"Above the throne there are five other levels – heart, spirit, secret, hidden, and most hidden – resembling these five, reflected like a mirror, five facing this way and five that way (Sheikh 'Ali demonstrates with his open palms, one palm towards the listener one palm towards himself).

"Beyond this are three other worlds that are totally obscure, meaning that we absolutely cannot comprehend them, whether with our thought, our minds, our practice of *zikr*, or our sensory perception. For Allah in His Glory is beyond comprehension.

"The heart is a level among the levels of piety on the way to Allah, the lights and secrets of which are manifested in a part of the body, the form of which is a pump that pumps blood in the body. In this area, not in the part of the body itself but around it, man feels something of the revelations of secrets, disclosures, and lights."

Sheikh Ali paused to drink tea then continued; "The heart is in man. It is a level among levels of the spirit, meaning a circle of the circles of the spirit. Above it is also the spirit; it is a level in which the spirit finds and comprehends itself.

"And then there is what is secret. At this level man understands that he is nothing and that Allah is the foundation of all things. In this stage man might lose his way and believes himself to be Allah, and believes himself to be nothing because Allah has totally taken him over and therefore is him.

"After this he ascends to the hidden and knows that he is one thing and Allah is another. That he is mortal and Allah is permanent and that there is a difference between the created and the Creator. Then he is elevated beyond this and knows that he is a manifestation among the manifestations of the Beneficent, and that the attributes of Allah are all reflected in him through ability, will, and knowledge. This is the station of the most hidden. The first of all these endless levels is the heart, the instrument of contemplation *(fikr)* and *zikr* (remembrance by repetition).

"Allah is eternal, but I perish. I have a beginning and He has no beginning. I need Him but He does not need me, and so a feeling comes from my heart. This is the station of the hidden that is a level of the levels that reside in the heart. This heart is a container, a vessel, and the levels of which the first is also called the heart is different. Then there is the spirit, the secret, the hidden, and the most hidden – all reside in the heart as a vessel. For the spiritual world has a connection to the physical world, but in reality this material that includes heart, spirit, secret, hidden, and most hidden is comprised of gradations of the spirit. It is not the pump, but its locus is the pump, just as water is contained in a glass. The pump is the locus of the spiritual of which al-Ghazali speaks. So the question is: Does this spiritual entity that is inside the pump have emotions, feelings? Yes, it has emotions.

"These emotions have been the subject of Sufi thinking and are seen as ten levels. These emotions include a feeling called repentance, which is when man feels the need to turn away from what is not Allah, as if his preoccupation with the universe is a sin on his part from which he wants to turn away, an ugly feeling.

"There are ten stations and a section called states. A station is an unchangeable emotion and the states are passing emotions that come and go. Man ascends from one station to the next and does not return to a lower station. If a man does return to a lower station it is a major catastrophe, like returning from faith to unbelief.

"The states come and go. The Sufis have given them names such as depressed, happy, union, and separation. The spiritual heart has emotions and these emotions are of two kinds, unmovable and passing.

"According to the Sufis the heart has two doors: a door to creation, and a door to Truth, therefore to Allah. There is also what is earned, and what is given. By his nature man's heart is open to creation. He needs food, drink, clothing, a dwelling place, a companion, and he needs to live in the world according to its laws. This is the door of creation. It is in the nature of man that this door be open.

"When *zikr* is achieved, it opens the other door, the door of Truth, and this happens in three stages. In the first, the door of Truth is closed. In the second, it opens, but the door of creation closes from the intensity of *zikr*; as if *zikr* is a wind closing the door of creation and opening the door of Truth. In the third, the door of creation also opens, and the heart has two open doors. The fourth case is when both doors are closed and this is what is called madness. This is someone who is neither into worship nor into the world – that is, he knows nothing at all. He has exited from the circle of responsibility.

"When the door of creation is opened, blocking the door to Truth – that is from a lack of *zikr*, and from man's nature.

"So what opens and what closes? This is the answer; the door of creation opens naturally, and the door of Truth is opened by *zikr* and *fikr*. The door of Truth opens little by little until it is wide open.

"An important issue to mention here is that of what is earned and what is given. We can open the door through *zikr*, but Allah can also open the door without *zikr*. The Sufis speak of a person who is a seeker and another who is sought. There is one who is on the way and one who is attracted. All these terms lead to the same meaning, namely that there is something man can do that leads to his heart being opened, and there is also a gift from Allah that opens the heart and has nothing to do with the person's effort.

"The Prophet used to say: '*Allahumma*, let there be in my heart light, and in my hearing light, and in my seeing light, in my hands light, to my right light, to my left light, and let me be light.'

Sheikh 'Ali sipped his tea and I used the opportunity to ask a question. "Moses threw his staff and it became a snake. He was commanded to pick up the snake. He did and it again became a staff. Then he was told to place his hand on his heart. When he removed it the Name of Allah was written in light on the palm of his hand. Can metaphysical light be transformed into light perceived by the senses?"

Sheikh 'Ali leaned forward and said; "All Spiritual things can be transformed into things of a sensory nature. On the Day of Judgment death comes in the form of a ram. Death here is a concept but it becomes materialized. There are two kinds of secrets and two kinds of lights. We spoke of the realm of *al-mulk* and the realm of *al-malakut*, circles of the creation. In each there are secrets and lights. The secrets of *al-mulk* are of the senses. Meaning the benefits of medicinal plants, the laws of building and engineering, of mathematics, and hydrology – all these are secrets that man discovers every day in the realm of *al-mulk*. There are also sensory lights: electricity, the sun, moon, stars, lasers and so on.

"There are also lights and secrets of *al-malakut* – lights and secrets that are non-sensory. But anything from the realm of *al-malakut* can enter the realm of *mulk,* can be transformed into something perceived by the senses.

"Creation is comprised of two sections: *al-mulk*, which is perceived by the five senses, and *al-malakut*. That realm which may be sensed by the five senses is what we are in now. In *al-malakut* it is the spirit ascending the circles that is the perceiver and not the senses."

As Sheikh 'Ali readjusted himself on the couch covered by a cloth with an Islamic design, I asked; "There is a saying of the Prophet Mohammad: 'All things have a polish. The polish of the heart is the Remembrance of God.' What rusts the heart?"

"In the Qur'an there are descriptions of what ails the heart. There is the layer of scum on stagnant water, the cover, the locks, veils, pride, and so on. These can be removed through faith, others by repetition of the Names of Allah, and others by contemplation.

"The Sufis link this to the seven levels of the self *(al-nafs)*: domineering, censorious, inspiring, tranquil, contented, pleasing, and pure. They have linked these to the Beautiful Names of Allah and to the gradations of man's attempt to remove rust or scum. Seven Names are used: *la illah illa Allah, Allah, Hu, Al-Hayy, Al-Qayyum, Al-Haqq,* and *Al-Qahhar*.

"Disagreement exists about this as some Sufis choose *Al-Aziz, Al-Wahid, Al-Wadud, Al-Wahab, Al-Basit,* and *Al-Muhaymin*.

"There are various formulas given by a sheikh as to the manner and frequency of the repetition of the Names. The invocation of the Names of Allah satisfies the heart and opens the door of Truth."

I felt refreshed, like walking in the rain beside the Ka'bah.

The Awakening

Safer Baba and I are drinking *sahlep*, a hot beverage made from the dried root of wild orchids, in the hope of finding warmth from the biting chill of March in Istanbul.

"Let's make a pact," he says. "Whoever wakes up first, wakes the other."

He recites a *hadith*. "Every malady has a cure except one." When asked which malady had no cure, the Prophet Mohammed answered, "Old age."

Afghan Bread and Hot White Coffee

The Prophet's Mosque in Madinah is now larger than the city was when he entered. The Prophet Mohammed loved Madinah and left his light among the desert date palms and the small mosque that has grown to allow a million believers to pray under its roof today.

I arrived in Madinah a few days before my friend Hussein and checked into a small hotel, now razed, a short distance from the mosque. It was a few months after the religious fanatic Juhayman al-Otaybi took over *Haram al-Masjid* in Makkah in November of 1979, causing the government to close the mosques after night prayer. It was late. I prayed on the street in front of the green dome.

The call to *fajr* prayer broke the silence of darkness. I washed, dressed and walked the short distance to the mosque as if in a dream where hundreds of people were slowly converging into one space.

After prayer I stopped for warm Afghan bread and hot white coffee flavored with cardamom seed in a small café then continued toward my hotel. Morning light nudged the darkness.

Approaching the hotel I noticed a man selling perfume. His shop was a large cloth spread on the pavement. Small glass containers of perfume would make good gifts, and they were easy to pack. He sat on the cloth and was serving another man so I hunkered before him and waited my turn. This is when I felt the beauty of his presence. Light emanated from him. His movements were ethereal, as if everything he did was part of a cosmic dance. His white beard complimented his *thobe* and turban. He spoke in a gentle but authoritative tone, addressing me in Turkish. I explained that it was not a language that I knew well. Then he spoke to me in English. How did this simple perfume seller on a Madinah street become well versed in English?

"I would like the scent of roses."

"You must take the best quality."
He placed a little on my finger; some dropped and he said, "Rub it into your scarf."
It was the best rose from Taif. "I'll take five small bottles."
He had yellow and green plastic containers and placed four of the bottles in green ones then began shuffling through the box. I said, "It is all right, you can put the last one in a yellow container."
"No you must have a green one."

Each movement of his hands was like a *mudra*. I was so taken by his light that I didn't want to leave. I had to see him again.
"Are you from Madinah?"
"Yes, I am a Madinah man."
"Are you here everyday?"
"Yes."

Now I could leave with some comfort. I gave my *salams*, received his and stood. I felt as though I were in the middle of a *zikr*. A few steps from him sat a large Nigerian man selling *miswak*.

That night I had a peaceful sleep, until I awoke feeling a presence in the room. I sat up and saw the perfume seller standing at the foot of the bed.

"Whenever you need me I will be there for you," and then he was gone. It was not a dream. For all these years, whenever I had a spiritual difficulty, I have felt his presence and can see him as clearly as that day in Madinah.

The next day Hussein arrived from Jeddah and I related the story. After *fajr* we went to the spot on the street where the perfume seller had been sitting. He was not there. We approached the Nigerian *miswak* seller and realized he was blind.

"It is Friday," said Hussein, "many men do not work on Friday." We searched for him the entire week. He had disappeared. Perhaps behind a cloud of Light.

A Dream Worth a Hundred Pieces of Gold

Thirty years ago in the garden of his house in Uskudar, among the fruit trees and engraved brass trays filled with plates of sliced oranges and glasses of Turkish tea, Safer Baba turned to me and said, "story."

"During the time of ignorance in Makkah a merchant travelled to Damascus on business. Being a merchant was a good profession. Nine tenths of Allah's sustenance comes from business.

"In Damascus the man dreamt a full moon came to him and he hugged it to his chest. He felt it was a profound dream so he went to a priest and asked him to interpret the dream.

"The true priest charged him ten pieces of gold for the interpretation and said, 'This dream is worth a hundred pieces of gold.'

"If the dream comes true I will willingly pay the other ninety.

"Know that a sun is going to rise. A man will come and be the last Prophet and you will be his trustworthy friend and take over for him when he dies. That sun will change the face of the world. Here is a letter for him.

"The letter read, 'O master, I believe you are the last Prophet and if I am alive when you read this I will come to you and if I am dead please intercede for me.'

"Abu Bakr al-Siddiq was the merchant.

"Years after he heard a voice like thunder from a hilltop. 'Come to the invitation of Allah and say *La Illa ha illa Allah, Mohammed Rasul Allah*.'

"The next morning Abu Bakr saw the Prophet. They had known one another since childhood. The Prophet lifted him from the ground by his shirt.

"When are you going to believe in me ya Abu Bakr?

"Ya Mohammed we know you as a most noble and trustworthy man but every Prophet has performed a miracle.

"Fifteen years ago you travelled from Makkah to Damascus and were told a dream. You have worn that letter on your chest for the last fifteen years.

"Ashadu ana la illa ḥa illa Allah wa ashadu ana Mohammed Rasul Allah."

I am being filled with the deeper meanings of Sufism and feel like a huge clay vessel and each drop of knowledge placed in it creates an echo in my heart. I realize that I know so little, perhaps the water left on the head of a needle that is dipped in the ocean compared to the ocean.

We interrupted the conversation to make *wudu* and afternoon prayer. Later while drinking tea Safer Baba taught me how to catch a monkey.

"You dig a small hole, place a thin-necked bottle in the hole and fill it with nuts. The monkey will reach in and grab a fistfull of nuts but will not be able to remove his fist from the bottle. The monkey hunter approaches and captures his prey. A smart monkey realizes that if he lets go of the nuts he can slip his paw from the bottle.

"Freedom exists when you let go of desires."

I Held the *Taj* and Safer Baba Wrapped

Dervish *tekkes* in Istanbul are often hidden behind green doors on trafficked streets or in gardens surrounded by fruit trees. I went to numerous *tekkes* with Safer Baba to rewind the green ribbons that wrapped the *tajs* of the sheikhs of the Sufi orders. With time the ribbons frayed. Many *tekkes* were no longer "alive with *zikr*" so there were few men who knew how to properly wrap the green cloth around the base of the *taj*. As we sat on the floor near each sarcophagus Safer Baba mended the *taj* and showed me how to fold and wrap the cloth so that a short length of ribbon hung on the left side. I held the *taj* and Safer Baba wrapped. Either fish or cut bait. A beautiful scent permeated the rooms.

The Khidr Construction Company

I am building the house I will live in. It is adjacent to the rented one I live in now. The new one, that I realize I have been constructing for some time, will be attached by a walkway so I can observe myself in the old house while building the new. It is a tower house so I can see everything and be alone to do my work.

As I observe parts of the house I live in diminish in strength, it has become necessary to consider alternatives. My eyes are not as acute as before, my hearing is slowly getting less tuned, I ache in former places of pleasure, and although I feel my mind is sharp, my thinking even better than when I was younger, I find that there is a loss of memory on a daily basis. A friend suggested that it was Age Activated Attention Deficit Disorder, perhaps the forerunner of dementia or Alzheimer's, but I think, at least for the moment, it is a lack of interest in certain mundane and ordinary things in life and a refocus on what is more important. Like Walter's house in Wingdale, it will be constructed and razed in the same lifetime.

I placed a sign on the edge of the land that says, "The Khidr Construction Company," so when anyone approaches they are aware that things may be unusual. When I became a septuagenarian sounds became muffled or loud. Hearing loss accompanied a blurred picture of events. I know now why in my youth eyeglasses were called "cheaters."

Outwardly the old house does not seem so bad. A little paint here, some mortar there, the sanding of still harsh edges, but I can breathe better in the new house and felt it was to early for my breath to stop nourishing the house that I live in and cause it to crumble like the mud-brick house on the Hopi Indian reservation.

The triangular metal "Man at Work" sign on the edge of the land reminds people to approach with an understanding that inside was a man working on himself and getting his passport in order.

The walls of the old house were cluttered with paintings and photographs. The new ones are bare but I did hang one picture on the wall near my heart. It was a handwritten calligraphy of the Name of Allah.

In the meantime I am building new memories and unfreezing old ones.

The Increasing and Diminishing Population

There are over six billion people in the world. Yet, when one of them dies it is a unique event. There is going and returning and there is going and not returning. There is going and returning and finding, and there is going and returning and not finding. With this thought in one's mind and heart one bids farewell to another. Every departure, even for what may seem as a short time, is filled with a concern of the heart.

When a person dies they take their unique face. Allah has not created two faces alike. They take the thousands of memories that have filled their minds and hearts. Personal memories that no other being can share. Those memories that sometimes were climbed like mountains. Others that clung to one's ribs and some that sank into an expanding heart and adhered themselves with a cosmic glue to the Names of God that have always been there.

These personal memories depart with each of us.

The Journey

All of mankind, whether one is a believer or an unbeliever, secular or spiritual, will experience the journey of birth to death. One's entrance is accompanied by pain and one's departure is due to death. This world eludes those who attempt to capture it and pays homage to those who are indifferent to its allurements. It is a teacher to those who learn from history and blinds those who are attracted by its false charms. The healing of man is from "the treasury of the invisible."

Life begins in the womb as a drop for forty days. Then forty days as a sticky attached clot followed by forty days as a piece of flesh after which God sends an angel to blow the spirit (*ruh*) into the being.

The child remains in the womb for an apportioned time–until God wills him to come forth. It is *sunnah* to recite the call to prayer in the right ear of a newborn baby, and the *iqama* in the left ear to remind the child of its primordial nature according to which God has made people.

One should instill goodness in children for goodness is a habit.

PUBERTY

God has lightened the load between birth to puberty. One is not obliged to pray, fast, or perform other *shari'a* obligations. The *hadith* states: "The pen is withheld from recording the deeds of three people. A child until he reaches puberty. A sleeper until he awakens. A madman until he recovers."

At puberty a child becomes accountable. Two noble guardian angels record good and evil deeds and this record will be presented to him on the Day of Judgment.

A child must be encouraged, reminded and explained about religious obligations such as the five pillars of Islam and the need to avoid what has been prohibited.

YOUTH

During youth, energy is abundant and strength increases. This is both a good and a hazardous stage for one is drawn to worldly desires.

A *hadith* states that one should seize the opportunity to make use of five things before five other things replace them. "Youth before you grow old. Health before you may fall sick. Leisure before you are occupied. Wealth before you grow poor and life before you die."

In youth one acquires merit, knowledge, and attains leadership.

MATURITY

A young person moves to the "Age of Maturity," the peak of one's lifetime and the attainment of one's full power.

Ibn Qayyim al–Jawziyya, known to some as "the scholar of the heart," a thirteenth century Islamic jurist and physician who authored *al-Tibb al-Nabawi*, expresses the division of the human lifespan:

1. Childhood ends at age fifteen.
2. Youth extends to age thirty-five.
3. Maturity ends at age fifty.
4. Seniority ends at age seventy.
5. Decrepitude terminates in death.

In Maturity one may expect to attain wisdom given by God to those fit to receive it. At age forty the Prophet Mohammad received revelation from Allah.

Some scholars say that by forty a man's goodness should be dominant.

"Did He not grant you a life long enough for him who reflects to reflect therein? And the warner came to you." (Qur'an 35:37)

Sheikh 'Abdul Wahab writes: Life is narrowed after forty, and heedlessness, distraction, and playing are inappropriate for him who nears the Battleground of Deaths.

Imam al–Shafi'i upon reaching the age of forty began walking with a stick and when asked about it used to say: "It is to remind myself that I am a traveller."

SENIORITY

One then moves from Maturity to Seniority. Strength recedes. The earliest signs of weakness appear. The Messenger of God called the years between sixty and seventy "The Battleground of Deaths."

The Prophet Mohammed said: "The reaping of my Nation is between sixty and seventy."

Allah has said: "Did We not grant you a life long enough for him who reflects to reflect therein? And the warner came to you."

God has left no excuse to a man whom He allows to reach sixty. He has left him no way of excusing himself saying that the end came too soon and his life was short.

When Prophet Mohammed considered the lifespans of his nation short in comparison to others and therefore his people would have less time to spend in obedience and in preparation for the Hereafter and would miss many of the rewards of God, then God gave them *The Night of Power*, which is better than a thousand months. (Qur'an *97:3)*

In Seniority people's dominant state is to revert to God, to gather provisions for their life to come, renounce the things of this world and do their utmost in obedience. It is the age of dignity, reverence, and the total avoidance of jest and levity. White hair appears at this time.

The Prophet Mohammed said: "For someone whose hair turns grey while a Muslim it becomes a light for him." White hair is a reminder of the nearness of one's time and the necessity of folding up the carpet of hope. It is said that white hair brings with it the allusion that one's time has come. It is the banisher of hope.

Omar asked his servant to remind him of death every day. One day the servant arrived and Omar said that he was no longer needed.

"Why? When I reminded you I also reminded myself and this was good for me."

"I now have grey in my beard and a reminder is no longer necessary."

The Prophet Mohammed said: "The one who does not show respect for our elders, and compassion for our youngsters, and does not enjoin a good and forbid an evil, is not of us."

And he said: "Whenever a young man honors an older person, God sends him someone who will respect him when he reaches that age."

DECREPITUDE

At this stage weakness enters all one's senses, limbs, and faculties. The *hadith* states: "Let none of you wish for death, for either you are doing good and this may increase, or doing evil and thus enjoying the chance to make amends. The most intelligent are those who remember death and prepare for it best."

This period most commonly ends with a fatal illness and uncommonly with death without illness.

One should observe one's actions. If an action would please you if Death were to find you doing it then continue doing that action. And if you are performing an action that would displease you if Death were to find you occupied with it, then abandon this now.

The Prophet Mohammed said: "The likeness of myself and the world is that of a rider travelling on a summer day. He finds a tree, rests beneath it for a while, then goes on, leaving it behind."

Seek the protection of God from every hope that distracts you. When the heart fills with the sensation that one will remain long in the world, then most of its attention will be devoted to making one's worldly affairs prosper; one will become heedless of the Hereafter and of gathering provisions for it, until Death takes one by surprise and one meets God bankrupt of good works.

Work as if you will never die, and pray as if you will die tomorrow. Those who don't learn from the lessons of others, become lessons for others.

These are some memories of one man.

POSTSCRIPT

Some World Conditions

In 2014 the average cost of a new car is $32,086 and a gallon bottle of milk can be purchased for $3.50. A cry of despair and cracking of hearts worldwide is sounded as a result of the bombing of occupied Gaza by Israel, who indiscriminately kills more than a thousand innocent women, children and the elderly as the world responds with useless rhetoric.

The Middle East continues to suffer from the recent Arab Spring. Al-Qaeda and DAASH are militant Islamist groups. Islam is misrepresented by most of the world. Africa is in turmoil. Ukraine and Russia are at war.

Saddam Hussein is dead. Muammar Gaddafi is dead. Hosni Mubarak has been overthrown and is confined to a military hospital in Egypt.

It is a generation where few read books and the attention span of the young is limited to the approximately 25 words of a *tweet*. Everyone has a phone in his or her pocket.

There is little water, food or electricity in Gaza. *Le Reve*, a painting by Pablo Picasso, sold for $155 million. The Boston Red Sox won the World Series. Germany won the World Cup in soccer. Technology has occupied our lives but has not enabled people of the world to become friends. These were some of the conditions of the world when Alia Rose Friedlander entered in July of 2014.

Through Love all that is bitter becomes sweet,
Through Love all that is copper becomes gold.
Through Love all dregs will turn to purest wine;
Through Love all pain becomes medicine.
Through Love the dead become alive,
Through Love the king becomes a slave.

Jalaluddin Rumi

Acknowledgements

Some words were taken from Jorge Luis Borges, Jalaluddin Rumi, and a number of Sufi masters who have guided me with their writings and their presence. I have referred to sixty notebooks kept between 1960 and 1990, with references and stories from many sheikhs, that revealed what was in the sleeve of my past.

The solitude that comes when one is writing a book is food for the heart. Few works are completed without help, consideration and advice from others. I am grateful to my dear friends Abdallah Schleifer and Haroon Sugich who read and commented on various versions. To Nadia Naguib and Krystina Friedlander who read early pages. Their comments were fruitful and encouraged me to look deeper into the ocean of my memories.

I thank Nadine Aboulmagd who watched the growth of the book, especially the Arabic and challenged my phonetic interpretations. Nilufer Usta who recognized a seed that could grow and bear fruit. My gratitude to Emine Eroglu, the publisher of Sufi Kitab, who had the vision that this would be a worthwhile endeavor and allowed me to reenter my life through thoughts that I imagined to have frozen or disappeared. An exercise I encourage everyone to experience.

To Nuri whose integrity and manner of thinking has always challenged me to be better. To Hatice who has blossomed as a person and an artist, for putting up with the many hours I remained in thought, in silence, or buried in words. I am appreciative to Omer Colakoglu for his thoughtful translation and am thankful to Batul Salazar a distinguished editor who made the time to read the final manuscript.

I bow to the many teachers who have led me to the path, nudged me onto the path, or kicked me onto the path. I thank you for your guidance and patience.